"I need a shieldmaiden."

Bryn was bent over, digging out a rock wedged under one of her horse's shoes. At the sound of that voice, deep and rich and so familiar, every muscle in her body froze. Pain and longing and a million other emotions she refused to feel twisted through her soul. Moving as slowly as a thousand-year-old woman—which was actually how old she was—she carefully set the mare's hoof on the ground and straightened but didn't turn around to face him. "Well, you'll need to keep looking, then."

"Brynhild."

"Just Bryn, thanks. Go away, Siegfried." The gods knew he'd never show up here unless it was to fuck up her life. No, thanks. She might once have been a shieldmaiden, a valkyrie. She might still be able to shift into a raven and soar into the clouds. She might be older than dirt. But all of that meant she had an even lower bullshit tolerance than she did back in the day when Siegfried was the love of her life. Also her betrayer, her tormenter, the man who cost her mortal life. The man she'd betrayed in turn, a blood-soaked vengeance she'd never been able to cleanse from her stained, battered soul.

That was a long time ago, but some wounds never really healed, did they? She tried not to think about it. Ever.

Reclaimed by the Immortal Viking Shifter

CRYSTAL JORDAN

CJ BOOKS

Copyright © 2025 by Crystal Jordan

Published by CJ Books

All rights reserved.

No part of this publication may be reproduced, distributed, or transmitted in any form or by any means, including photocopying, recording, or other electronic or mechanical methods, without the prior written permission of the publisher, except as permitted by U.S. copyright law. For permission requests, email contact@cjbooks.com.

This is a work of fiction. Names, characters, places, brands, media, and incidents are either the product of the author's imagination or are used fictitiously. The author acknowledges the trademarked status and trademark owners of various products referenced in this work of fiction, which have been used without permission. The publication/use of these trademarks is not authorized, associated with, or sponsored by the trademark owners.

Book cover by GetCovers

Reclaimed by the Immortal Viking Wolf was originally published as an e-book in © 2015, with a second edition in © 2024.

Reclaimed by the Immortal Viking Bear was originally published as an e-book in © 2016, with a second edition in © 2024.

First print edition 2025

Contents

Reclaimed by the Immortal Viking Wolf

1. Chapter One — 2
2. Chapter Two — 9
3. Chapter Three — 18
4. Chapter Four — 21
5. Chapter Five — 27
6. Chapter Six — 32
7. Chapter Seven — 41
8. Chapter Eight — 48
9. Chapter Nine — 55
10. Chapter Ten — 63
11. Chapter Eleven — 69
12. Chapter Twelve — 78
13. Chapter Thirteen — 84
14. Chapter Fourteen — 87
15. Chapter Fifteen — 90
16. Chapter Sixteen — 97
17. Chapter Seventeen — 102
18. Chapter Eighteen — 105

19.	Chapter Nineteen	112
20.	Chapter Twenty	115
21.	Chapter Twenty-One	122
22.	Chapter Twenty-Two	128
23.	Chapter Twenty-Three	132
24.	Chapter Twenty-Four	136

Reclaimed by the Immortal Viking Bear

1.	Chapter One	148
2.	Chapter Two	157
3.	Chapter Three	164
4.	Chapter Four	170
5.	Chapter Five	184
6.	Chapter Six	197
7.	Chapter Seven	204
8.	Chapter Eight	208
9.	Chapter Nine	215
10.	Chapter Ten	220
11.	Chapter Eleven	227

About Crystal Jordan	237
Also by Crystal Jordan	238
Excerpt from Claim Me	239

Reclaimed by the Immortal Viking Shifter is a contemporary paranormal shape-shifter romance based on Norse mythology. If you haven't read anything about Vikings, I can only warn you that their history was pretty brutal.

Please be aware that the stories in this book involve betrayal, deception, infidelity, sexual assault, drugging someone into sex or marriage, violence, abuse of power, revenge, kidnapping, the murder of a child, parents losing an adult child, and suicide. All of these things happen a thousand years before the start of these stories, but they are discussed during the book. There is also mention of cannibalism in these stories. If these are sensitive topics for you, please read with care (and the knowledge that these couples get a second chance at happily ever after).

~**Crystal**

Reclaimed by the Immortal Viking Wolf

Crystal Jordan

CJ Books

1

Ravencrest Farm, Virginia

"I need a shieldmaiden."

Bryn was bent over, digging out a rock wedged under one of her horse's shoes. At the sound of that voice, deep and rich and so familiar, every muscle in her body froze. Pain and longing and a million other emotions she refused to feel twisted through her soul. Moving as slowly as a thousand-year-old woman—which was actually how old she was—she carefully set the mare's hoof on the ground and straightened but didn't turn around to face him. "Well, you'll need to keep looking, then."

"Brynhild."

"Just Bryn, thanks. Go away, Siegfried." The gods knew he'd never show up here unless it was to fuck up her life. No, thanks. She might once have been a shieldmaiden, a valkyrie. She might still be able to shift into a raven and soar into the clouds. She might be older than dirt. But all of that meant she had an even lower bullshit tolerance than she did back in the day when Siegfried was the love of her life. Also her betrayer, her tormenter, the man who cost her mortal life. The man she'd betrayed in turn, a blood-soaked vengeance she'd never been able to cleanse from her stained, battered soul.

That was a long time ago, but some wounds never really healed, did they? She tried not to think about it. Ever.

She stroked a hand down the horse's silky neck. Unhooking the cross ties, she snapped a lead line on to the mare's halter, and walked her to her stall.

No sound gave away the fact that he'd followed her, but she was keenly aware of his presence, his nearness, his ability to throw her off-balance. Tingles skipped over her skin, and she tried to ignore the reaction.

His voice came from directly behind her when she latched the stall. "I've used Siegfried as my surname since I came to America. A hundred years ago. Maybe more."

"Okay." She infused as much disinterest into the word as she could manage.

"Erik is what you can call me now."

"I prefer to call you gone." She set off down the wide, concrete barn aisle. The sun would set in about half an hour, so she had to wrap up for the day. One more horse needed to be brought in. She whistled as she approached the paddock gate, and Rogue's Gallery came galloping up. This paddock was designed specially to keep often unruly stallions in—the double fences were several feet higher than normal, for starters, with several other security features that discouraged her boys from trying to get out. Rogue slid to a stop just before he reached the inner fence, rearing up and whinnying.

She snorted. "Settle down, show-off."

The stallion snorted back, shaking his head. The second she opened the gate, he shoved his nose against her shoulder, demanding to be petted. She scratched behind his ears, and he nickered in appreciation. "Ah, now. That's my boy."

"He looks like my Grani," Erik noted. "Same color, anyway. Gray as stone."

Yes, and she hated to admit that she might have a soft spot for Rogue for just that reason. "Grani was a warhorse who died a millennium ago. Rogue here is a thoroughbred. He had a great racing career, and now I keep him for stud."

She clipped on the lead rope and then had no choice but to face her unwelcome guest.

Whoa. Her lips parted, surprise spurting through her. What a change. He was still enormously tall and built like a honed Viking warrior, a berserker who could conquer an army with one hand tied behind his back. It was his hair that caught her attention. Or rather, the lack thereof. He'd shaved his head, and the look was so different she blinked. She'd seen him once or twice over the last thousand plus years, never of her own will, but when Odin and Freya had summoned them at the same time, there was nothing Bryn could do about it.

This was the most dramatic change he'd ever made to his appearance. He'd always worn his hair long, no matter what the current fashion of the time dictated. His silver eyes, framed by absurdly long lashes, somehow seemed even more dramatic, more intense. Before this moment, she wouldn't have believed it possible.

That gaze pinned her in place like a bug under a microscope, and it took effort not to squirm. She wasn't used to that. Most men she met were like spoiled toddlers, and it had been years—maybe a decade—since one had interested her in doing anything other than yawn.

A decade. Shit, she might be regrowing her hymen at this rate.

And thinking about sex while staring at Erik was a mistake. She shook herself and glanced away. Somehow with the shaved head, it was easier to think of him as Erik instead of Siegfried. Though he was both now, wasn't he? Erik Siegfried. The new name suited him.

"Why are you still here?" She brushed passed him—careful not to make actual contact—and led Rogue to the smaller stallion barn.

"Are you serious?" he asked, incredulousness dripping from the question. "You've seen the signs, Brynhil—Bryn. You have to know what they mean."

Hurricanes, earthquakes, winters that were far too short, summers that burned far too hot. Mortals thought it was climate change, but a valkyrie could sense the difference. Signs of the end times. The Vikings called it *Ragnarök*—the Twilight of the Gods—but it had been given many names by many cultures. Armageddon, eschaton, apocalypse, Satya Yuga, the appearance of Maitreya. It was all the same as far as she was concerned—a prophesized final chapter before a supposed golden era began.

She shrugged as she finished putting Rogue away, and then she turned to Erik. "Ah, but you're the dragon-slayer who's supposed to kill the baddies who want to take over the world. I suggest you quit bothering me and get to it."

His smile was sharp and unamused. "Trust me, I'd like nothing more than to kill the baddies, preferably before they do the kind of damage that will land us in *Ragnarök*. Unfortunately, I need a shieldmaiden's help."

"I'm not the only one left." Though, it had been a century or two since she'd been in contact with any other valkyrie. Freya hadn't summoned her in a long time, and Bryn was just fine with that. She had her farm, her horses, and a quiet existence she enjoyed. "Go pester someone else."

"Damn it, Bryn." He scrubbed a hand over his head, looking as if he'd like nothing more than to throttle her. Interesting. He'd always been so obnoxiously calm and patient back in the day.

It annoyed the shit out of her that she liked this less stoic side of him. She widened her eyes innocently. "What?"

"I need your help." He spread his hands in a gesture of helpless frustration, his brows snapping together.

"No." There. Simple, easy. An idiot should get that message through his thick skull.

The growl he emitted was more wolf than man, reminding her that berserkers could shift forms as easily as valkyries. Again, that less civil side of him was...too alluring, too tempting, tugging at something deep within her. Something she'd rather crush under her boot.

Executing a quick about-face, she headed across the stable yard to the tidy two-story Colonial she called home. He stayed hot on her heels, of course. The persistent bastard. "Why *me*, Erik?"

He shoved his way through her back door, refusing to let her slam it in his face. Yeah, she could have gotten into a wrestling match with him, but they both had superhuman strength and it would have just resulted in the door being reduced to splinters. Plus, it wouldn't keep him out. The only way to get him to leave was to *convince* him to go. Diplomacy had never been her strong suit, so this was going to be such fun.

He snapped, "Why you? Because a *völva* came to talk to me."

"There's a sentence that strikes fear into the most stalwart heart," she drawled as she stomped over to the fridge and yanked it open. Despite the mockery in her tone, *völva* were no laughing matter. Prophetesses, witches, and power-hungry bitches all rolled into one nasty package. The few times Bryn had had to deal with them only made her loath to repeat the experience.

"I've never sought the company of a *völva*, no. They're not my favorite kind of women. But not listening to them is a stupid idea, so I listened, and here I am." When she didn't respond at all, he let out a breath. "You haven't changed a bit. Stubborn as a mule. More beautiful than the sun and the moon. Damn it."

Glancing back, she saw him staring at her ass. The breath seized in her lungs. His eyes had burned to molten quicksilver, lust stamped clearly on the harsh angles of his face, and heated awareness flashed through her. There was no controlling her response to him, a lightning-strike of utter craving. Her nipples tightened, goose bumps shivered over her flesh, and her pussy fisted on emptiness. She straightened but couldn't make herself confront that burning need, so she pulled open the freezer as if she had some interest in the contents. The wash of frigid air hit her overheated cheeks.

"Did the *völva* specifically say I was the shieldmaiden you had to come to?" She'd kept up her weapons abilities, adding martial arts and firearms to her repertoire as they'd been introduced to Western culture. She was a valkyrie, which meant knowing how to fight was part and parcel of her existence. That didn't mean she wanted anything to do with whatever he had in mind.

A long beat of silence passed. "No, she didn't specify."

"Alrighty, then." She closed the freezer, turned around, and flipped her long braid over her shoulder. "It's been *great* catching up. Bye, now."

"Sorry, sweetness. That's not going to happen." Shaking his head slowly, a smile kicked up one corner of his lips. He had a deep dimple in his right cheek. Gods, how had she forgotten that?

Then what he'd said hit her. Sweetness? Where the hell had that nickname come from? She scowled. "You can save the world without me. I'm not interested."

Two strides took him across the kitchen, blocking her avenues of escape. She could always shift to her raven form and take flight, but she refused to run or cower. The refrigerator's door handle bit into her back as she glared up at him.

He bent forward until his lips almost brushed hers. Anticipation flowed like white-hot lava through her veins. His scent hit her, musky and masculine—no need for any kind of cologne. He smelled exactly the way she'd always thought a man should smell. Need throbbed within her, and her pussy was soaking wet in seconds, the muscles in her thighs trembling. His body heat surrounded her, seeping into her. He was all muscle and sinew and tempting hard angles. She licked her lips and clenched her fists at her sides to keep from reaching for him. Her mind warred with her body, and she wasn't entirely sure which would win.

When he spoke, his breath whispered over her skin. "You're not interested, Bryn? Are you sure about that?"

"There are different kinds of interest." She was ridiculously proud of herself for managing an even tone.

He displayed that dimple in a blatantly unfair move. "I want *all* of your interest."

"Too bad." Because her slutty little long-dormant hormones were all for whatever he wanted, but the tiny scrap of rationality she possessed had zero interest in any trouble he'd bring to her doorstep.

"Mmm." His gaze searched her face, looking for gods-knew-what. "Well, let's start here and worry about the rest later."

"Wha—"

His mouth cut off her question.

A jolt of shock went through her, and it took a split-second for her brain to catch up to what was going on. That kind of delayed reaction would have gotten her killed on the battlefield. But then he shoved his tongue between her lips, and her thoughts scattered. The flavor of him flooded her taste buds, coffee and sugar and something uniquely *him*. She couldn't prevent a moan as utter unstoppable want licked through her. He shifted them to the left, so she was trapped between his fiery heat and the icy metal of the fridge door. His big body settled against hers, every hard angle fitting against her softer curves. He pinned her in place, not giving her a chance to think or escape. He forced her to *feel*, and fear fluttered through her at the realization. One of his hands closed over her breast and twisted her nipple. Hard. A needy, greedy sound wrenched from her throat.

He wedged his other hand between them, popping open the button on her riding breeches. The fabric had just enough stretch for him to delve in without pushing her pants down. His fingers edged under her panties and slipped into her curls. Her torso arched against him—in encouragement or protest, even she didn't know. He stroked over her slit, toying with her slick lips. Her breathing turned to ragged gasps, her heart pounding so loudly all she could hear was the rush of blood in her ears.

Two thick fingers pierced her in a swift thrust that had her rising on tiptoe and bunching her fists in his T-shirt. The heel of his hand ground into her clit, making her shudder.

Oh, gods. Oh. Gods.

No one, but no one, had ever gotten to her as fast as he had. It was madness. He kissed his way along her jaw and down to her ear, nipping at the lobe. Then he unerringly found and scraped his teeth over a hot spot just under her ear that always lit her up like a firecracker. *How* had he remembered that? Continuing to tease her nipple, he twisted with just enough pressure to send streaks of pleasured pain zinging through her. Sensation swamped her, left her senses reeling. Her sex clenched, orgasm building high and hot within her. Her hips moved with his hand, low groans pouring from her mouth into his. *More.* She needed more; her body demanded the surcease he was offering.

He pressed down on her clit, curled his fingers inside her until he hit her G-spot, and pinched her nipple. It was more than enough to send her flying. Her entire body froze, and then her pussy pulsed in rhythmic waves around his thrusting digits. Fiery bliss exploded within her, and tingles skipped down her limbs. She threw her head back against the fridge, crying out with completion right there in the middle of her kitchen. But even as ecstasy ripped through her, she wondered what the fuck she was doing. This was insane. Her hands were still balled in his shirt, so she hooked a foot behind his ankle and shoved hard.

With a grunted curse, he landed on his ass, sprawling across her scuffed wooden floor. For a moment, utter shock flickered across his expression. Then he leaned back on his palms and chuckled, the sound rich and rough at the same time. "Yeah, I deserved that. Totally worth it though."

Ah, shit. Sanity was overrated. Really, it was the laugh that did her in. That, and the dimple.

She jumped him.

2

Odin's blood, she was fucking gorgeous.

Bryn came down on top of Erik, her long legs straddling his hips. She was a tall woman, a warrior, built with lean, graceful lines. Her breasts were small and pert, and an active lifestyle made her ass a work of art. He'd wanted to get his hands on it from the moment he'd seen her bending over in the stable—one look and lust had hit him like a punch to the gut. Stupid, foolish, but there it was. He hadn't meant to touch her, but he'd been unable to resist temptation. Which had always been his problem with her, hadn't it?

He cupped his hands around the firm globes of her backside, groaning at how good she felt, how being near her fired his blood. But she wasn't into savoring the reunion. She jerked his T-shirt out of his pants, and he had to release her buttocks to let her get the shirt over his head. Though he couldn't complain at having her hands on his chest, stroking his skin, tweaking his nipples. Gods, yes. His cock jerked, chafing painfully against his fly. He needed to be inside her, thrusting into her tight, silken depths. No matter how many years had passed, he'd never found anything that felt as good as being inside her. It was a truth he'd never admit aloud, not with how badly they'd betrayed each other, but he'd made his peace with the past long ago. He doubted she could say the same, considering the lack of welcome he'd gotten.

Too bad, but dealing with the past was a problem for later.

A braid held back her magnificent white-blond hair, and it tumbled over her shoulder to brush his chin. He remembered the feel of her locks flowing through his fingers like water. Slipping the tie off the end, he unwound the plait and let her hair fall into his face. Perfect, the slight tickle somehow erotic. The pale locks formed a curtain that contrasted with the pure black of her eyes, so dark it was difficult to tell where her iris stopped and her pupil started. There was something about those uncanny eyes that pierced a man straight to his soul.

"Too many clothes." She yanked his belt open and unzipped his jeans. He lifted his hips so she could pull his pants and underwear down to his ankles. His shoes were next, and he let her struggle with getting everything off him.

Normally, he'd be more aggressive, but there was something undeniably arousing about watching Bryn strip him. His cock was an iron bar, pulsing with need only she could quench. He'd almost forgotten how *good* it was to have her fingers dancing across his flesh. Or maybe he'd just tried to put it out of his mind so the knowledge that he couldn't have her wouldn't drive him mad. She grasped his cock, stroking it from base to crown. He jerked in reaction to her touch, and sweat beaded on his forehead. Hers had never been the delicate hands of a pampered lady, but she was still all woman—soft and strong at the same time. He liked that.

He felt his wolf fangs slide down and claws tipped his fingers, and for once he didn't need worry about his lover seeing them. Bryn wasn't a normal human. For good or ill, she knew exactly who and what he was. He ran the razor-edge of a talon along the neckline of her shirt. "I want you naked too."

"Oh, really?" She cocked her head, the movement bird-like, reminding him of her raven side.

He realized that he'd never seen her in her bird form. That would probably change soon. Because, whether she liked it or not, their fates were tied together for the foreseeable future. The prospect seemed a lot less painful with her perched over him, her cheeks flush, her eyes glazed with lust.

She swirled a fingertip around the head of his dick. "I never would have guessed you were interested in me being nude."

He rocked his pelvis upward, panting for breath. "I know I'm subtle, but you're a perceptive woman."

"Subtle, yeah." Her eyebrows arched, and she nodded sagely. "Right."

Slipping the buttons free on her shirt, she let the fabric slide off her shoulders to pool behind her. Her bra quickly followed, and a growl soughed from his throat. Her rosy brown nipples were puckered, begging to be sucked. He reached for her, but she shook her head and rose to her feet. She untied her ankle boots and toed out of them. Then she peeled off her tight breeches, baring her impossibly long legs. Ah, gods, he wanted those legs cinched around his waist while he fucked her.

The scent of her arousal was a heady aphrodisiac, curling into his nostrils. It did nothing for his control that she stared openly at his cock. A bead of precum slipped down the length of his erection. When she licked her lips, his restraint broke. He was on her in a split-second, dragging her to the floor. As soon as she was down, she bucked and flipped him onto his back. He had no problem with that, because every naked curve of her pressed against him.

Finally.

He grasped her hips, yanking her down on his dick. A little sound of surprise from her was cut short by a deep moan. Her head fell back, and her nails dug into his shoulders as he sank into her with one swift plunge. The fit was so hot and slick and tight, he thought his skull might explode.

"Bryn...*gods.*"

He felt the prick of her talons, sharp as a raven's claws, and he could see the bird rippling just below the surface of her skin. He loved that she had to fight the beast within herself just as he had to. The sting of pain just underscored the pleasure rocketing through him, and he couldn't hold back an animalistic sound of ecstasy. She pressed forward, taking him deep, grinding her clit downward.

Sweat slipped down their skin in slow beads, gluing them together. She rode him hard, and the slap of their flesh echoed in the room. Their gasps and groans, the creak of the floorboards beneath them...it was a symphony of sheer carnality. He rocked upward to meet her every movement, his muscles burning as the speed and force increased. As ever, they pushed each other to their limits, shoving past all possible boundaries.

He gripped her firm ass tight enough to bruise as he worked her on his cock. Then a wicked thought wisped through his mind, and he grinned. He eased his fingers inward, teasing the pucker of her anus. Her breath caught, those dark eyes going wide. Then he pierced her ass with two fingers, stretching her passage. Her breathing became even more ragged, and the scent of her desire amplified. His cock throbbed, and it was all he could do not to come then and there.

He shoved his fingers into her ass in tandem with their thrusts, and low cries wrenched from her throat. Her head fell back, and he couldn't resist leaning forward to nip and suck the length of her neck. The flavor of her was salty sweat and sweet woman. It added to his excitement. Little shivers ran through her, and he could sense how close she was to orgasm. Still not close enough for him. The feel of her sex clenching around his cock each time he penetrated her was just too much.

Wrapping his free arm around her waist, he used it to pull her down to the base of his cock, going deeper than he had before. He scraped his fangs across the sensitive area under her ear, slammed his fingers into her ass, and knew the moment her control broke. She screamed, her body bowing in his embrace. Her inner muscles milked his dick and—thank all the gods—he could loosen his tenuous hold on his own restraint.

Come jetted from his cock, filling her. He groaned, long and loud, shudders wracking his body. Continuing to stroke into her with his hand and dick, he dragged out both of their pleasure as long as possible. This was far too good to end too quickly. Another climax shook through her, and he couldn't help the satisfaction he felt at having pleasured her so well. She finally collapsed against him, spent. He sucked in air, struggling to get enough oxygen.

Resting his forehead against her chest, he slowly came down from the high. "Awesome."

"Mmm-hmm." Her voice was vague, and her fingers idly stroked the back of his neck.

While she was still soft and languid, he lifted her off of his cock, gathered her close, and rose to his feet. He'd rather not give her the opportunity to recall she didn't want him there. Perhaps it was underhanded, but he had a planet to save.

He needed her.

Maybe on more levels than he could admit, but right now he had to focus on stopping the apocalypse. Everything else would have to wait.

But first he had to convince her that hiding out in rural Virginia wasn't the best way to deal with what was coming. He mounted the stairs, and a quick look around at the top revealed her bedroom easily enough. Turning right, he strode to the end of the hall, deposited her on the rumpled bed, and climbed in beside her.

"What time will your farmhands be back?" He'd seen the two men leave in a rickety pickup, just before he'd pulled into her long gravel driveway. He hadn't caught the scent of anyone else on her property.

She stirred, but didn't bother to open her eyes. "Not until Sunday night. They're brothers, and I gave them the weekend off to go celebrate their mom's birthday in DC."

"Nice boss."

"Tough, but *reasonable* boss," she corrected, meeting his gaze. "No sane person would ever call me nice."

And he would be the one to know that, wouldn't he? Considering she'd told her jealous husband how Erik could be killed. He'd slain a dragon as a young mortal, the blood coating him and making him indestructible—except the one spot on his shoulder where a leaf had gotten stuck. Which meant he'd *had* to be stabbed in the back in order to die, so there was a certain irony to how she'd betrayed him.

Then again, her husband had had every right to be enraged. Erik's behavior had been less than honorable, toward Bryn and her husband both. He'd earned his ignominious death, but then she'd killed his son as well. Sigmund had been just three years old, a baby. That, Erik had never been able to forgive. Though he'd never asked her *why* she'd done it either, had he? As hard as it was to be fair about something like that, even a millennium later, he knew better than anyone that the myths surrounding their relationship were loaded with half-truths and ugly speculation.

"Maybe I'm not sane." He propped himself up on an elbow. "Because you were pretty damn nice a few minutes ago."

"Ha." She rolled her eyes. "I'm going to be not nice pretty soon here."

"Kicking me out?" He cocked a brow.

She sat up, pushing her hair over her shoulder. "This was a bad idea, you have to admit."

"Nope, not admitting anything." He stayed where he was, keeping his pose relaxed. "But I also didn't think we were quite done."

Pulling her knees to her chest, she wrapped her arms around them. "We were done a long time ago, Erik. This was just...chemistry."

"True, but if the chemistry is this good, why stop after only one round?"

"Because you're not here for a simple shagfest." Her sharp gaze speared him. "This is just your way of trying to wear me down."

The smile he gave her was unabashed. "Guilty."

"It won't work." She sighed. "I'm too damn old to be that stupid."

"There is that." He rolled to his back, folding his hands behind his head. "We're both fucking ancient."

A ghost of a grin crossed her lips. She'd never been much for smiling or laughing, so he'd treasured every time he'd gotten her to lighten up. He doubted the years had made her less somber.

"So, what?" He stared at the carved casing above her window as if it fascinated him. "You're assuming the prophecy is right, and somehow I'll kill a bunch of powerful giants and survive *Ragnarök?* You think I won't need any help?"

Her chin rested on her knees. "The gods are supposed to stand alongside you."

"When's the last time you saw one? A god *or* a goddess?" He reached up and tugged at the small rune stone that hung around his neck. It marked him as one who served Odin, and Bryn wore a similar stone that marked her affiliation with the goddess Freya. The stone was supposed to be a way he could call on the god, if needed. Of course, gods and goddesses only answered if they felt like it. Odin hadn't answered the last few times Erik had called. He'd once been the god's right-hand man, a confidant and advisor as much as a warrior. Odin liked his berserkers to walk the world every now and then, living as mortals did, but he always brought them back to Valhalla after a couple of decades. Until now. Erik had been mostly left to his own devices since the end of the nineteenth century, and what little contact he'd had with Odin had tapered off to nothing in recent years. It was more than a little troubling.

Bryn licked her lips. "I haven't tried to get in touch with Freya in ages, nor she me. I haven't spent much time in the gods' realm for...maybe eight or nine *centuries* now. I prefer staying away from Asgard, and she knows it."

"No one has been to Asgard, not for years," he countered. "I've tracked down a few berserkers, and not a single one of them has had any contact with the gods. Odin, Thor, Frey, Tyr, Heimdall—none of those who are prophesied to die during *Ragnarök*."

"There are few who believe in our gods anymore. Maybe they've retreated to Odin's hall to enjoy their eternal retirement. Valhalla can hold one hell of a party." The forced note of hope and cheer in her tone made Erik give her a skeptical look.

"Really, Bryn? That's the argument you're going to go with?"

"Shit, I don't know." She forked her fingers through her hair. "How do you know they're not doing the same thing we are and just hanging out with humans?"

"You think they could resist the urge to meddle enough to *hide?*"

She inclined her head to concede the point. "Laying low was never their strong suit, true, but you shouldn't make assumptions with no evidence. If you're not a god or goddess, you can't go to Asgard unless called. You don't know what's going on there, which means they could all be just fine."

"Or they could all be dead, picked off one by one to change the prophecy." Unlike many of the other deities humans believed in, Viking gods weren't all-knowing, all-powerful, or invincible. Those omniscient gods might also exist; he had no way of knowing for certain, he just knew he'd never met one face-to-face. Viking gods and goddesses, though? He'd met most of them, liked a few of them, and shagged several more. Goddesses, that was. He hadn't lived so long that he was off females. Some immortals got bored enough to swing both ways. More power to them, just not his style.

"If you're against the gods, why change the prophecy?" Bryn's blond brows drew together, but at least she was listening. "The major deities are *supposed* to die."

"And take the monsters with them—the great dragon Jörmungandr, the giant wolf Fenrir. The giants of Jötunheim want to use those monsters to rule the realms of humans and gods. If the gods die early, there's nothing to stop them." He swallowed hard, voicing the awful truth that had been choking him since that *völva* had turned up on his doorstep. "There's no one to fight beside me."

"So you think this is a big conspiracy?" Doubt dripped from her words, and her dark eyes searched his face.

"I can't afford not to think that way, and one of the berserkers I found has collected some evidence that might convince even you." His friends weren't far behind him. He'd texted them the address once he'd confirmed that, yes, this was the woman they were looking for. Only then had he actually spoken to her. He was smart enough to know he'd need backup. Bryn never went down without a fight. "How can we not assume something might be wrong if *five* immortals haven't heard from the deities they serve in decades?"

"Berserkers serve Odin, valkyrie serve Freya. That's only two deities," she pointed out.

"The two who rule the halls of the valorous dead." He kept his tone as matter-of-fact as possible. Emotion was never going to convince her, just cold fact. "There's been lots of war in the human world during the last hundred plus years, and more than a few of the dead warriors would have had some Viking blood in their veins. You think that wouldn't have kept the valkyries busy, taking those fallen to Valhalla?"

Her gaze fell away. Ah, yes. She had no easy argument for that, did she? He almost wished she did. This wasn't something he enjoyed being right about. And he was pretty damn sure he was right.

"If the giants win during *Ragnarök*, the gods become their slaves and humans become their *food*. You've lived among mortals for a very long time, and you still care enough to let your farmhands off to celebrate something as trivial as a birthday. You can't tell me it doesn't bother you, especially since former humans like us are as likely to fall into the brunch category as we are to fall into the slave category. A pretty shieldmaiden like you? Oh, they'd have fun with you." He hissed in a breath and shook his head. "I'm not sure which would be worse—being eaten alive or being raped to death by a giant."

She swallowed hard. "Don't be an asshole."

"The truth isn't pretty, Bryn. You, of all people, should know that." Yes, he was being harsh, but the picture he painted was all too feasible, and the thought of such a fate befalling the woman beside him made bile flood his mouth. He couldn't stand by and just let that happen. Not ever. Deep down, he didn't think *she* could stand by either. It wasn't in her nature, no matter how idyllic her life was now.

"I..." She shook her head. "I need to go flying."

When she moved to rise, fear gripped his gut. If he let her go now, he might never be able to find her again. He felt like he'd spent an eternity trying to catch up to her, which was an unsettling thought. Snapping his fingers around her wrist, he hauled her back down to the mattress, rolled on top of her, and made sure she didn't think about going anywhere for a long, long while.

3

THE NEXT MORNING, BRYN snuck out of her own room, leaving Erik sleeping in her bed. Yeah, there wasn't much dignity in creeping out like a misbehaving teenager, but it was the only way she was going to escape him. She carried her clothes with her, dressed quickly in the hallway, and tiptoed barefoot down the stairs, making sure to skip the second step because it creaked.

Before she went anywhere, she had to feed her horses, so she headed straight for the back of the house. As much as she wanted to fly off into the sunset, her ponies were counting on her to make sure they didn't starve to death. If Erik and his Seer were wrong and the world didn't end, she still had to make a living, right? Not to mention she loved the four-legged beasties.

After she passed the door to the living room, she froze, backed up, and did a double take. There were three large men occupying her space. One guy was flipped upside down and leaning up against a wall. Another was sprawled across the couch and looked to be taking a nap. The last one was sitting at a small table, using it as a desk as he hunched over a laptop.

His brows were drawn in a heavy frown and there was something oddly familiar about him, but it was hard to tell with the harsh glow of his monitor casting shadows on his features and only the weak pre-dawn light coming through the window.

"I assume you're friends of Erik's?" Not a difficult guess considering the guy standing on his head had a rune stone necklace dangling around his chin.

Couch-boy opened one eye, and a thick New Orleans drawl that practically oozed chicory issued from his mouth. "Yep. We heard a party going on upstairs, and we figured cock-blocking y'all was just bad form. So we made ourselves at home."

"You're out of milk now, love." She looked down as Mr. Handstand started talking. This guy had a cute English accent. "Sorry about that. We'll send Holm out to fetch more later."

Since she had no idea which one was Holm, she just gestured at English and New Orleans. "Great. You can both get your feet off my sofa and wall."

English dropped lightly to the ground and New Orleans sat up, swinging his legs around. Once upon a time, she'd known all of the berserkers in Valhalla. But she'd been wandering the human world for a long time, unable to face the man who was still sleeping upstairs. She'd been consumed with pain and rage for so long. Luckily, Freya had been understanding and given Bryn her way, only calling her back in when she was needed for a specific task. Of course, if Erik was right, the goddess's prolonged silence might mean she was now dead or on the run from conspirators.

When nobody offered names, Bryn arched an eyebrow. "And you are?"

"Valbjorn Makan. Val." English held out a hand to shake. His grip was firm, but he didn't try to make it a pissing contest by crushing her fingers. "Pleased to meet you, Ms. Ravencrest."

New Orleans didn't stand up, just gave her a nod. "Holm Sutherland." He gestured to the last man. "And that's Ivar."

The man at the computer grabbed the sides of his seat, and that was when she realized he was in a wheelchair. He slid back and spun to face her. "Ivar the Boneless. You've heard of me, I presume?"

"Yeah. I've heard of you." Coldness tingled in her fingertips and she felt the blood leave her face in a sickening rush. Well, that explained why he looked vaguely familiar. He was her grandson. Hers and Erik's. With her platinum blond hair and his silver eyes, this man was a perfect cross between the two of them. She swallowed hard. "There's coffee and bagels in the kitchen. Help yourselves."

Spinning on a heel, she exited the room.

Ivar's deep baritone followed. "We fed your ponies for you—I found a list in the office of what to feed all of them. Holm drew the short straw and had to muck their stalls."

"Awesome. Thanks." She didn't pause, just walked to the kitchen, grabbed her ankle boots off the floor, and shoved her feet into them. Erik's and her discarded clothes from the night before were missing, but she didn't want to think about what might have happened to them. She didn't want to think about anything at all. Out the back door, she headed straight for the barn. Keeping her mind deliberately blank, she checked the horses, found them properly cared for. Good. Then she went into her office, opened a window, stripped naked, shifted into her raven form, and launched herself skyward. She had to get away from here.

Her past had truly come to roost.

4

"So, you didn't warn her I'd be showing up, huh? Real classy, Grandpa." Ivar hadn't even let Erik get all the way into the living room before the chastisement rang in his ears. Of course, he wasn't moving all that fast considering he had to keep a grip on the towel around his waist.

He closed his eyes, partially because of the grandpa crack, and partially because, yes, he probably should have mentioned to Bryn that one of the berserkers he'd run across was their daughter's son. They'd both been dead long before Ivar had been born, but that didn't mean Bryn wouldn't be sucker punched by their rather traumatic past when she met him. "Shit."

"Never seen anybody go so pale so fast unless they were actually bleeding out." Ivar crossed his arms over his muscular chest, narrowing eyes exactly like those that looked Erik in the mirror every morning. He should be used to it, but it was still unsettling.

"I get the picture," he said shortly. "I should have told her that her long-lost grandson would be stopping by."

Not that it wasn't strange to be staring at his grandson and have the man look almost exactly the same age that he did—forever in their late twenties. It made it impossible to really think of him as a grandson, so Ivar had become something of a...not brother-figure, but perhaps a beloved distant cousin.

Dropping the attitude, Ivar sighed. "You think me being here will make it easier or harder to get her on our side?"

"With Bryn?" Erik scrubbed his free hand over his shaved pate. "I have no fucking clue. If I could predict her, my mortal life would have ended a bit differently."

The other man spread his arms and shrugged. "Ah, but only those who die gloriously in battle get to hang out immortally ever after in Valhalla. Maybe she did you a favor."

Erik cocked an eyebrow. "Is that how you think about the person who did you in?"

"Nah, but I took him with me." Ivar grinned. "His God may have saved his soul, but Odin had my back, so I guess we're both good with our respective afterlives."

"Right." Erik rolled his eyes.

Holm piped up from where he lounged on the couch. "It sounded like you two had one hell of a reunion last night."

Yeah, like Erik wanted to share any details on that. Holm had a way of saying exactly the *wrong* thing in any situation. He spent his life with his foot in his mouth, which was probably why he preferred to hide away from other people in some backwater bayou in Louisiana. But he'd come to help when Erik had called, no questions asked. Erik appreciated the loyalty and vote of confidence, so he ignored the tactless comment and kept his focus on Ivar. "When did you guys get in?"

"A little after midnight," Ivar replied.

Erik had vaguely noticed their arrival some time during the night, but since he'd only smelled allies, he'd let them take care of themselves and glutted himself on the feel and scent and taste of Bryn. It might have been his last chance.

"Where is she?" The sweet aroma of her was fading, as if she'd come and gone.

"I saw a blackbird fly out of the big barn a little bit ago. I'm betting that was her," Ivar gestured at the open living room window, but he frowned at his laptop screen. The man was a gadget freak of the highest order. It was his research—aka hacking—that had made it possible to track down Bryn. She could have been anywhere in the world, living under any assumed identity, but Ivar had narrowed their possibilities down to a handful of women. They'd divided the list between them, and Erik had hit the jackpot.

"Yeah, that probably was her." A chilly morning breeze came through the window, and Erik shifted his hold on his towel. Frosty balls were not the way to start the day. Nor was waking up alone, abandoned by your companion.

Holm grinned at Erik's discomfort, which earned him a stony stare. "Think she'll be back? Or has she flown the coop for good?"

Refusing to admit he'd wondered the same thing when he'd leaped out of bed, Erik managed a casual shrug. "Her farmhands won't be back until tomorrow night. She wouldn't abandon her animals."

"Glad she has her priorities straight," Holm drawled.

The words were mild enough, but Erik felt his hackles rise anyway, wanting to defend her. He told himself to get a grip and moved toward the door. "I'm going for a run—I'll be back in an hour or so. Send up a flare if you need me sooner."

"Will do." Ivar gave a distracted wave, closing his laptop.

"Hang on."

Holm's voice made Erik turn back. "Yeah?"

The other man propped his elbows on the back of the couch. A shit-eating grin curved his lips. "Your clothes are in the dryer…you know, in case you were wondering. Val was nice enough to wash them for you."

"Tell him I said thanks." Where Val had taken himself off too, Erik didn't know. Somewhere close by, from the intensity of his scent.

Ivar tucked his computer into the backpack slung across the handles of his wheelchair. "I'm going for a drive. I dug something up that I think could help us. I'll be back whenever I'm back. You know how to reach me."

"Sure, fine. Whatever." Right now they were just hanging around waiting for the end times to show up, which was maddening and boring all at once. The *völva* had said it would be soon, but soon could be an hour from now or a week from now. Seers could be damn annoying when their visions didn't provide real details.

He'd found exercise helped burn off the frustration in the last couple of weeks while he'd tracked down Holm and Ivar, both of whom he'd kept in touch with over the past decade or so. Ivar had known Val since they were mortals, so that had added another member to their merry band of misfits, and then Ivar had managed to unearth Bryn's location. Still, weeks of uncertainty, not knowing when or even *if* he'd find the shieldmaiden before the apocalypse hit, had stretched his patience to the limit.

Discarding the towel on the kitchen counter, he shifted into his wolf form in the space between heartbeats, his body twisting and reshaping until he stood on all fours. Shaking from head to tail, he settled into the familiar form. He nosed out of the screen door and then shot off the porch at a dead run. He headed for the wide green path that cut between two pastures.

Every now and then, he caught Bryn's scent. A glance skyward didn't reveal a raven in flight, but he knew she was nearby.

The run let him think, and while he should be focusing on *Ragnarök* and saving the world, that tantalizing scent of Bryn kept his mind on her instead. Even when they'd first met, when he'd gone in search of her castle, she'd already been a legend. He'd just slayed a dragon and claimed the beast's treasure and its enchanted ring—Andvaranaut—which could turn anything into solid gold. He'd been told if he bathed in dragon's blood, he'd become indestructible, so he'd been cocksure and certain there was no prize beyond his reach.

He'd gone looking for further adventure and found Bryn. He remembered the first time he'd seen her, deep in an enchanted sleep, her tower surrounded by elemental fire. The castle had been little more than a myth then—one that said a man who knew no fear could pass through the fire and find a reward beyond riches within the stone walls. Many had tried and failed, but Erik had managed it. Looking back, he thought he'd been too young and stupid to know he should be afraid, but he'd found his greatest treasure nonetheless.

The moment her midnight eyes had opened and met his gaze, he'd known she'd own his soul forever. That was it for him. Done. No other woman would ever do.

Stretching his forelegs in front of him, Erik raced along the path as if pouring on more speed might help him escape the memories. The world became a blur of green grass and white fences, streaking past his vision. He came to the edge of Bryn's farm and bolted into the woods beyond.

But there was no way to outrun himself, was there?

After they'd met, they'd talked for hours, days. He'd regaled her with his victory over the dragon, and revealed his one vulnerability where the dragon's blood hadn't touched. Of course, he hadn't realized then that telling her meant he had *two* vulnerabilities.

She'd told him she was a valkyrie, and she'd displeased Odin by using her magical ability to choose the victor in battle to pick a man Odin didn't favor. As retribution, the god had made her a mortal woman, trapped her in the tower, and cast a sleeping spell on her, so that any man who desired her might claim her virginity. Knowing she'd be defenseless in sleep, just before she'd succumbed to the god's spell, she'd thrown out a ring of fire that would only let in a fearless man. If she was to be claimed by an unknown man, he should at least be brave enough to be worthy of her admiration.

Ah, Bryn. If only I'd remained worthy.

But, fool that he was, he'd craved more exploits and renown, so he'd given Bryn his ring as a token of his promise to return and asked her to wait for him. She'd agreed—not that he'd given her much choice.

More than once, he'd wanted to go back and slap the shit out of his younger self. He should have found the closest temple and married her immediately.

Instead, he gone to the royal court of Burgundy and offered his sword to King Gunnar's service. There was fame to be found in their ongoing wars, and his reputation as a dragon-slayer and daring feats in battle made him a respected advisor to the king in short time. Unfortunately, it also drew the unwanted attentions of the king's sister, Princess Gudrun. Erik had spurned her advances as gently as he could, but it was the king's mother, Grimhild, that proved his ultimate downfall. Grimhild was a powerful sorceress, a *völva*, and she wanted the riches he'd claimed from the dragon's horde to remain in her family. She concocted a vile potion that made him believe he was in love with Gudrun and wiped his mind of any other woman he'd ever met.

Erik had gone to Gunnar and begged for his sister's hand in marriage.

Erik had spoken of his beloved valkyrie one too many times before the spell kicked in, and Gunnar had decided he wanted the legendary beauty for his own. So he agreed to let Erik marry his sister if Erik helped him claim Brynhild. They'd gone to her castle, where she'd kept that wall of fire burning so that none but her brave love could approach.

Gunnar couldn't get through the flames—too weak and cowardly—though Erik hadn't acknowledged that at the time. He'd had only one focus then: marrying Gudrun. He'd thought he might die if he couldn't, known that he'd do *anything* to wed her. Everything else was irrelevant, crowded out by the single goal that possessed him.

So he'd passed through the fire in Gunnar's stead, promising that Bryn would remain untouched, and swearing that he'd give her one of Grimhild's potions to make her believe it was Gunnar who'd made it through the fire, not Erik.

The only thing he hadn't counted on was how the passion between Bryn and him would explode out of control. Even believing he loved someone else, Erik couldn't stop himself from touching her, taking her. Again and again and again. He'd never told Gunnar the truth of his actions, and hadn't known until much later that the night he'd spent in Bryn's bed had resulted in a child. Erik had always told himself that Aslaug was Gunnar's daughter.

The woman he'd loved became his sister-in-law instead of his wife. When the potions wore off, the irony of it had left bitterness coating his tongue every time he'd seen her. The ugly truth had spelled his doom. His and Bryn's and his young son's.

Erik shook his head, dragging himself back to the present day. He slowed to a stop and let his head fall forward, panting for breath. A glance around revealed a small clearing of sweet-smelling grass and wildflowers. Bryn certainly had chosen a beautiful patch of country for her retirement.

He wished he didn't have to drag her back into the fray, but he couldn't regret that circumstances had pushed them into contact again. No matter how love-hate their relationship had become, there was a part of his soul that would always belong to her. He'd tried for centuries to excise that treacherous part of himself, but he'd never succeeded.

Somehow that didn't seem so bad now.

A shadow passed over the meadow, and when he looked up he saw her. His raven, his shieldmaiden, his Bryn. She swept past, headed in the direction of home. A growl rumbled in his chest, anticipation and longing tangling inside him, for once defeating the bitterness of the past. There was much they still had to hash out, and he thought he'd start with the issue of her ditching him in bed this morning. Talking about bed might land them back there, and that was just fine with him. Being near her had made the future more inviting than ever before.

He rose to his feet, running back to her.

5

THE WIND RUFFLED OVER Bryn's feathers and she banked into an easy turn, descending in slow circles toward the long stretch of her main barn. She swooped under the roof into the wide aisle, shifted midair and landed neatly on her feet. Combing her fingers through her hair, she tried to straighten it into some semblance of order.

A low growl made her stiffen and turn, prey before a predator. The massive wolf prowled inside the barn, and a few anxious whinnies echoed from the stalls. Even though it could have been any of the berserkers, she knew down to her bones this wolf was Erik. It was unsettling to realize how attuned to him she was after less than a day in his company.

She cleared her throat. "You're scaring my horses. Knock it off."

His body twisted, fur retracting, and then Erik stood before her. Their eyes met, and something electric passed between them. She'd swear the air crackled around them. A breath shuddered into her lungs, fire ripped through her body, and her pussy went slick and hot, clenching on emptiness.

He stared at her, his gaze raking over every single inch of her. By the gods, he could rev her up with a simple glance. This was bad. Terrible. He was naked, she was naked, and they were alone. Not only was he naked, but he was hugely, flagrantly aroused. So was she, but at least her body could hide it better.

Then his nostrils flared, and she knew he could smell her readiness. A reminder that this wasn't a normal man. This was an immortal, a berserker, half-wolf, and he had abilities no human could claim.

Then again, even when he'd been a mortal man, he'd been able to strip her of all defenses with a single look.

His eyes narrowed, and that was when she realized he was irritated. "For the record, I didn't enjoy waking up alone."

"I had work to do." She lifted a brow.

The look he gave her chastised her for the lie, but his tone was deceptively mild when he spoke. "You could have woken me. I would have helped."

"Maybe I don't want your help any more than I want to offer you my help. Too many strings attached."

Dropping his gaze to her breasts, lower, to the juncture of her thighs, he licked his lips. She shivered, recalling his mouth on her flesh the night before. He took a step toward her, and she had to muster every ounce of self-discipline to stand her ground. Her heart hammered, but not from fear. Anticipation sang through her.

"If this isn't what you want, say no," he ordered, but the expression on his face dared her not to.

She couldn't have even if she wanted to, even if she could have resisted such a blatant challenge. Lust speared her, the need more intense than any other lover had ever managed to make her feel. That made her uneasy, but it didn't stop the throb of want that passed through her. Her nipples tightened, her pussy contracted, some muscles within her loosening, others tightening as her body readied itself for sex. Good sex. The most amazing sex of her entire existence. She'd wanted to tell herself she was just romanticizing the memories, but the sizzle of chemistry the moment she'd seen him again made a lie of that.

She lifted her chin, staring him down as she gestured to their surroundings. "I'm not interested in concrete road rash, splinters, or getting hay wedged up my ass."

Which left very few options for getting it on.

With his head tilted, his eyebrows drew together in consideration. Without saying another word, he wrapped an arm around her waist and dragged her forward until his back was against the wall and she was plastered to his front. Cupping her hips, he lifted her so her legs naturally wrapped around his trim waist. She gripped his shoulders and held on tight.

Her breath caught at the feel of his skin against hers. He was rough satin, all hot skin and crisp curls that abraded her nipples.

"Kiss me," he demanded.

Instead of obeying, she tightened her legs and lifted herself, then took his cock deep in one swift downward plunge, letting gravity impale her on his thick shaft. Years of riding horses had given her some amazing leg and ab muscles, and she put them to good use now. She shimmied upward, then dropped down, letting him stretch her, fill her to the limit. He was so big, it would have been painful to take him if she hadn't been so wet. They both moaned, and she felt raven's claws tip her fingers, digging into his flesh. His fangs flashed as he smiled, and then his grip became bruising as he helped gravity along.

Their skin slapped with every plunge, and sweat made their flesh glide together. Their gasps and groans echoed down the long aisle, and she knew any of his friends could walk in at any moment, that they were basically fucking in public, but she was beyond caring. Everything about this—him—was just a little forbidden, and that made it so much sexier. Her thighs burned with the strain of riding him, but she couldn't stop, had to have that carnal surcease.

He shifted his grip, banding an arm under her ass, and then one hand came up to tunnel into her hair. He jerked her forward so he could claim the kiss he'd wanted. His tongue filled her mouth, and their lips melded. She felt the scrape of his fangs against her flesh, and excitement poured through her. The wildness in him called to the wildness in her, and her talons curled into his shoulders, raking down his arms. He groaned into her mouth, settled his shoulders more solidly so he could push his hips further from the wall. Then he pistoned into her harder, faster, their movements growing rougher.

She kept up with him, taking him deeper, loving the thrill of it, the feral edge to their coupling. Heat roared high within her. She was so close to exploding, she could taste it. She threw her head back, a low cry breaking free, the sound *almost* a raven's call.

"Come *now*, Bryn," he ordered.

He swatted her ass, and the sting sent her jolting forward. His dick slammed so deep, pinpricks of light burst behind her lids, and she tumbled over into orgasm. Her channel clamped down on his cock, pulsing in rhythmic waves. Goose bumps broke down her limbs, and each of his thrusts pushed her to another peak. It was almost more than she could take; she could only hang on and experience the overwhelming rush.

He shoved into her pussy one, two, three more times, and then he shuddered against her, flooding her with hot fluids. Their lungs heaved for breath, and that was the only noise that broke the silence. Even the horses seemed to have gone still. He let his head fall back against the barn wall, but he didn't loosen his hold on her. "Bryn, I—"

Whatever he was going to say was lost as they both noticed the sound of approaching footsteps. Deliberately loud footsteps, she thought, and then Val called, "Uh...Erik? Bryn? Ivar rang me, and he said he's got some news for us. Looks as if the end is nigh. Though if I was doing what you're doing, I couldn't be arsed about it either."

He didn't come around the corner of the barn, so he couldn't get an eyeful of her buck-naked ass. Maybe she should be embarrassed to be called out twice in as many hours for banging Erik. But she was too old to regret good sex—she knew firsthand that a shag this good didn't come around very often. Should she be fucking her former whatever-the-hell-he-was? Probably not, but the world was ending, so who cared? She might as well get some play before it all went to pot.

Erik closed his eyes. "How urgent is it?"

A pause, then Val answered, "He should be pulling up to the house right about now. Yes, there, you can hear his van. I'd wager you have maybe five minutes before he comes looking for you, mate. But he's impatient like that, so no telling how big the emergency actually is. He didn't say much over the phone."

"We'll be there in five minutes, then," Erik replied.

"Cheers." And then the other man left much more silently than he'd approached.

Bryn unhooked her legs and dropped to the floor, biting back a moan as his cock slid free. She headed for her office and the clothes she'd left there. Erik followed her, tracking her like a convict who might escape. That didn't annoy her at all. Nope. Not her. "You can go back without me, Erik. I don't need an escort."

"You're getting one anyway, so I can make sure you don't fly off into the sunset and disappear." He crossed his arms, making his sculpted biceps bulge.

She reared back, and she went from annoyed to pissed off in under two seconds. "Oh, that's nice. Your pillow talk blows, for the record. Should I remind you that you're trespassing on *my land* right now? I could have your ass tossed in jail. Wouldn't that throw a wrench in your plans to save the world, trying to talk the humans into letting you go without revealing any of your superhuman powers?"

"I'm not even going to dignify that with a response. The bottom line is you're involved in this whether you like it or not. You don't really have a choice, you know." His tone was less than civil, flashing that new edginess. In the old days, he'd only ever lost his cool in bed and in the intense heat of battle when his berserker side came out to play.

"Yeah, and fuck you very much for pointing that out." She thrust both hands into her hair, wrenching the tangled locks into a braid, and yanked a hair tie out of her desk drawer to fasten the plait. Then she stuffed herself into her clothes and shoved her feet into her boots, not bothering to lace them as she stomped toward the back porch.

"This isn't my fault," he barked.

"You could have found another shieldmaiden," she snapped, silently enjoying the fact that he winced as his bare foot hit a sharp stone in the yard. "Tangling with you has never served me well, Siegfried. It ends in lies, betrayal, and death."

"Erik." He folded his arms and jutted his chin, like this was an essential point to make.

She went in the screen door and let it spring closed behind her. Yep, it was petty, but good lay or not, the asshole had brought the apocalypse to her tranquil safe haven. She had no reason to be nice. "I note you didn't address the actually *important* part of what I said, but Siegfried is your surname now, right?"

"From you, I prefer Erik." He opened the screen, a dark scowl on his face. "We both know you don't mean my last name when you say Siegfried."

She grunted. Yeah, there was a lot of history tied up in their names. A lot of history that tripped over legends that were only half-truths. It was one reason why she went by Bryn instead of Brynhild. She didn't really want to be reminded of who she used to be. Of course, him being here did nothing *but* remind her.

6

The woman was fucking impossible.

Erik wanted to strangle Bryn half of the time. He'd commanded *armies* of men, and he couldn't keep one damn woman in line. Typical. He ran a hand down his face. Of course, that was part of her appeal, wasn't it? So many women cowered before a man as dangerous as him, but not Bryn. No, not her. She was every bit as dangerous, and he liked that far more than he should. There was a praying mantis appeal to fucking a warrior woman—you might die in the process, but it'd be the ride of your life.

He grabbed his recently discarded towel, wrapped it around his waist, and strode behind her into the living room, glaring at the back of her head. She paused in the doorway, blocking his path unless he wanted to bowl her over or walk around her. He walked around her because tripping her was a little too juvenile. Though still tempting. Holm and Ivar were waiting for them, but he had no idea where Val had gotten off to.

"There's an emergency?" she asked.

"Not an emergency, per se," Ivar answered. "I found someone who has news *and* will be able to help us."

Bryn's eyebrows lifted and she stated the obvious. "I don't see anyone else. Also, Holm, get your feet *off* my coffee table."

Dropping his heels to the floor, Holm offered her a charming smile and drawled, "Yes, ma'am."

Ivar met Erik's gaze and shrugged. "You said you needed a shieldmaiden, and I thought, why not look for more than one? So I did some homework, and I found something almost as good."

"Almost, but not quite," came a dry tone from the doorway. Erik closed his eyes and didn't bother to turn around to greet the new female. He'd already caught her scent, so he knew exactly what Ivar had found.

This was going to go *so* well.

The woman gave both him and Bryn a wide berth as she went to stand beside Ivar. She pushed up a pair of sunglasses and set them on the top of her head. She was of medium height, had medium-brown hair and medium-brown eyes, and wore a shapeless dress.

Holm nodded a greeting. "And you are?"

"Nauma." While she was just passably pretty, her voice was low and throaty and well-suited to a phone sex operator.

Arms crossed over his chest, Holm's brows rose as he repeated, "And you are?"

A brief smile fluttered at the corners of her lips. "A handmaiden. Freya's handmaiden. Once mortal, but I was...promoted, I guess. More of a pity promotion, really, but there it is. Or, here I am, rather."

He shook his head.

"I know," Ivar sighed. "She talks a lot."

Holm shot him a glance from the corner of his eyes. "Talking a lot is fine, as long as it makes sense."

"I am a handmaiden of Freya." Her words were slow and measured and *just* this side of insulting. How she managed that, Erik wasn't sure.

"Well, another immortal is a good thing," Ivar assured her. "We need all the help we can get. Thanks for hopping on a plane when I called."

"Not sure how much help I can be." She shook her head. "Don't expect much in the way of brawn because weapons are not in my repertoire."

Ivar grinned broadly, slapping a hand against the arm of his chair. "Brains trump brawn any day, sweetheart."

"Nauma?" Val came into the room, looking as if he'd been poleaxed. "I thought I smelled...so I tracked the scent." He blinked. Rubbed his eyes. Blinked again. "You're alive."

Her face went pasty white, her hands clasping and unclasping in front of her. "Hello, Valbjorn."

He shook his head. "I…You…*How?*"

"Freya's got a soft spot for pathetic saps who die for love." Her shoulder jerked in a shrug. "She made me a handmaiden. Because there's no way I'd ever go valkyrie."

"I see." But it was clear he didn't.

The silence stretched into something awkward. Since neither Ivar nor Nauma had bothered to mention it, Erik broke in with, "Ivar, you brought a *völva* here."

Ivar frowned. "She's a handmaiden."

"She's both, actually." Nauma managed a knife-thin smile. "Just to stop any debate on the subject."

"You told me you weren't like your mother." Val scowled, his eyes narrowing.

"I didn't know." She smoothed a crease in her dress. "The first time I had a vision was the day I died. Even then, I didn't fully realize the extent of my abilities until after I was a handmaiden. Freya found my visions useful, so…it kept me in favor."

"How did you know she was a *völva*, Erik?" Bryn spoke for the first time since the other woman had walked in. Her tone was measured, like the calm before a storm. Bryn hated *völva*. He didn't like them much himself, considering they'd both ended up with the same spiteful, avaricious witch for a mother-in-law after she'd drugged them into marrying her son and daughter.

He kept his answer short and to the point. "This is the *völva* who told me I needed the help of a shieldmaiden."

Bryn bared her teeth at the handmaiden in a terrifying rendition of a smile. "So, you're the one I can blame for him showing up on my doorstep? Or rather, for this entire pack of berserkers invading my home?"

A quiver ran through the smaller woman, but she didn't turn tail and run the way any sane person would—then again, she *was* a Seer. They weren't quite right. She lifted her chin. "Planning to kill the messenger? I can't change what I am, even if you don't care for my kind. The important part is that I'm here and *I'm* willing to help. Can you say the same?"

Bryn snorted. "If you're so eager to help, why didn't you just come with Erik in the first place?"

"Visions don't give every little detail. I knew I had to track Erik down and tell him what he needed to do." The *völva* spread her hands. "I didn't know I'd be further involved until Ivar's phone call."

"It also seems you didn't know Val would be along for the ride," Erik observed.

"My visions of my own future are usually incomplete and annoyingly unhelpful." Her lips twisted in an ironic grin. "The curse of being a Seer is we're rather short-sighted when it comes to ourselves."

"That's tragic." Bryn rolled her eyes. Yep, no love for *völva*. This little surprise probably pissed her off even more than springing Ivar on her. She planted her hands on her hips. "I take it you've all decided there's going to be a sleepover at my house?"

"We can camp outside, if you like," Ivar offered with a winning smile. A smile that looked a lot like Erik's, now that he thought about it. And that was probably an uncomfortable reminder of their genetic connection too. Well, fuck. Ivar continued, "This wouldn't be our first night in a tent."

No, since most of them had been on raiding campaigns before, they'd spent days at sea in boats with barely any cover from the elements and nights on land in tents. Camping outdoors in the mild Virginia weather would be a cakewalk after that.

Bryn flipped her braid over her shoulder. "I don't have enough bedrooms for all of you. There's a bunkhouse out behind the barn. Ivar, you can take the downstairs bedroom here so you don't have to deal with the bunkhouse steps. There are fewer getting up to the main house." She jerked her chin at the *völva*. "You can have the spare room upstairs. I think there's a saddle on the bed, but that's easy enough to move."

Looking a little ill—which Erik guessed had to do with sleeping so close to a valkyrie with a reputation for bloodshed and a serious hate for *völva*—Nauma asked, "What about the cottage on the other side of the driveway?"

"That's my stable hands' house." Bryn bent over to tie her boots. "The guys will be back tomorrow night."

"They live together?" Nauma's eyebrows winged upward. "Gay?"

"Brothers," Bryn grunted.

"Ah." The handmaiden shifted from foot to foot, looking as if she'd rather be anywhere but here.

Erik sighed. "Val said there was news. Is Nauma it?"

"No, but she comes bearing news." Ivar straightened in his chair. "Or at least some information about why *Ragnarök* is happening now."

The *völva* took a breath and nodded. "The basics are this: there are two eclipse seasons each year, one every six months, each lasting a little over a month. Some seasons have more eclipses than others. This one is going to have three—solar, lunar, solar. In certain parts of the world, North America being one of them, these eclipses will be visible."

A solar eclipse would fulfill part of the ancient prophecy. Erik tilted his head. "The sun will be consumed."

"Yes."

Bryn crossed her arms, looking thoroughly unimpressed. "A bunch of eclipses doesn't necessarily mean dick. Loki hasn't escaped yet, has he? And what about the dragon? Jörmungand still sleeps."

Ivar raised a hand, maybe to ward off an argument between the women, maybe just to get their attention. "I suspect all the high-magnitude earthquakes in the last few years are part of a ruse, caused by Loki, to awaken the sleeping dragon."

"Where *is* the sleeping dragon?" Val asked. "Does anyone even know anymore? People used to think it encircled the circumference of the world, but obviously not."

Ivar shrugged. "I think it's at the center of the world, encased in the lava core. All the huge earthquakes are meant to disturb its slumber."

"Shit." Holm summed up what everyone else was thinking.

Snorting, Ivar spread his hands. "Yep."

"The more important issue is—where will it come up?" Bryn asked the question, but Erik noted she didn't look directly at Ivar. Everyone else was, but not her. Was being near their grandson so painful for her? Erik doubted she'd admit it even if it was excruciating.

"A fissure at the bottom of the ocean, maybe." Nauma ventured the first guess. "They cut deeper than anywhere land-based. It'd be the easiest escape route."

"A volcano?" Val closed one eye, as if that might help him concentrate. "Mauna

Loa, Mount Fuji, Tambora, Lakagígar. There are several big active ones."

"And even more huge dormant ones," Erik pointed out.

Bryn huffed out an impatient breath. "Both options basically mean the dragon could come up anywhere on Earth."

Again, it was Holm who offered the unanimous opinion. "And ain't that a bitch?"

A bit of tension-breaking laughter went through the group, and Erik tightened the fit of his towel. Not that he gave two shits about nudity, but he didn't know everyone else well enough to say if they cared. Val and Nauma, he'd only met a few weeks ago.

He didn't want to ask the next question, but he did anyway. "Loki might be causing the earthquakes, but he's still imprisoned, right?"

Ivar tapped a button on his ever-present laptop and turned it toward him. There were massive lists of files, all labeled by date. "I keep tabs on Loki."

He opened one of the files and a grainy video showed. A man lay chained to a rock, and a woman sat next to him. She held a bowl over his head, catching venom from a snake mounted over the man's face. The giant Loki and his wife. Loki had gone to Odin's hall and insulted all the gods, trying to cause strife in Asgard. This was the trickster giant's punishment.

Ivar ran a finger along the side of the screen. "I have video on Loki at all times. Set that up the moment I could get an inconspicuous camera near him. Fortunately, he's bound here on Earth because there's no way to get a signal from any other realm. No audio, but I can see him, his wife, and anyone else who stops by to visit."

"Does anyone?" Bryn asked sharply.

"Visit? No." Ivar shook his head. "He's guarded 24/7, of course. No one else even tries to get close."

Erik arched an eyebrow. "You don't trust his guards?"

Ivar just gave him a steady stare. "I don't trust much of anything or anyone. It pays to be cautious."

"Agreed." Erik rubbed the back of his neck where stress was drawing the muscles tight. "Have you tracked any other gods?"

"Not many. Of the major gods, only Heimdall." Ivar's expression turned frustrated. "Of the major goddesses…Thor's wife, Sif, spends a good deal of time on Earth. Though she *is* an earth goddess, so that's to be expected. The skiing goddess Skadi hits the slopes every winter all over the world, which makes her pretty easy to spot. I also have a bead on a couple of giants who like to come to Earth. That's it."

The video showed Loki's wife moving away to empty her bowlful of venom. In the time she was gone, the snake dripped his poison onto Loki's face. The giant jerked on his bonds, writhing in agony. Though the sound was muted, it was clear he screamed.

Nauma pressed a hand to her chest. "How long has he been that way?"

Glancing at her, Ivar lifted a brow, his words dry. "Chained by the ironized entrails of his son, getting poison dripped on his face unless his wife catches it in a bowl first?"

She winced. "Yeah. That."

"Beyond the reckoning of human time, I think. So, many thousands of years. Does he realize it's been that long? Or have the days just blurred?" Ivar shrugged. "I don't know, but it's plenty of time to build up some bitterness. If he gets loose, *Ragnarök* is on like Donkey Kong."

Bryn snorted. "Such a Viking way to put it."

He winked. "Nothing wrong with liking technology. Just because I was born before the fun gadgets were invented, doesn't mean I can't enjoy modern amenities."

"You used to invent a few fun gadgets of your own," Val noted, wagging his finger at his old comrade.

Ivar's lips curved in a smug grin. "Still do."

Val's gaze lit. "Show me."

Swiveling in his chair, Ivar motioned to Erik. "Show the man."

Waving down at his bare chest and towel, he rolled his eyes. "I don't have it on me. I'll get it."

It only took a few minutes to fetch his bag from the back of his SUV, but he took the opportunity to yank on a pair of jeans, T-shirt, and sandals. He didn't bother with underwear. Ivar wasn't the most patient soul on the planet, so Erik decided it was prudent to move his ass.

Besides, he wanted to show off his new toys.

He grinned and jogged back up the porch steps, setting his duffel on the coffee table. Though he was betting Bryn would try to kick him out to the bunkhouse with Holm and Val, Erik was going to do his best to make sure his bag was parked in her bedroom until it was time for them all to leave. They might rub each other the wrong way at times, but that happened with strong personalities. Plus, they also rubbed each other the right way. No reason not to enjoy some more of that.

Unzipping the duffel, he pulled out a gun and a palm-sized metal cylinder. He ejected the clip from the handgun and gave it to Ivar. "You explain this one."

Ivar took it, but gestured to the cylinder. "Nah, show them the good stuff first."

"That's the good stuff?" Holm's tone was somewhere between dubious and bored.

"Just watch, numbnuts."

Holm sat up, his heavy brows snapping together. "My nuts are anything but numb, limp dick."

"Considering I'm looking at you, yes, my dick is limp." Ivar looked him over in what could only be called an insulting manner. "You just don't do it for me, Swamp Thing."

"Children, I'm going to box your ears if you don't behave." Val flicked his fingers at Erik. "*I* want to see the good stuff."

Erik held up the cylinder, checked to make sure no one was standing too closely, and hit a concealed button at one end. A flattened, tightly linked chain unfurled from the other end, and he swung it in a quick arc.

"Well, that's interesting, but—"

Erik flicked his wrist the way Ivar had shown him, and the chain solidified into a Viking sword. "It's unbreakable, designed to cut down even a god or a giant."

He flipped the sword around his hand, set it on a fingertip to show its superb balance, thrust and parried with the air. Flaunting his skills just a little. Yes, because there were women in the room. Apparently, there were some things a man never grew out of. Flicking his wrist again, he let the sword revert back to a razor-sharp chain, and then hit the button to retract it. He grinned when even Bryn let out a soft, "Ooooh."

"I got the initial idea from *Star Wars* lightsabers." Ivar sighed with satisfaction.

"Nerdgasm, I know, but…it fucking *worked.*"

"How do you know it'll cut down a giant?" Bryn reached for the weapon, and Erik made sure his fingers stroked over hers as he handed it to her. She gave him a smirk to let him know he was as subtle as Thor's war-hammer, but he just winked back.

Erik answered her question, though he knew it was directed at Ivar. "Another immortal I ran across a while back. The blacksmith, Volund. He forged legendary swords, even those used by the gods. I introduced him to Ivar, figuring they could create some advanced weaponry for me."

"Viking meets James Bond?" Val asked, smoothing his accent into a posh Bond-like tone.

"Something like that." When he'd met the smith, Erik had been more interested in surviving the coming fight than looking cool with gadgets. "The chain-sword is one of their inventions. As are the bullets."

"Bullets." Val snagged the clip out of Ivar's hand, thumbing one of the bullets free. He held it up to the sunlight that streamed through the window, squinting at the metal casing. "Looks normal."

"It's supposed to." Ivar had all the appearance of a sugar-addled kid let loose in a candy store. "But, like the sword, it can put a hole through a giant. Evens the odds for us a bit, don't you think?"

White teeth flashing in a smile, Val flipped the bullet in the air like a quarter and caught it neatly. "It's brill, mate."

Angling a glare at Holm, Ivar demanded, "Still think it's not the good stuff?"

"It's not bad." Holm fought a grin and lost. "It's only the good stuff if you have enough for the rest of us."

Ivar laughed, grabbed the wheels on his chair and pivoted, then rolled out the door. "Let me give you a tour of my van."

Everyone followed. Except Bryn.

Erik didn't realize she was absent until they'd reached the van, but his gaze met Ivar's, and a small flash of hurt in the other man's eyes told Erik he wasn't the only one who'd noticed.

The question was—was it Ivar she didn't want to be around or Erik?

7

Letting the world-saving misfits go play with new weapons—and, yes, Bryn could admit she wanted to play too, but mostly because they were shiny toys and she *was* a valkyrie—she retreated to the barn to take her horses out to their pastures. Because her stable hands were out of town, she'd already decided the ponies could have a leisurely weekend without a lot of exercise riding. Sure, she could ask the berserkers for help, but she'd rather they were indebted to her for trespassing and using her home as their personal B&B than be indebted to them by begging assistance.

She just...needed a moment or forty to process. There was a *völva* in her house. As a breed, they were meddlesome, troublemaking, and power-hungry. She'd admit this particular *völva* didn't come across as power-hungry, but the rest was spot on. Bryn suppressed a twitch at the thought. Those bitches loved to find your weak places and lay them bare with their prophecies. In that, Nauma seemed to fit the mold perfectly.

Bryn would deal with the *völva*. Just like she did with everything else.

No matter what shit rolled downhill and piled up on her, she shoveled her way out and got on with things. She was, at heart, a no-bullshit, practical creature. Which mean that, yeah, she knew she was going to get dragged into this fight. First, because Erik was right—she *did* care what happened to humans—and second, because she didn't want to end up a giant's appetizer. They liked to play with their food before they consumed it, and they preferred their meals alive and kicking when they ate. Letting them win the coming fight wouldn't end well, for mankind in general, or for her personally.

She checked the rifle she had in the barn. Though it was cleaned regularly, she broke it down and made sure it was in perfect working order. Maybe Ivar had bullets for this caliber. She fought a flinch as she thought of him. Ivar. Another person she wasn't thrilled about having around. Looking at him was a piercing reminder that she hadn't gotten to see her baby girl grow up, that she'd never seen Aslaug get married and have babies of her own. Bryn should have been able to hold Ivar in her arms when he was a tiny thing, not this hulking gadget-junkie in a wheelchair.

She swallowed hard and forced those thoughts from her head. Should, could, would…that way lay madness. Snapping the clip into her rifle, she carried it across the yard to the back porch, thought about leaving it propped against the house, and decided to take it in with her.

Walking in the door, she almost tripped over Ivar. Of course. Then again, it wasn't as if Erik or Nauma would be so much better. "Oh, sorry. I'm not used to anyone being in the house except me."

"No problem." He wheeled backwards to let her pass. "Erik tells me your stable boys are away until tomorrow."

"It almost sounds ominous when you say it, like look at all the time we have before the unsuspecting humans return." She congratulated herself on keeping her voice light and easy. Sad when standards got that low, but she was uncomfortable and trying not to be.

Sidestepping him, she couldn't make herself look directly at him and focused on laying her rifle across the table as if the task required her full attention. She needed to get over this weirdness with him. She knew that, but he was just…a reminder of everything that had been wrong and right about her mortal existence. She'd put all that behind her, and the last day had churned up memories and emotions she didn't want.

"Ominous, huh? Should I rub my hands together maniacally for effect?"

"Please don't." She reached into the fruit bowl and snagged an apple.

The silence stretched until it was weird, but she had nothing to say to this stranger who shared her blood. Or maybe she had too much to say and just didn't know how.

"Um. I'm reading a book about Erik. And you." He held up something, and she glanced at his hand to see what it was. One of those ebook readers. Figures he'd eschew the old-fashioned paper version. "You know, Tolkien thinks you and Erik will survive *Ragnarök* and be like the next Adam and Eve."

She rolled her eyes. "Awesome, just what I always wanted."

He tapped the Kindle against his thigh. "Tolkien calls Erik the World's Chosen. Because he's going to defeat the baddies and stuff."

"After everyone else is dead, just in time for me to be stuck alone with him for all eternity, popping out babies to repopulate the planet." She went to the sink and washed her fruit. "Yeah. I see this going *so* well."

"Well, you know Tolkien was a scholar on cultures like ours. He translated *Beowulf* from the original language." He made a humming noise. "Good translation too."

"Peachy." She crunched into her apple.

Ivar's voice went soft. "Do you really hate him that much?"

"Tolkien?" She propped herself back against the edge of the counter, pretending to think. "Bit of a rip-off of ancient mythologies for his fiction, but otherwise, he was okay."

"Bryn." Ivar's tone was scolding.

She sighed. "It's all water under the bridge. Leave it alone."

Because once upon a time, that fate would have sounded absolutely perfect to her. Erik, her, an eternity of togetherness, and their beautiful babies to hold in her arms. But that was a long time ago.

"Is it really water under the bridge? Somehow, I don't think so. I think—" He cut himself off, and she heard him drum his fingers on the face of his ereader. "Look, I have no idea what it's like to be handed the kind of destiny you have. I have no idea what it's like to be a myth in my own time. Sure, people were justifiably terrified of me when I was leading my armies during invasions, because I was a damn good strategist, but...that's not the same as what you and Erik have had thrust upon you. No one tried to box me into a fate I didn't ask for."

She'd bet he hadn't asked to end up on four wheels instead of two legs, but she didn't say that aloud. He'd clearly adapted to his disability long ago, which couldn't have been easy before accessibility became a concept. She took another bite of the apple, chewing it slowly.

When she made no response, he sighed. "You know, they say the Sleeping Beauty fairy tale is based on you. That has to be weird."

"I've heard that." She focused on the toe of her boot, bouncing her heel against the floor. "They also say the Arthurian legend is based on Erik. The once and future king."

"And the treacherous, backstabbing wife. Though would that be you or Gudrun?"

"Gudrun." Her grip tightened on the apple so hard, a chunk broke off and fell to the floor.

"She didn't plot to kill him," he mused.

Ah, salt on the wound, how it burned.

Bile coated her tongue, and she tossed the remainder of her apple in the trashcan. "She and her mother Grimhild set the wheels in motion that led to his death. And mine."

"Or we could blame it all on the ring and the treasure. They say Andvaranaut was cursed, and anyone who possessed it would suffer with strife and bad luck."

"The ring *was* cursed, but Grimhild's greed and her family's scheming played a big-ass role in what happened. Curses can be broken, but you can't fix evil." She'd sacrificed her life to break that curse, though the myths rarely spoke of that, did they? Instead they painted her as a petty, vengeful woman scorned. Boohoo for her, right? She was hardly the only person to ever be unjustly vilified, so she didn't complain, especially when she was somewhat less than innocent anyway. She scooped the fallen bit of fruit off the ground and tossed it too. Then she grabbed a sponge and wiped up the mess on the floor.

"My mother said you somehow broke Andvaranaut's curse, and that she and Erik's other daughter Svanhild were able to live their lives without that curse hanging over them because of you."

That one sentence made something deep inside Bryn crack, and she wiped shaking hands down her thighs. "Who...who told her that?"

"Gudrun." His chair creaked as he shifted his weight. "Something about your death affected her deeply, and she would never hear an unkind word said about you."

The irony of that burned through her, since the woman had never had anything *but* filthy, vicious things to say about her when they'd been living in the same castle.

But it wasn't Gudrun that interested her. She licked her lips. "Did Aslaug…was my daughter happy? Did she have a good life?"

Freya had kept Bryn busy in Asgard for the first century or two after her death. But, like Odin, Freya preferred those who served her to spend some time amongst the mortals every now and then. During that first sojourn on Earth, Bryn had convinced Freya to leave her with the humans instead of making her live in Valhalla, where she might have to see Erik. But all those years in Asgard meant Bryn had never known what had become of her daughter. She could probably look it up on the internet, but she found it was easier to sleep at night if you didn't ask questions you didn't really want the answers to. So why was she asking it now? Apparently, she'd turned into a masochist in the last twenty-four hours.

"She looked exactly like you," Ivar said.

"Yes." Aslaug had had the same pale hair and midnight gaze, and Bryn remembered so clearly the way her heart had clenched like a great fist the moment those solemn, dark eyes had blinked up at her. Gods, she had loved that child, known that she would do *anything* to protect her.

"She acted a bit like you too. Not a shieldmaiden, but definitely no bullshit, no pity, no standing around wringing her hands like a helpless half-wit." He popped a wheelie with his chair. "My father dismissed me as worthless when he found I couldn't walk, but Aslaug? Ha! Mother told me that I could be every inch the warrior dear old dad was, and told me that whining about my problems would get me nowhere. She was the one who shoved a bow and arrow into my hands the first time and insisted I learn how to use it. She was the one who sent me off on my first raid and demanded I not only come back alive but that I bring her great treasure."

"Did you?" Bryn scrubbed her hand across her eyes, not sure if she wanted to laugh or cry. Her daughter had inherited more of her personality than she'd realized, considering she'd only been part of her life for the first three years.

"Of course." He chuckled softly. "Disappointing Mother was something my brothers and I *never* did. We'd sooner cross our father than her, and Ragnar's reputation for ruthlessness was well earned."

"Was he good to her?" Bryn knew better than most that in days gone by an unhappy husband had the right to unleash his wrath on his wife in any way he saw fit.

"Yes, he was. They had their arguments, but he never beat or raped her, if that's what you're asking. They had a good marriage." Ivar's tone was matter-of-fact, and Bryn felt his gaze on her, but she couldn't bring herself to meet his eyes. Too many emotions might come exploding out if she saw even a hint of empathy in his expression. He continued, "To answer your first question, I believe she was happy. I was too young and self-involved to think much about it at the time but, except for the few times she and Father were at cross-purposes, she always seemed content with her lot in life."

"Good." She swallowed hard, trying to tuck those unwanted, unwieldy feelings away. "Okay, I need to grab a quick shower. Excuse me."

She tried to beat a hasty retreat out of the room but almost collided with Holm. He grinned and sniffed the air a bit, no doubt smelling exactly what she'd been up to with Erik earlier. "You know, you don't have to shower on our behalf. Actually, I rather like—"

"You'll only finish that sentence if you want to die slowly and painfully," she snapped, glad to have someone to vent her spleen on, to let out some of the emotion that was threatening to strangle her. If looks could kill, the one she gave this man would have ended him. "Also, don't for a second presume I do anything on your behalf. Now, move."

He blinked, stepped aside, and bowed gallantly. "Of course. My mistake."

And then she got the hell out of there. Though not before she heard Holm remark to Ivar, "I can see why Siegfried likes her. She's got sharp edges."

Gods, wasn't that the truth?

But those sharp edges had protected her through a lot of years where women were men's *property*, viewed as mindless twits, and used as little more than brood mares.

She was glad that fate hadn't befallen her daughter, that someone who'd known Aslaug could separate fact from fiction. When Bryn had sacrificed her mortal existence, all she could do was pray her baby girl would have a good life, knowing she'd never be able to protect her again, but also knowing that ending the curse would be the very best thing she could do to ensure Aslaug had the kind of future Bryn wanted for her.

She hadn't failed entirely. Thank all the gods.

In that one thing, she hadn't failed.

8

Sweat poured down Erik's skin, stinging his eyes and streaking in rivulets down his limbs. He ignored the discomfort, keeping his gaze locked on his opponent. At the moment, it was Holm, but he'd already gone two rounds with Val. They were practicing with the new weapons Ivar had given them.

They each carried the modified Viking chain-sword in one hand, but preferred different weapons for the other. Val liked the deadly elegance of a wicked knife, Holm preferred the brute force of a battle axe, and Erik had opted for a second chain-sword—one in serrated chain form, the other as a sword, but he switched up which was which to throw the other berserkers off. So far, the tactic was working.

Ivar whipped himself around to keep track of the fights, serving as a wisecracking coach and obnoxious referee all in one. "Keep your axe up, Holm, or your sorry ass is gonna—"

Erik slashed out with the chain before Ivar could finish, leaving a neat slice across Holm's shoulder. The other man grunted, cursed lividly, and danced backward, but not before Erik whipped out with his sword and slapped the other man's buttocks with the flat of his blade.

"Oh!" Ivar hooted. "And a little bitch slap to keep it interesting."

"Can I kill him? Please?" Holm begged as they stopped fighting for a moment, his gaze beseeching Erik. "Put him out of all our misery. You know you're thinking it too."

Val smothered a laugh. "So much for being a southern gentleman."

"Only since the 1700s, y'all," Holm drawled, swiping a forearm across his sweaty brow. "Remember, I'm a Viking. A very *good* Viking—meaning a very *bad* man."

A horse snorted loudly, and Erik glanced to the right. Bryn was riding in a ring nearby, exercising that big gray stallion. They seemed to be doing some sort of fancy training maneuvers—dressage, he thought it was called—but he didn't think he was imagining it that every time she went past the fence closest to the fight, she slowed down. Maybe that was part of her dressage routine, but he sensed her attention focus on them. It should be unsettling how in sync he was with her, but he found he liked it. Not that he'd tell her or anyone else, but in his own head, he couldn't deny he liked the way his senses sharpened whenever she was around. He liked the way she kept him on his toes, though he doubted there was much about him she enjoyed except what he did to her in bed.

Ah, well. He enjoyed the hell out of that too.

"Kick his ass, Erik." Ivar's demand yanked Erik back to the skirmish. "He threatened your family, Grandad."

"Easy on the Grandad crap." Erik fended off a swing of Holm's battle axe, but the hit vibrated up his arm with bone-rattling intensity.

"Come on, that was pathetic, Erik." Ivar stabbed a finger at him. "Defend your bloodline, man. You should be wiping the ground with his face. He can't fight for shit. I'd say he fought like a girl, but we all know Bryn could beat both your asses. Maybe she should be defending my bloodline."

Holm opened his mouth to retort, but Val beat him to the punch. "You don't want to challenge Ivar the Boneless. He will kill you. I've seen him in battle."

Ivar bared his teeth in a terrifying grin. "Let's go, gentlemen. You need to keep your skills up for what's coming."

Spitting on the dirt, Holm eyed Erik. They began circling each other, trying to find an opening for attack. The slight pause in the fighting had given Erik's body time to remind him of all the bruises, the aching muscles, the little nicks and cuts he'd earned during these bouts. Fatigue dragged at him, but Ivar was right, they needed to be sharp if they wanted to have a hope in hell of beating giants.

Erik clenched his jaw, shoved the pain away, and brought an overhand swing down on Holm's sword. Sparks flew through the air as their blades clashed, and Holm's eyebrow lowered in intense concentration. His axe came within a hairsbreadth of ending Erik's favorite body part, and the wolf within him snarled as he whipped out of the way.

Holm smiled, fangs flashing. "Careful, Twinkletoes. I'm gonna have you singing at a higher pitch."

In answer, Erik flicked his wrist up, wrapping the chain around the axe's handle. Throwing his weight back, he ripped the weapon out of Holm's hand and sent it flying across the yard. Then Erik slammed his foot into Holm's wrist, and the sword went the way of the battle axe.

Erik made an exaggerated kissy face at his opponent.

"Fuck you." Holm laughed, dropped low and swept his leg out, catching Erik below the knees, and they both went down. Holm ended up on top, wrapping a beefy hand around Erik's wrist and slamming it against the ground. His fingers went slack for just long enough to lose his grip on the sword hilt.

Shit.

Holm's knee hit his ribs, and the breath whooshed out of his lungs. Black spots swam in front of his eyes, but he managed to keep hold of the other chain-sword. They wrestled for the final weapon, fists and elbows jabbing. Pain exploded through him at each hit, but Erik brought his heel down on the back of Holm's knee, and that leg buckled. He used the leverage to throw Holm over onto his back. In the space between heartbeats, Erik pinned the other man. A snap of his wrist and the chain solidified into a blade, which he had at Holm's throat, digging in just enough to leave a thin cut. Holm froze under him, growled, and slapped a palm to the ground, ending the match.

"All right, good work." Ivar clapped twice. "I think we're done for the day."

Erik rolled to the side and collapsed beside Holm, both of them panting for breath. "You okay?"

Holm slung an arm over his eyes. "Fine, you?"

Using the sleeve of his shirt, Erik swiped the sweat from his face. "I could use a stiff drink."

Holm grunted an agreement. "I need a change of clothes and a shower first, but then I'm in. I have a flask in my bag. Moonshine."

Amusement trickled through Erik. "Homemade?"

"Is there any other? That bottled, commercial shit that says *moonshine* on the label is for weaklings. My moonshine puts hair on your chest." Holm thumped his sternum for emphasis. "So good it'll knock you on your ass and bring tears to your eyes."

"A ringing endorsement if I've ever heard one." Val offered them both an arm and hauled them to their feet.

Bryn strode toward the house, offering a curt nod as she passed. She didn't stop to chat, barely looked at them. He thought her gaze lingered longingly on the chain-swords, then she met his eyes, and for a second he'd swear her expression softened, and something deep in his chest warmed. He winked at her, and a little smile curved her mouth, but then she went through the screen door without a backward glance. And what did that mean? Was that a fuck-off-and-die or a come-find-me-later? He had no clue. It was two steps forward and three steps back with her. The only problem was, he wasn't sure where the steps forward were leading anyway. If he didn't know what direction he wanted them to go, he doubted they'd ever get there.

"I can smell baking bread." He took a deep breath. "I think food is calling my name first."

Ivar snorted. "I doubt it's the bread calling your name."

Erik set a hand on Ivar's shoulder and leaned down to speak in the man's ear. "That's none of your business, is it? Also, no matter how hot she is, she'll always be your grandmother. Think about that."

"You're gonna give me nightmares, man."

"You're welcome." He scrubbed a palm over Ivar's hair.

Ivar propped an elbow on the arm of his chair. "So you're getting the one who got away, huh? You figure there's no reason not to start repopulating the planet together a little early? Should we send out wedding invitations?"

"It's not like that." Or was it? Was that what he wanted from her? A second chance with the one who got away? He froze for a moment, and then slowly bent over and picked up his two weapons, retracting the chains into the hilts.

"It's exactly like that, Erik. I see how you look at her when you think no one notices, and I see how she looks back."

"Stay out of it, Ivar." Because what else could he say? He knew he craved Bryn like an addict after a fix, that being around her made him feel alive the way nothing and no one else ever could. He knew prophecy dictated that they'd be together, but the past shaped the future, and there were still too many unanswered questions between them. There was still too much suspicion and distrust to make a real relationship. Could that be changed? Did he want it to be changed? He wasn't sure. He only knew he'd take any chance he had to get his hands on her. Whether he could open his heart again, he didn't know yet. Whether he wanted *her* to open her heart again...even the thought sent a kind of pained longing through him.

Yes. No. Maybe.

Fuck it. So much of their history was tied up in unforgiveable acts. Some that were beyond their control, but even understanding that didn't remove the sting of betrayal. He blew out a breath, though his stomach churned with an onslaught of memories.

He walked toward the house, leaving the other men to their own devices. He'd barely made it into the kitchen when Nauma started talking. Then again, a few minutes in her presence showed that she was rarely at a loss for words. He far preferred Bryn's more reserved personality.

"She went upstairs. Says she's not hungry and skipping dinner." Nauma's voice grew stiff. "I'm not a bad cook, you know."

"I'm sure you're right." He tried to keep his tone as soothing as possible.

Her lips twisted. "Not all *völva* are like your late mother-in-law."

"Thank the gods." The fewer people in the world like Grimhild, the better. Though her abuse of power had ended with Andvaranaut's curse raining hell down on her family, so he hoped she'd choked to death on her regrets.

Nauma's smile was a thin slash, her brown eyes troubled. "I should hope Bryn starves, but mostly I feel bad about her going hungry because of me."

He sighed, not sure how to word this in a way that didn't offend. "Nauma, it's not about you. Or not just you. It's me too. It's Ivar. It's all of us invading her space. It's *Ragnarök*. Try not to take it so personally. We all have our coping mechanisms. Hers include isolating herself from anyone."

Sudden sympathy filled her gaze. "Makes it easier when people die, if you didn't care about them too much to begin with."

"Yeah." On the one hand, he could understand it. On the other, he hated that he seemed to be included in the people Bryn wanted to shut out. Even if he wasn't sure he wanted in, he also knew he hated being out. It made no damn sense, but there it was.

"I'm not sure if that's sad or just *sane*." Nauma stirred a big pot of beef stew, her brow furrowed. "I've never been in a battle, so I can only speculate on what kind of mental processes you guys go through."

"We all do what we have to do to survive, mentally and physically." He considered the food she'd set out on the table—fresh baked bread, peach cobbler, salad. "Would you mind if I took some food upstairs? Maybe I can tempt her into eating."

She pulled a couple of bowls out of the cupboard and dished out stew. He wasn't sure where she procured a tray, but soon two servings of everything were being pushed into his hands. She gave him a wry look. "I think you want to tempt her into other things, but…I have a feeling that not letting her shut everyone out is a good thing."

Something about her inflection made him focus on her more intently. "Would this *feeling* be—"

"Not an official vision," she hastened to assure him, but then she hesitated. "Though I'll be honest and warn you that ignoring my hunches has always ended disastrously for me."

Disastrous. His gut clenched. Knowing everything Bryn had been through, he loathed the idea of her going through more. But the world might be ending, so they were all going to be put through the ringer, including her. If they failed to stop the apocalypse, no one on this farm except Bryn and him would survive. He hated that thought, hated that those he cared for would die, hated that innocent people would be killed in a war between gods they didn't even believe in. They had to stop this. They *had* to. But if he were honest, *Ragnarök* had little to do with why he didn't like being shut out by Bryn. Everything inside him rebelled at any distance between them. He hadn't spoken to her since the day she'd had him killed, had only seen her from afar a few times since then. But now that he'd had her in his arms again, he found he couldn't give it up. He needed to be near her and maybe, for a little while, allow them both to not be quite so alone.

He smiled at Nauma. "Well, your gut instinct and mine are saying the same thing."

"Have a lovely evening. The rest of us will manage just fine without you."

"You'll let us know if there are any *Ragnarök* updates."

It wasn't a question, but she answered anyway. "Of course. Visions from me, techno-alerts from Ivar…we'll call you."

Val stepped in the door, his gaze going directly to Nauma. A gamut of emotions crossed the man's face, from blatant hunger to agonized suffering and back again. Nauma seemed intent on ignoring him. It appeared that the history between those two was as tortured as the one between Erik and Bryn. He shook his head and left the room. There was nothing he could do to help them. He wasn't even sure there was anything he could do to help himself, in the end, but that was his problem to deal with.

9

When Erik reached Bryn's bedroom, the door was closed. He shifted the tray to one hand and knocked.

He heard bed springs creak, light footsteps, and then the door opened. She already wore pajamas—a loose pair of drawstring pants and a tank top. He tried not to focus on her obvious lack of bra and the beautiful things that thin shirt did to her breasts.

Her gaze swept him from head to toe before she jerked her chin at the food. "What's that for?"

He mustered up his most charming smile. "I'll trade you some dinner *and* delicious dessert for a shower and a bed to sleep in that won't have Val and Holm shaking the walls with their snoring."

Her head cocked to the side. "Do they actually snore?"

"I have no idea." He winked. "But I stowed my bag in here this morning, so I had to come back. And I came with an offering of home-cooked goodness."

"Smart man." A smile fluttered at the corners of her lips, but she sobered quickly. "I'm not really fit company right now."

"I'm sure I've seen you in worse moods," he said mildly. "Killing moods, in fact."

"True." She dipped her chin to concede the point.

"You really don't want to try any of this? It smells amazing." He waved a hand to waft the scent of food towards her. If he wasn't mistaken, there was a very tiny rumble from her stomach. "I know I worked up an appetite today, and I bet riding horses for hours did the same for you. Though if you're really not interested, I'm pretty sure I can finish it all myself."

Her tongue flicked out to run along her lower lip. "You could just leave mine here."

His body tightened, and he couldn't help the image that formed in his mind of other things he'd like her tongue to be doing. "Sorry, no. I'm not your butler. All of this is mine, and I'm willing to share what I have, if you're willing to share what you have."

"My shower and my bed." Her expression turned dubious.

He shrugged lightly. "Or you could go down and hang out with the team, eat with all of them. I'm sure they'd be happy to have you at the table."

"I'm not that hungry." But she couldn't hold his gaze, glancing to the side.

"You're avoiding everyone, let's be honest." He sighed. "You know, the first time I saw you, you were surrounded by a wall of fire."

Frowning, she shook her head. "Yeah, so?"

"You were already something of a legend then." And her legend continued to this day, no matter how she tried to avoid it.

"So were you, dragon-slayer." She propped her shoulder against the doorjamb. "Isn't that tray getting heavy?"

"I have preternatural strength so, no, not really. And don't change the subject." He gave her a pointed looked. "That's how you still are, isn't it? Always throwing up barriers between yourself and everyone else."

She stiffened, her jaw jutting. "Those barriers have helped protect me from some pretty awful stuff. And I haven't exactly done well the few times I dropped them, have I? A lover who discarded me like I was no better than dirty laundry, a husband who had no problem having me drugged so he could take your sloppy seconds." Her eyes widened dramatically. "Yeah, those were some great life choices. I can't imagine why I don't drop those barriers more often."

A direct hit. He tried not to wince and forced a smile. "Why don't we talk about that over dinner?"

Her lips pursed as if she'd tasted something sour. "I'm not interested in talking."

Neither was he, but he had a feeling they both needed to. It was far past time they started clearing the air between them, especially if they were going to be shackled to each other for all eternity. "Then how about I feed you and just wring you out in bed?"

"You? Wring *me* out?" Her laugh was derisive. "What delusional fantasy are you living in?"

He leaned forward until his nose was an inch from hers, invading her space. His gaze locked with hers, and he let a challenging grin curve his mouth. "I dare you to let me try."

He felt her muscles tighten, but she didn't step back. Not his Bryn—she never backed down. Her expression went regally cool, reminding him of the queen she once was. "Really? You think I'm going to fall for that?"

But the sweet scent of her arousal reached his nose, and his cock hardened in response. The wolf in him writhed with the need to claim her. He sensed her breathing and heart rate elevate and, if he glanced down, he was almost certain he'd see her nipples had tightened. But he kept his gaze on her face and let his smile widen. "No, I think you're curious enough to want to know exactly how I intend to go about wringing you out."

Her lips compressed as if she was trying to hide a grin. She stepped back and held the door open. "I'm holding you to that."

"Please, do."

"First, though...you need a shower." Her nose wrinkled as he walked by and set the tray on the mattress. "Before you sit on my clean sheets. Seriously."

"So fastidious." He dropped a quick kiss on her mouth, nipping at her full lower lip, then headed for the bathroom.

He took the fastest shower of all time, not wanting to give her a chance to change her mind. He dried off, hung his towel, and was back in the bedroom within seven minutes. She was still spooning soup into her mouth, using the broth as a dipping sauce for her bread. He stood there for a moment, just watching her. She was so unbelievably gorgeous, it stole his breath every time he looked at her. Not that she'd ever cared much about her looks, and he thought that had always made her even more beautiful in his eyes. His late wife—damn her perfidious soul—had wielded her beauty like a weapon, using it to bring men to their knees. When it hadn't worked with him, she'd resorted to dirtier tactics.

Bryn's eyebrows arched. "What are you standing there for?"

"Enjoying the food porn."

She chuckled, and an automatic smile formed on his lips. He loved when she laughed.

He stepped over to the bed, careful not to overset anything on the tray as he sat on the mattress. She handed him the remaining bread and bowl of stew and he grinned in return. "Thanks."

She tossed her hair over her shoulder, creating a cascade of blond silk. "Well you need to carb up if you're going to *wring me out*."

"Sure." He held his grin in place, propped his shoulders against her headboard, and tucked into his dinner.

As Nauma had promised, she was a very good cook. The soup was flavorful, and he probably could have eaten an entire loaf of the bread by himself.

They ate in companionable silence, and he realized how rarely he'd had the opportunity to spend quiet time alone with Bryn. He wouldn't have pictured her ever being so restful, but contentment spread through him—sweet and warm and entirely unfamiliar. It was...nice. The word seemed tepid to describe the feeling within him, but he could get used to this. For once, the stress and pressure of being the World's Chosen fell away and he could just *be*. If anyone understood what getting such a massive destiny shoved on to his shoulders felt like, it was Bryn. She knew the worst of him and had every reason to loathe him, and yet she was still here, sitting beside him.

It was a relief in many ways.

Death had given him a hero's welcome to Valhalla, but few knew the real truth behind his demise. No one wanted the secrets that made a hero less than perfect, especially not one who was supposed to father the whole human race after *Ragnarök*. He was supposed to be flawless if he got to be the only man left standing at the end of days. But Bryn knew how they'd wronged each other and how it had ended both of their lives. She knew his flaws, and she still seemed to think he was up to the task he'd been given.

Her spoon scraped the bottom of her bowl, calling his attention back to the present. She set the dish aside and pulled her knees up to her chest, resting her chin on the bony plateau.

"Do you hate me, Bryn?" The question was out of his mouth before he could call it back.

She blinked, glancing at him out of the corner of her eye. "Why would that matter, after all this time?"

Let it drop, Siegfried. But he couldn't. Now that the words had been spoken, he needed to know. "You hated me back then. What I'm asking is—do you still?"

A sigh trickled out of her, and she wrapped her arms around her bent legs. "No, I don't. I wouldn't have slept with you otherwise. I'm not sure I like you, but I don't *hate* you. I know what the prophecy says about us repopulating the planet, but I'm not sure how much stock I put in that part. We're good in bed together, so that makes part of fulfilling the prophecy fairly easy. However…we both have dominant personalities. I just don't buy us not killing each other pretty quickly. That would end the repopulation movement a bit prematurely, wouldn't it?"

He grunted. "Growing older has made us both more and less tolerant."

"Ha. Yes, exactly."

"If it helps…I've been kicking my own ass for a millennium for having left you alone and not marrying you the moment you said yes."

"It helps, and it doesn't. We could play woulda, coulda, shoulda forever, but that's a game you can't win and always just leaves you feeling like shit." Her hands curved around her bare ankles. "After you left, I called back the ring of fire. I knew men took my being alone as a challenge to try and force me to marry them. While I could handle one or two or three men on my own, if they brought their army with them…I would have been screwed. Literally and figuratively. So I called back the fire. I knew the only man who could get through it was you."

"Then I spiked your wine with a potion to make you think it was Gunnar and not me." His smile held no amusement. *"After* I'd spent all night with you, screwing like minks. *After* I'd promised Gunnar not to touch you.*"* He shook his head. "I should have known something was wrong, when I was so in love with Gudrun, so desperate to wed her, and yet I couldn't resist you. The moment I saw you, I had to have you, had to claim you and make you *mine.*"

"Wow, great. I'm your sexual Kryptonite," she replied dryly.

"When the potions wore off and we both realized what had happened—" He swallowed, balling his fingers as old rage flooded him. "I was so fucking angry. It was all I could do not to wring their necks."

She reared back, shooting him an incredulous look. "You brushed it off, told me to forget about it and be content with the good life I had."

"Of course, because when the potion wore off, I realized how badly *I* had betrayed you, how dishonorable I'd really been." He forced his hands to relax, pressing them against the comforter. "The shame was eating me alive. I *needed* you to be content, does that make sense? That was the only way I could live with myself, if you were happy with the life you'd ended up with."

"You are such an idiot." She shook her head. "How could you think I'd be any less angry than you were? How could you not see that I felt even *more* angry, *more* betrayed? It wasn't just them who drugged and used me, it was you. The man I loved more than anything. Enough to basically imprison myself behind a wall of flames. Again. Did you think that was easy? I said I'd wait for you, and I kept my promise."

"I know. I'm sorry." Old regrets threatened to consume him and burn a hole through his soul, but he battled them back. He couldn't undo what had been done, and loathing himself accomplished nothing.

She turned her head and met his gaze squarely. "Do you know the potion didn't just wear off for me? Your wife taunted me, humiliated me, because she got you and I didn't. She called me your concubine, your whore."

A strangled noise was all he could manage. Maybe that label was bandied around these days, but back then? For a lady—a *queen*—to be called a whore was an insult that could start a war.

"She said shit like that to me every time we were alone together, rubbing salt on that wound daily." Her crack of laughter was painful to hear. "When all the men were out on raids, she was fucking relentless."

There had been a lot of raids after the elixir wore off. It wasn't for the glory anymore; it was to escape the castle so he didn't have to face Bryn—his sister-in-law, his queen, the woman he'd still loved—day in and day out, so he didn't have to look at his deceitful wife, so he didn't murder his mother-in-law.

Bryn had more than earned her reputation as a shieldmaiden while they were away, defending the kingdom against three different sieges. Gunnar and he *could* be gone so often because they knew the country was safe in her hands. He'd never known Gudrun had made her life miserable.

Her fingers clenched into her pajama pants. "I wanted to kill her, but…she was telling the truth, wasn't she? You *had* made me your whore."

"No, I didn't mean…" Who the fuck cared what he'd meant to do? He'd still done it. He closed his eyes, horror blooming inside him. *Gudrun, you heartless bitch*. Had he known this back then, he might not have been able to restrain himself from throttling his wife. "No wonder you wanted me dead."

Bryn leaned back, her head thunking softly against the headboard. "I tried to let it go, tried to be Zen about it like you wanted. But she wouldn't let me."

"Shit." He scrubbed a palm down his face. "I'm so sorry for my part in what happened. I should never have left you in the first place. I'm sorry I let Gudrun and Gunnar and Grimhild come between us."

She let her hands lift and fall. "That was one fucked up family."

A gusty laugh escaped him. "Right?"

"They wanted the dragon's gold." She pinched the bridge of her nose. "It was all greed, and wanting what wasn't theirs. We weren't theirs, your gold wasn't theirs, but they took everything."

"But I have my own portion of the blame. I can't lay it all on their doorstep. Yes, I was drugged and used, but there were certainly more honorable choices I could have made, especially when it came to you." Then he confessed the darkest part of his truth. "I should never have touched you, but I can't regret it."

Her eyes rounded, then narrowed to dangerous slits.

"Hate me if you want, but I will never regret having had the chance to touch you. I don't think I'll ever be able to pass up that chance if you offer it. Even under the influence of a potion, even thinking I was in love with another woman, even *engaged* to that woman, I couldn't resist you. I'll never be able to." He swallowed. "I'm sorry that you were hurt, I'm ashamed that I broke my word to my best friend—and to you, though I didn't know it at the time—but touching you? No. I don't regret that."

She folded her arms over her breasts. "You're splitting some very fine hairs on that one."

"I know. Was what I did wrong? Hell, yes. No question about that. But there are only some parts of it I feel guilty for. Maybe that makes me a terrible person, but that doesn't change how I feel." He tapped a fingertip against his chest. "Good or bad, I have to live with what happened. I choose *not* to feel bad about the best sex of my entire life."

She was silent for a long moment, and he sat, tense, waiting for her to come at him swinging, bloodlust in her eyes. But she heaved a deep sigh.

"I think we can do better. In fact, I think you promised to wring me out tonight." She gave him an arch look. "Are you backing out on me?"

"Not a chance."

She nodded crisply. "Good."

"Otherwise I can take my ass down to the bunkhouse?"

"I thought that went without saying." Amusement flashed in her dark gaze.

"Dessert first." He reached for the cobbler. He had some interesting ideas about what the warm peach syrup at the bottom could be used for.

But even as his body revved up for the sex that was coming, he couldn't help but notice that, as many times as he'd said he was sorry, she *hadn't* said she forgave him.

He shouldn't let it bother him, but it did anyway.

10

An odd noise woke Bryn just before dawn, sending a shiver of foreboding down her spine. She bolted upright in bed, her hand coming down on Erik's bare back.

"I heard it too," he breathed. He eased his arm across the mattress, silently lifting his pistol off the nightstand.

It came again. Somewhere between a sob and a choking sound. The voice was female, and close by. Nauma? Was someone in the other woman's room? Bryn slipped out the long, slender dagger she hid between her mattress and box spring. Unsheathing the blade, she left the leather casing on the bed and rose. Adrenaline flooded her body, her senses sharpening as she eased down the hall, her feet placed carefully on each wood plank so her passage was soundless. Erik followed one step behind her, and then they set their backs against the wall on either side of the *völva's* closed door.

"I smell no one else." His words were almost soundless, but she heard him anyway.

She dipped her chin to acknowledge him, though the news made her no less cautious as she set a hand on the knob. He tapped his chest and pointed to the door, indicating he'd go in first. She nodded again, twisted the knob and shoved it open.

He went in, leading with his gun, and she spun in behind, each of them checking the room for intruders with military precision. Erik said, "Clear."

"Clear," she confirmed. Then she approached the bed. Nauma had been still when they entered, but now her back bowed, and she writhed on the mattress. Her hair and nightgown were sweat-soaked. That sound came again, but from up close, it seemed even more plaintive, rising to a high keening wail that lifted the hairs on the back of Bryn's neck.

"What's wrong with her?" Erik stayed near the foot of the bed, looking wary.

"I don't know." Bryn leaned closer, reaching out to check her forehead for a fever. "Maybe she's sick?"

"Can immortals *get* sick?" he replied dubiously. "I didn't think so."

"Well, if you have a better—"

Nauma's eyes flew open, the brown irises gone an eerie white, and Bryn jerked back a step. The *völva's* torso bowed in an unnatural arch, and the lights in the room flared to blinding brightness. It felt as though a vibrating, suffocating *power* filled the room, like a million bees buzzing in the confined space. Nauma sucked in a breath, and it was as if the entire room drew in air, the curtains flapping wildly in the open windows. "He's coming."

"Who's coming?" Bryn swallowed, her insides twisting tight. She set a tentative hand on the other woman's forearm. "Nauma, *who's* coming?"

She shook her head wildly, those milky eyes locking on Bryn. "Not now, not today. But soon."

"Who?" Bryn's fingers tightened on the dagger's hilt, trying to ground herself in reality. Her heart hammered, and her knees felt like gelatin.

Nauma blinked, and her irises cleared, the static energy in the room faded, and the light bulbs dimmed to normal. "What?"

Swiping a hand across her sweaty forehead, Bryn replied, "You said someone was coming. Not now, but soon. Who is coming?"

"Loki," Nauma said softly, staring at the ceiling. "I had a vision that he escaped."

Bile burned Bryn's throat, the sum of all her nightmares wrapped up in that one sentence. She felt an iron band cinch around her chest, forcing the air from her lungs. She gritted out, "In your vision...how did he escape?"

"Not sure." Nauma grimaced and licked cracked lips. "Someone is helping him. I think. No, I'm sure. Someone is helping him. There's a plan in motion to deliberately set off the apocalypse."

Bryn grabbed the glass of water sitting on the nightstand and handed it to Nauma. "The original prophecy says that his daughter, Hel, and the king of the fire giants, Surtr, will be at his side when he escapes."

"No. I mean, yes. They're on his side, of course. But there's more to it." The *völva* rubbed her bloodshot eyes, looking as exhausted as a warrior who'd spent three days in endless battle. "There are players who haven't revealed themselves yet."

"Traitors?" Erik asked.

"I hope not, but I fear so. My vision didn't show me that. Just Loki." She sat up slowly, squinting as if the light hurt her eyes. She scanned the room until her gaze landed on Erik, then she looked at Bryn. "Gods. Does he ever have clothes on?"

He didn't point out that Bryn was also nude, which she thought showed some serious restraint. He cast Bryn a wry glance. "Since when are Vikings modest?"

"Just put some damn pants on," Nauma hissed.

His eyebrows lifted, but he inclined his head and disappeared into the shadows of the hallway, presumably to do what she wanted. Bryn snorted. She didn't think the man had ever moved so quickly to obey *her* unless it involved doing something dirty in bed. *Völva* were uncanny like that.

A half-second later, a massive wolf came in the room. She didn't know which of the other berserkers it was, but it wasn't Erik. The way the wolf averted his eyes instead of ogle her nudity gave her the big hint about who it was. "Ivar?"

His muzzle dipped in a nod.

The wolf's fluid, animalistic grace showed no sign of his human disability. Magic was a funny thing that way.

Bryn wrapped an arm across her breasts, though there was little else she could do to make this grandson-grandmother moment less awkward for him. Frankly, she didn't care, but she could tell he did. "I take it you heard Nauma too?"

Another nod from the wolf.

The *völva* cleared her throat. "I was having a vision of Loki's escape."

Ivar jerked, every muscle in his body quivering with alertness.

"He hasn't escaped yet," she soothed. "But feel free to go check your security camera."

Ivar grunted, turning away, presumably to do just that.

"I'll go with him." Erik appeared as silently as he'd left, set his hand on Ivar's head, and scrubbed between the wolf's ears. The man was wearing basketball shorts and a baggy tank top. It looked good on him, the shorts clinging to his groin in very interesting ways. He noticed her attention and winked, a promise in his gaze that made her insides quiver in want. She'd never confess it to him, but he'd done a damn fine job of wringing her out in bed.

"Ivar," Bryn called, and the wolf glanced over his shoulder. "She said Loki has accomplices. Non-giants. People we might expect on our side."

"The men here are trustworthy," Erik said quietly. Ivar made a noise of agreement.

"Maybe." She didn't know them well enough to fully concur, but since Erik and Ivar's asses were on the line here too, they had good reason to be absolutely certain who they could trust. "But what about other berserkers, valkyries, handmaidens, gods or goddesses? Can you vouch for all of them?"

"Point taken, *hjartað mitt.*"

The two males left, but Bryn stood there with her mouth gaping. *Hjartað mitt.* My heart. He hadn't called her that since…before she'd married Gunnar. A hundred lifetimes ago. And she had no idea how she felt about his using the endearment now. As was always the case with him, she was a jumble of confusion. She hated that, but she could admit to herself that maybe she was a little too somber, and he lightened something inside her. But was the end of the world the time to lighten up? Shit looked pretty grim right now.

She snapped her mouth shut, and found Nauma eyeing her speculatively. Bryn gave her a sour look in return. "I really don't want any prophetic words of wisdom about us."

"You're beyond my help anyway." The *völva* threw her legs over the side of the bed and rose as slowly and creakily as an ancient woman.

"That's comforting," Bryn replied dryly, catching the shorter woman's arm to steady her.

The two of them shuffled over to the dresser so Nauma could pull out a new nightgown. "You're a valkyrie, and you trust your fighting ability, you trust your instincts, but you don't trust your heart, your emotions. You haven't since the day you found out he betrayed you."

So much for avoiding words of wisdom, but short of dumping the other woman on the floor, Bryn was stuck. "True enough."

Nauma straightened and turned to meet her gaze squarely. "For your own sake, you need to learn to forgive yourself for what happened. You've accepted that you can't change the past, and that's good, but you haven't forgiven yourself or trusted your emotions enough to love again since then."

Heat washed up Bryn cheeks in a rare blush. Nauma had pegged that one neatly, hadn't she? Bryn muttered, "Love isn't going to stop the apocalypse."

"Actually, I think it will," the *völva* said softly, her eyes flashing milky white for a split-second.

A prickling wave went down Bryn's spine.

Nauma tugged her arm away and took a few shaky steps toward the door and the bathroom in the hallway. "Think on what I said, shieldmaiden."

"I will, handmaiden." Bryn somehow doubted much else would be on her mind for a while. There was no way she'd get any more sleep tonight. Sunrise was only about a half-hour away, so she might as well start the day.

"Good." The *völva* nodded. "Now I'm going to wash the sweat off, get some grub, and then go for a morning flight. I haven't shifted into my dove form in far too long. Want to come?"

"I would, but I have to get down to the stables. The horses don't like to be kept waiting for their breakfast." Bryn shook her head with more regret than she'd have ever expected. Maybe she'd never love *völva* as a breed, but this one didn't seem too bad. Watching her have a vision gave Bryn a new perspective on Seers. The blue bruises under Nauma's eyes underscored how much her abilities took out of her—such power wasn't limitless or without cost.

Bryn went to her room, threw on some clothes, and headed downstairs to grab a cup of coffee and a blueberry muffin. Someone had already made a pot of caffeine, which was nice. Muffin in one hand, mug in the other, she walked past the staircase to Ivar's room. The door stood open, and she could hear Erik and Ivar talking before she reached the threshold. Every available surface in the room was covered in electronics, and Ivar was back in his human form, typing away at his laptop.

"Loki still tied down?" she asked.

"For now." Ivar's voice was an ill-tempered growl.

"Hey." Erik came over and dropped a light kiss on her mouth. He moved away before she had time to blink in surprise. Warmth suffused her chest, but she squelched the feeling. Erik used his own cup of coffee to gesture upward. "Did she say anything else?"

Bryn shrugged lightly, and kept her tone just as airy. "Apparently, love's gonna stop the apocalypse. Let's all hold hands and sing Kumbaya, shall we?"

"Love?" An arrested expression crossed Erik's face.

"I have work to do." Because Nauma was right. Bryn didn't trust her heart, didn't trust in love, knew how weak and helpless any kind of tender emotion could make a person.

And Erik was the one who'd taught her that awful lesson.

Even if he'd apologized, did that really change anything? Maybe. Maybe not. She wasn't sure she could trust him any more than she could trust what he made her feel.

11

Erik went with Bryn to the barn, figuring he'd rather help her than deal with Ivar in a foul mood. They fed the horses, walked them out to their respective pastures, and then mucked stalls. They worked easily side-by-side, and it took a bit of teasing, but he got her to chat with him. There was wariness and confusion in her eyes when she looked at him, but somewhere in the last twenty-four hours, he'd realized he wanted her trust back. There was a lot of shit they had to hash out between them, reprehensible things they'd done to each other, and yet...he'd decided they'd figure it out. If fate was determined to force them together, they had to find a way to get along outside of the bedroom. They had to face the demons between them. How and when, he didn't know, but adding the normalcy of working on mundane tasks together couldn't hurt.

He stepped out of the stall he'd finished cleaning and headed for the last one in the row, setting his pitchfork on top of the wheelbarrow and pushing the load along the cement walkway.

Bryn's voice came from the stall across the aisle. "If you emigrated to the U.S. a hundred years ago, you have to have been doing something besides being ye olde Norse hero."

Moving across the stretch of concrete between them, he lounged against the wooden half-door. "I served in both World Wars, bootlegged whiskey in between, then did some time as a cop in New York, New Orleans, and Chicago. Now, though? I'm a scholar of ye olde Norse heroes."

She glanced over at him, her lips pursing thoughtfully. "I could see that actually. You always were a thinker."

"It's from spending my childhood tending sheep." He shrugged. "Nothing to do but be in your own head."

"And fuck a farm animal when you got bored." She smirked.

Assuming an innocent mien, he pressed a palm to his chest. "I swear I was just pushing it over the fence!"

She doubled over in a belly laugh, leaning on the handle of her pitchfork for support. It was unusual for her to let loose like this, and he relished it. After a few minutes she swiped her damp eyes on the shoulder of her T-shirt. "I can't believe you just said that."

"I've always said whatever it took to make you laugh." Not that he'd ever been a clown, but he tried to catch her off-guard with the occasional witty comment. That approach usually worked best with her.

She sobered. "I know. I laugh more around you than anyone else."

He saluted and spun away to get back to work.

"I've cried more because of you than anyone else, too."

The words were low enough that he wasn't sure if he was meant to hear them or if she'd been talking to herself. Either way, he winced. He half-turned back to her, but then stilled. What could he say that he hadn't already said? And hadn't she also brought him boatloads of agony in his lifetime? He sighed and went into the last stall. The physical labor was good, gave him something to focus on, but didn't take too much concentration.

The light conversation they'd shared earlier evaporated into silence. What she was thinking, he didn't know, but his brain still focused on the biggest sticking point he had with her. He could apologize until he was blue in the face, and she'd forgive him or not, but was she equally sorry for the pain she'd caused him? Did she still relish having gotten him murdered? Worse, was she glad she'd killed his young son? Why had she done it? Just to complete her vengeance or something more? She'd spared his daughter with Gudrun—why not slaughter Svanhild too?

He heard Bryn finish and tip a bucket of horse manure into the wheelbarrow. "I'm going to grab a shower. Do you know where the dung heap is to dump this load?"

"Yep." He didn't look up, just kept cleaning out the stall.

She hesitated in the doorway for a few seconds. "Okay...see you later."

"Later." He was going to need to ask his burning questions, but was now the right time to bring up more personal shit? Or should he wait until everything had blown over?

He hadn't found an answer by the time he'd gone back into the house, showered, and put on some clean clothes. He was halfway down the stairs when Ivar's voice echoed through the house. "Everyone, you're going to want to see this!"

Erik heard the pounding of footsteps on wooden floors as people reacted to the summons. He continued down the steps, Nauma came pelting behind him, and he almost collided with Holm, who was rounding the corner from the kitchen. They jostled for a moment, and Nauma darted past them into the room.

"What's going on?" she demanded breathlessly.

Ivar glanced at the three of them. "Let's wait for everyone to—"

"We're all here, mate." Val waved Bryn into the room, and they lined up to hear what Ivar had to say.

The tension in the air felt as thick and suffocating as a wet blanket, and Erik could almost imagine each of them both hoping and dreading that the waiting would finally be over.

Ivar pointed to a silenced newsfeed on his laptop. Similar feeds were running on the TV and on two other monitors he'd rigged up. "A sinkhole opened in Illinois around midnight."

After a short pause, Bryn threw up her hands. "So?"

"It ate the house where I'd last tracked Heimdall. He was having an affair with a human woman." He tilted his head. "Well, maybe with the woman and her husband, but I didn't dig too deeply into any possibilities."

Several of them sucked in a breath at once. Shit. This was bad. There'd been natural disasters popping up all over the world the last decade or so, but he'd never heard of one deliberately targeting an immortal. Since giants were often connected with elements, it made a terrifying kind of sense that they might use that connection as a weapon.

Val asked, "So, Heimdall is...dead? Before the apocalypse started, even though he was supposed to die during the battle of *Ragnarök*?"

That was the thing about being immortal—it didn't make you invincible. It also didn't mean you couldn't die or be killed. It didn't mean you couldn't be permanently disabled, as Ivar demonstrated. The god Tyr got a hand bitten off by a giant wolf, and it hadn't grown back. Being immortal just meant you'd never die a natural death. So long as nothing bad happened, you'd just keep coasting along forever. But if you lived long enough, something bad *was* going to happen. Eventually.

Immortality had different effects on different people. Some of them clung to that life with a desperation, a fear that was unlike anything that a human could comprehend. Some immortals had lived so long, they'd gotten bored and almost welcomed death. Then there were ones like Erik—he didn't fear death, but he didn't flirt with it either. When it came, it came. He hoped it was a passing that he could be proud of, unlike when he'd shuffled off his mortal coil. Yes, he'd died in battle, and he'd taken the other guy with him, but...it had been a battle instigated by his dishonorable deeds. Not his finest moment.

"Heimdall might be dead. Or he might be just kidnapped." Ivar looked both helpless and angry at the same time. "I don't think the sinkhole itself would have killed a god. His mortal lovers, yes—their bodies were dug out by authorities this morning. But who or what was waiting for Heimdall when he crawled out of the hole..."

"Why would anyone kidnap or kill him?" Nauma sat on the arm of the couch. "He was pretty mild-mannered, as gods go."

"He was supposed to sound the horn to let Valhalla know the apocalypse was upon them," Bryn noted.

Erik finished that thought. "Someone just took away the gods' advanced warning system."

"Yep." Ivar nodded. "I'm reviewing footage from several news cameras to see if there's anything useful the humans might have accidentally picked up." He rubbed bloodshot eyes and sipped his coffee.

"How long have you been at this, mate?" Val set a hand on his friend's shoulder.

"About five hours. Since Erik and Bryn went outside."

Nauma gave him a no-nonsense look worthy of a kindergarten teacher with a naughty pupil. "Maybe it's time to take a break."

"Please, I haven't even gotten to the part where I mix NoDoz and Red Bull into my coffee yet." Ivar grinned. "That's when the party really gets started."

"That's so frat boy during finals week of you." Erik rolled his eyes. "My undergrad students would be so impressed."

Ivar grunted, his gaze glued to the monitors. The others gathered closer to watch the footage with him. Erik figured it was as good a time as any to get some caffeine for himself. If they'd be settling in for a while, he was going to need it. He left the room, but when he reached the kitchen, he found only dregs in the coffee pot. It took a couple of minutes to have a cupful, and he let the rest of the pot percolate when he returned to the living room.

He rounded the corner and saw Bryn shrug and say, "I'm getting some lunch. If I have to watch boring shit, I'm gonna at least be fed."

Waving his mug through the air, Ivar said, "I sucked down the last of the coffee pot."

"I can make more," she replied.

"Great. Bring me a cup while you're at it, darlin'," Holm called, plopping down on a chair. "And I'll take some of that lunch too."

Silence fell for a moment. Erik bit back a grin, leaned his shoulder against the doorjamb, and prepared to enjoy the show. Nauma arched her eyebrows, Val pinched the bridge of his nose, and Ivar shook his head, disgust on his face.

Bryn smiled, though only a fool would call it a pleasant expression. "Does this look like Valhalla, jackass? No. Which means this valkyrie doesn't fetch anything for fallen warriors, not beer, not caffeine, not food. You want something, feel free to get off your ass and get it yourself."

Holm drew back, offense on his face. He glanced around and seemed to realize he didn't have a scrap of sympathy coming from his comrades. Scowling, he inclined his head. "Noted."

That acidic smile flashed again. "Good boy."

"I made a new pot." Erik handed her his steaming mug. "You need this more than I do, clearly."

"Good boy," she purred and sipped the hot, liquid ambrosia.

He offered her a grin that was all kinds of wicked and suggestive. She winked and made sure to brush against him as she passed, sinful promise in her gaze that lured him like a Lorelei. There was no way he wouldn't follow her anywhere when she looked at him like that. Lust fired through his veins, a visceral reaction to her that would never die. He didn't want it to.

After she'd left, Holm sighed heavily and glanced at Erik. "Before y'all occupy the kitchen for a different kind of cooking, would you mind leaving some food in the dining room for the rest of us?"

Erik shrugged and turned to go. "I'll throw out some bread crumbs so you don't waste away of starvation."

He heard Bryn snicker and watched her slip into the kitchen. When he pushed through the swinging door, something was already flying at his head. Lightning-fast reflexes meant he caught it before it hit him in the face. A loaf of bread.

"You're in quite a feisty mood today." He chucked the bread out onto the dining room table and then turned back to her. "Need some help relaxing?"

Sauntering across the room, a provocative sway to her hips that made his tongue stick to the roof of his mouth, she shrugged. "After I've had some lunch, perhaps."

Oh, she wanted to tease, did she? The wolf inside him growled appreciatively at the new game. He grinned and felt his fangs scrape his lower lip. She opened a cupboard, and he prowled around the small table in the middle of the room. Her head tilted, bird-like, and he knew she was listening to his approach. A little shiver went through her, and he watched goose bumps break down her arms. He could hear her breathing accelerate, the air was spiced with her arousal, and anticipation punched through him.

Stepping close behind her, he curved his hands around her waist and brushed his lips over the nape of her neck.

"I like that." Her head bowed further. He nipped at the side of her neck, just grazing that sensitive patch of skin. She shuddered, but then she swallowed hard and a big breath whooshed out of her. "If Heimdall is dead or kidnapped, this is really it, isn't it? We're not talking prophecies or visions of what might be, but…"

"*Ragnarök*," he finished for her. He pulled her back so they were pressed together, and he held her close.

She stroked her fingers up and down his forearm. "I was hoping Nauma was wrong. Wishful thinking, I know, but I don't relish what's coming."

"Neither do I." He didn't mention that their fate—however bad it might be—was still supposed to be better than what lay in store for their compatriots in the living room.

"If this has to be it, then I'd like to go out with a bang." She rolled her head against his shoulder until her gaze met his, and there was no mistaking the look on her face or the tone of her voice.

"A bang, huh?" He extended his claws, scraping lightly over her midriff. His cock went rigid, and he could smell her desire increasing by the moment. "You want it slow and soft or hard and fast?"

"Hard." She squirmed against him, rubbing her ass into his groin. "Fast."

She didn't have to tell him twice. Retracting his claws, he wrenched open her pants, shoving his hand in so he could feel that sweet cream. Ah, yes. She was so wet for him. The noises she made, little mewls of pleasure, made lust scorch his insides. His dick pulsed with the need to bury himself within her. He could bring her to climax with his fingers, with his mouth, but he just couldn't wait. He had to have her, had to feel the slick grip of her tight sheath closing around his cock.

He swung her around until they faced the table, pressed his palm between her shoulder blades, and urged her forward over the flat wooden surface. She wore tall riding boots today, so this was the best position to take her in. Grasping the back of her breeches, he yanked them down to her thighs, baring her to his gaze. Her pussy was drenched, the pale curls darkened with moisture. He had his pants open in seconds, pulling his cock free. He rubbed the head up and down her slit, and she moved restlessly before him.

She glanced back over her shoulder. "This isn't hard or—"

He pierced her core, gliding in with one swift thrust that sank him to the hilt. But then he stopped, and grinned when she squirmed impatiently. His fingers splayed over the slender curve of her hips, and he drew back a hand to slap one cheek hard. He grinned at the lovely *crack* of sound. She choked on a breath and shuddered. He did it again, swatting the fleshy part of her thigh, peppering hot little spanks over the globes of her ass.

"Erik!" Her nails turned to raven's talons and dug furrows into the table, her back bowing as she moaned.

Every time his palm made contact with her backside, her inner muscles clenched around his cock. He couldn't hold back low groans, doing his best not to get *too* loud, but he heard the volume on Ivar's video increase to near-blaring. Erik grinned and shook his head, but didn't consider for a second that he should stop what he was doing.

"Erik, I...I can't..."

She tried to straighten, but he set his hands over hers, lacing their fingers together and pinning her to the table. She shivered, but didn't fight his hold. Instead, she pushed back into him, silently demanding he move *now*. He nipped at her shoulder, letting his fangs graze her skin. The salty flavor of her burst into his mouth, sinking into his psyche. It was a taste he'd never been able to forget, as familiar as breathing.

He'd dreamed of touching her so many times—even under the control of that fucking elixir, when he didn't understand why—he'd craved the feel of her skin against his. There was something about her that excited him on a level no other woman in a thousand years had ever managed to replicate. It was just as good now as it was back then. No, better. Because now there was no taboo, no shame—just the two of them glutting themselves on the best fuck of all time.

He pulled his hips away until he almost slipped free of her, then thrust in hard. The slap of their flesh together made him growl in appreciation. The wolf inside him had craved her from the first, had never had the man's reservations for how they might have torn each other's souls to pieces. The wolf didn't care about the past or the future, only the present. Only claiming the mate it wanted. He bit her shoulder again, sinking his fangs deeper into her skin, the tang of her blood rushing over his tongue.

A low cry broke from her, and she shoved back into him faster and faster. He moved with her, driving as deep as he could. Sweat slid down his face, stinging his eyes, but wiping it away would mean letting her arms go and...nope. He liked her right where he had her.

Her pussy flexed around him, and he had to clench his jaw to keep from coming then and there. He ground his pelvis downward, and moans spilled out of her.

"I'm going to come," she gasped, tugging at her hands. He refused to release her, tightening his grip.

"Yes. Come for me, Bryn." He pushed himself to greater speeds, hammering into her relentlessly.

Her body bowed upward, and her pussy pulsed around his thrusting cock. That was it, his control snapped. He exploded inside her, emptying every ounce of worry and tension into her. Groaning, he pumped into her until his dick began to soften. She relaxed against the table, her cheek pressed to the wood. Her eyes were closed, a tiny smile curving her lips.

It was one of the most perfect, peaceful moments of his life. He realized that he loved her. Still. Again. No other woman had ever fit him as well as her. The timing couldn't have been worse, and there were so many ugly memories and unanswered questions between them, but he couldn't deny the truth.

He loved her.

And with the world on the brink of doom, there wasn't a damn thing he could do about it. There might not be much of a future for them to have, even if they did want to spend it together. But he knew one thing—he would do everything in his power to hold on to her, to this.

12

They retrieved the untouched bread from the dining room and made sandwiches for everyone. After they'd disinfected the table, of course. Bryn figured it was only fair, considering the team had kept Holm muzzled while she got busy. That man couldn't open his mouth without inserting his foot up to his kneecap. For Erik's sake, she'd stuck to telling him off rather than decking him. Though Holm was no worse than many of the other males she'd dealt with in Valhalla, her tolerance for their he-man shit was at an all-time low. She doubted anyone was going to keep him from making sextastic wisecracks when they returned, but a well-placed comment about him being jealous because he wasn't getting any and might never again should shut him down.

Her stomach clenched a bit. *Ragnarök*. Somehow the thought of Heimdall being killed made it all too real. All too immediate.

Despite what the prophecy said, she honestly didn't expect to see the other side of this. As Nauma had predicted, Loki had accomplices, and it looked like one of them had done Heimdall in. Which meant the ancient *Ragnarök* prophecy might already be nullified, the deck stacking in favor of the giants instead of the gods. Wherever the rest of the gods were. Maybe they were dead already too.

She had both more and less information than she wanted.

"Come on." Erik kissed the side of her neck, and warmth pooled in her belly. She still didn't like this weakness she had for him, but she was starting to get used to it. Whether that was a good thing or not, she hadn't a single clue.

"I may need my mind taken off this later tonight." She brought his hand to her mouth, biting the base of his thumb. "Assuming something else doesn't happen between now and then."

His eyes burned silver for a moment, and that wicked dimple flashed. "Count on it."

"Mmm." She grabbed the tray of sandwiches and left him to bring the heavier tray loaded with glasses full of sweet tea. She'd grown addicted to the stuff since she'd moved to Virginia.

The crowd in her living room fell on the food like ravening beasts, making appreciative noises of gratitude with their mouths full. Vikings were never known for their manners, but they liked their grub.

"You're looking mellower, love." Val gave her an easy grin.

She ignored that, gesturing to the many screens playing the news. "Find anything interesting?"

Not looking away from the monitor closest to her, Nauma patted her mouth with a napkin before she answered, "Not ye—wait. Go back."

Ivar jolted, dropped his sandwich on his plate, and reached out to click a button that stopped the video. "How far?"

"Maybe thirty seconds." Nauma leaned further forward, squinting. "Can you slow it down to half-speed?"

"Yep." The video whipped backward, with the people bobbing and weaving in awkward jerks. Then it started again and the people moved as though trapped in molasses.

After about ten seconds she tapped the screen. "There."

He froze the video and enlarged the image, sending it to the largest of his monitors. The slightly grainy picture showed a nondescript woman with stooped shoulders, a sour expression, and frizzy dishwater blond hair. Ivar glanced back. "You know her?"

Nauma nodded firmly. "She's a valkyrie."

"What?" Bryn bent closer to the screen. "I don't recognize her."

"It's a wig." The other woman tapped a nail against the blond frizz. "Picture her with long, shiny black hair."

Bryn shut her eyes for a moment, holding the mental image and making the necessary color shift. She looked again. "Kata. The ice-blue eyes give her away."

"Yep." The handmaiden grinned in satisfaction, though Bryn noted she had lines of exhaustion bracketing her eyes and mouth.

"Good eye." As compliments went, it wasn't much, but Bryn wasn't accustomed to needing to flatter anyone but her horses. A sugar cube and pat on the rump usually did the trick. Not so much with humans.

"Thank you." Nauma shrugged demurely. "I had a feeling there was something important on the video, so I paid closer attention."

"Well, I'm happy about you feeling your feelings." Holm flashed a charming grin at her, and Val gave him a resentful glare.

She snorted. "Thanks, I think."

"Frey," Bryn blurted out, her memories of the other valkyrie finally snapping into place.

"Excuse me?" Erik stirred beside her, his hand coming to rest on her waist.

"Frey," she repeated. "Kata is banging Freya's twin brother. Or she was about a hundred years ago." They'd gone off to some hidden corner of Odin's hall to fuck and, unfortunately for all of them, that was also the spot Bryn liked to retreat to when she needed a break from the throngs of immortals in Valhalla. She'd beat a hasty retreat, but not before she'd gotten an eyeful of the two of them getting down and very, very dirty. "But…Kata was never the type who slept around, so it probably wasn't a casual one-time screw. I always got the impression she was a little too controlled for that, you know?"

"Yeah, I remember that about her too." Nauma worried her thumbnail between her teeth. "She was never one who was rude, didn't seem to look down on me as a handmaiden or anything, but…she wasn't warm and fuzzy either."

"Difficult to get to know, yeah. Not that I tried hard." Since Bryn wasn't the warm and fuzzy type either. "I showed up when summoned and then got back to the mortal realm. Not enough time there to make friends."

"Me too. After the first few centuries, it was just easier to keep my distance." Nauma leaned back in her seat and sighed. "Quieter, less drama-filled. Freya wanted me more for oracle consultations than handmaiden duties, so…no need to be on site all the time."

"I hear you." Bryn hated the drama too, especially right after she'd gotten there, fresh from the drama of Grimhild and Gudrun. There was nothing Bryn had wanted so much as to be alone somewhere and lick her wounds.

"Can we get back to the sinkholes and bad guys? For just a sec, ladies? Hmm?" Ivar's tone was saccharine enough that Bryn wanted to smack him. He really was in a pisser of a mood today.

"Snide," Nauma chided.

Bryn widened her eyes in agreement. "Right?"

He pinched the bridge of his nose. "Kata. Frey. Focus, please."

She spoke slowly, as if to a toddler. A stupid toddler. "We recognize her face, but don't know her well. That's basically what we just said."

His reply was in the same condescending tone. "You know her well enough to know who she's sleeping with."

"That was more me walking into the wrong room at the wrong time. This wasn't something you could misinterpret either. Like full-frontal fucking." She made a face as if she'd tasted something nasty. "Never wanted that view of Frey's junk."

Nauma stuck out her tongue. "The gods are always less impressive than they like to claim."

Bryn quirked her eyebrow, but said nothing. Yes, she'd seen a few. Most were no more than average in their endowments. But that wasn't information she felt the need to share.

Val shot from his seat, rounding on Nauma. "Exactly how many gods have you been ogling?"

"Who said it was just ogling?" She licked her lips suggestively.

His face turned purple, fists clenching, jealousy written plainly on his expression. He turned on a heel and slammed out the door.

"Nice." Holm looked impressed. "That's faster than I've managed to piss anyone off in a while."

She wrinkled her nose. "I don't belong to him—haven't in a million years. I guarantee he's fucked everything that walked."

Ivar winked, ran a hand down his muscular chest, and appeared more chipper than he had all day. "And maybe a few things that don't."

"No!" Nauma's mouth went round with mingled horror and delight. "You and

Valbjorn? *Really?*"

"No, I'm just messing with you." He grinned like a pirate, and she swatted his arm. After a moment, his face sobered. "I met Val after what happened with you, and I could always tell that...something bad had gone down. Seriously, truly, tragically bad."

She swallowed, glancing aside. "He never...made any mention of caring about me. It was probably just guilt because some wimpy little princess died saving his skin."

"Keep telling yourself that if it makes you feel better." He flicked dismissive fingers. "I have some research to do to track down Frey and this Kata chick. Go away."

"With pleasure." Holm heaved himself out of his chair and sauntered off.

Erik cocked his head to the side. "Someone's coming up your driveway."

The distant rumble of a familiar truck reached her ears. She glanced at the clock on the mantel, found it was later than she'd thought. "My stable hands are back. I'll go talk to them about my...houseguests. And let them know I might be leaving town soon."

"You can trust them to look after the place?" Erik set a hand on her shoulder, support radiating from the gesture. "I know how much you care for your horseflesh."

She fought the dual urge to shrug away from him and lean into him. Wow, she really was a hot mess these days. "Yeah, they're good people. I've left them alone here before when I went on buying or selling trips. They'll take good care of my ponies."

The truck brakes squeaked, and with the number of extra vehicles parked outside, she knew her guys would want to check in with her first. She headed for the porch and heard Erik and Nauma fall into step behind her. After a second, she heard the whir of Ivar's wheels rolling over the hardwood floor. Apparently, they were having a welcoming party.

She pushed out the screen door onto the front porch. Holm was lounging on one of the rails, looking like a massive lion sunning himself. There was a sight to greet her farmhands, who were approaching with surprised expressions. She couldn't say she blamed them—she'd never had a guest here in the five years they'd been working for her.

"Tom, Greg, this is Erik. He's an old friend. And this is Holm, Ivar, and Nauma. There's another one around here named Val." She came down the porch steps to join the farmhands. "Let's head to my office—I need to discuss a few things with you. You know how you guys have been saying I should get off the farm more often and take a vacation? Well, you're about to get your wish."

They eyed the newcomers warily, but since they were both former jockeys, they were about 5'4 and 125 pounds each soaking wet. They had a wiry strength that kept race horses in check, but they were no match for a Viking berserker. The humans might not know exactly what they were dealing with, but they could see when a guy moved like he knew how to handle himself in a fight.

Then again, she moved that way too, didn't she?

She waved her employees towards the barn. "Come on."

Now she just had to invent explanations the mortals would believe. Shouldn't be too hard. She'd been lying about this kind of stuff for millennia.

13

After dinner that evening, Bryn helped her farmhands settle the horses for the night. They walked back across the gravel drive together, she waved them off to their cottage, and loped up her front steps. There was no sign of anyone else, so she headed for the living room. Maybe Ivar had managed to hack some international database and locate Kata. If she was even living on Earth. If she'd remained up in Asgard, Frey could take her back and forth at will. That would hose any chance of finding her.

Bryn rubbed at her temples, trying to ward off the headache that wanted to form. If the tension got to her, the horses and mortals on this farm would notice. That would make working difficult, and it wouldn't help her stress level. She blew out a breath, tossed her braid over her shoulder, and strode into the living room.

Only Ivar sat there, scowling at his computer screen. No need to poke the angry wolf, so she tried to back out quietly.

His silver eyes—Erik's eyes—flicked to her, pinning her in place. He sat back in his chair. "Since we met, you rarely look me in the eyes, and you always make a run for it as soon as humanly possible. Is it the wheelchair that bothers you, or just me?"

Straightening her shoulders like a soldier under review, she met his gaze squarely. As uncomfortable as the question might be, she didn't even consider not answering it. "Neither, really. It's that you remind me of things I'd rather not think about." Like another pair of silver eyes that had once gazed at her with helpless dismay, pain and terror mingling on that sweet little face. She shook the awful memory away. When Ivar appeared ready to question her on that topic, she went back to his original question. "So...since you brought it up, what's with the wheelchair?"

"As you saw this morning, when I shift into a wolf, I don't have any problem walking. Full mobility. A magical benefit of being one of Odin's chosen, I guess." He shrugged. "As a human, I was born with a very mild form of *osteogenesis imperfecta*, aka brittle bone disease. So I can't use my legs, but otherwise I'm pretty normal. Back in the day, I could use a long bow and designed a kind of chariot-like wagon that let me get in the thick of battles. Viking leaders had to fight—none of this weak-ass Monday night quarterbacking like they do now."

"Buncha dickless wonders in charge these days." She wrinkled her nose.

"I know, right?" He flashed a quick smile, and then patted his wheelchair affectionately. "Technology has come a long way since then. It's much easier to get around. Though I do kind of miss being carried on a throne by a legion of minions."

She stifled a short laugh. "And throngs of slave women to peel you grapes?"

"Good times, good times." His grin turned wicked, and the look reminded her so much of Erik, she had to look away.

"I should go and—"

Ivar interrupted. "Have you ever talked to him about it?"

She didn't pretend to misunderstand him. It wasn't as if Erik and her history was some big secret. Misunderstood and misinterpreted maybe, but not a secret. "Some. Not everything. It'd just stir shit up."

"Or clear the air."

"Look, I'm not the type who needs to feel her feelings about every damn thing. What happened, happened." And it would mean confessing her worst sin, baring her soul in a way she never had before. She...didn't think she could do it. "Nothing can change the past. Let it go."

"But you haven't let it go, have you?" Ivar set an elbow on the arm of his chair. "I'd say Erik has done better with that than you."

"Good for him. It's not a competition." Because if it was, she'd have lost. She didn't need to say so though. The scars on her heart were no one's business but her own.

"You still love him." He jabbed a finger at her. "Even after everything that happened. That's what kills you."

Yes. The reflexive answer that sprang to her mind rocked her to her core. She felt as if the wind had been knocked out of her, and it was all she could do to stay on her feet. Having someone shove it in her face so blatantly meant she hadn't had time to form an internal excuse. She tried never to lie to herself, but this truth had the power to rip her to bits so small there'd be no picking up the pieces again. She swallowed hard, clenched her trembling fingers. "You have no idea what you're talking about. You don't know me."

He continued as if she hadn't spoken. "You can't forgive yourself for loving him. Still. Deal with that and maybe Nauma's prediction will come true. Maybe it'll save our collective asses. Think about that, all right? It's not just about you anymore, hiding out alone in bumfuck nowhere."

Spinning his wheelchair neatly, he rolled out of the living room and down the hall toward his bedroom.

"Pushy bastard, isn't he?" Erik stepped from behind the wall next to the doorway.

She let out a breath. "How much did you hear?"

"All the parts you wish I hadn't."

Well, fuck. She almost wished a sinkhole would open up and swallow her whole. At the moment, it felt like Heimdall had gotten the easy way out.

14

Erik wasn't sure if Bryn was going to cry or punch him. Maybe both. The look on her face was guilt, shame, and anger. Anger at herself or him, he didn't know. Again, maybe both. He took a deep breath and girded his loins to broach the topic he'd been avoiding since he'd arrived.

"There is one part of the past I haven't managed to get over, despite what Ivar might think."

"I'm sure." Her face went pale, her lips compressing into a tight line.

"You killed my son. Sigmund died at your hand." There, he'd put it into words. If there was to be any trust between them, any future, they had to excise the wounds they'd inflicted on each other. This one was like a gash that became an infection that spread and spread, but never healed.

She flinched and her expression was utterly devoid of emotion. "So the legends say."

"Why?" He reached a hand toward her, but she stumbled back to avoid him. That hurt. He forced himself to continue. "I don't want to hear what other people think your reasoning was—I want to hear it from you. *Why?* Was it just vengeance? Was it worth it?"

Her dark gaze dropped to the ground. "He would have tried to avenge you when he grew up. That meant my daughter—*our* daughter—was in danger. He'd unleash his wrath on her." Her mouth worked. "I couldn't let that happen. The endless cycle of revenge, the curse of Andvaranaut, had to end with us. With me."

"So you threw yourself on my funeral pyre, breaking the ring's curse and ending your own life in the process." There was more to the story than this. He could tell she lied—or didn't give him the whole truth. Frustration welled inside him, and he fisted his fingers to keep from shaking her. This would haunt them forever if they let it, didn't she understand that? Look how long it had haunted them already. Avoidance helped nothing.

Her shoulder twitched in a shrug. "So the legends say."

"Damn it, Bryn—"

Her head shot up, fire blazing in her gaze. "You lied to me, humiliated me, handed me over to Gunnar like I was...nothing. A whore you could use and discard after you'd fucked her over. So, telling Gunnar what you'd done and letting him assassinate you for betraying us both...yeah, a lot of that was retribution. Don't expect me to apologize for it either, because I won't."

This was territory they'd already gone over, and it was clear she was spoiling for a fight rather than being willing to talk about the day Sigmund and she died. He reined in his temper, and forced his tone to reasonable levels. "I'm sorry. I didn't mean to betray you."

His mildness had the opposite effect he was hoping for. Her gaze sparked with fury and she jammed a fingertip into his chest. "Maybe, but you knew you'd betrayed him when you slept with me and knocked me up."

Stay calm, Erik. Stay calm. He drew in a slow breath, let it ease out. "I didn't know Aslaug was my daughter. How could I? There were no DNA tests back then, and she looked exactly like you."

"You never bothered to ask after Grimhild's elixirs wore off," she fired back. "With the timing of Aslaug's birth you had to know it was possible you fathered her."

He shook his head. "Denial. I told myself she had to be Gunnar's. Not until I met Ivar did I accept the rumor that Aslaug was mine."

"Your delusions aren't my fault or my problem." She spun on a heel and made to exit the room.

He caught her arm before she could pass, knowing his grip was bruising and not caring. "It wasn't either of my daughters I asked about—they both got to grow up and have kids of their own. It was my son I wanted to know what happened to. You're not telling me everything, Bryn. Stop feeding me half-truths."

"I killed your son." She lifted one knee and yanked a knife out of her boot, the lamplight gleaming off its wicked edge. She waved it in his face. "This was the blade I used to slit his throat. Then I set his body on fire. Isn't that enough detail for you? What kind of sick fuck wants a blow-by-blow of how his baby was murdered?"

Erik staggered back in shock, not even resisting when she ripped her arm out of his grasp and bolted up the stairs. He heard her bedroom door slam in the distance, and then the rattle of pipes as she turned on the water for a shower. Still he stood there, staring into space, unable to fit what he knew of Bryn together with a woman who would butcher a helpless innocent. She had loved his boy; everyone at court knew it. They called him her *skuggi*, her shadow, because when Erik was away fighting, Sigmund followed Bryn around like an adoring puppy. Even when she'd seethed with rage at the rest of royal family, she'd never taken it out on any of the children.

She hadn't done it. No matter what she said, Erik didn't believe her.

Perhaps it made him a fool, but every single thing within him rejected the idea that the woman he'd held in his arms, who didn't want the human race to be wiped out, who still cared about the insignificance of a mortal's birthday—*that* woman would never have murdered a boy she loved. Because Bryn felt things fiercely and always had. Even here in her isolated retirement, she was fierce in protecting that seclusion. She was intense in her passions, unstinting in her loyalty, and absolutely relentless when crossed. But her sense of justice hadn't expanded beyond ending Erik or she would have turned her wrath on Gunnar, on Gudrun, on Grimhild. Not on Sigmund, never on Sigmund.

He had doubted before, but no longer. Whatever had happened, it had been distorted. Whatever had happened, she was letting him—letting everyone—believe the worst of her. He needed to know why.

Now more than ever, he wanted the truth, even if he had to pry the details out of her.

15

During her shower, Bryn managed to slam the door on the memories Erik had tried to tear loose. She locked them away where they belonged—she was good at that. She'd had a lot of practice. She wrapped herself in hard-won calm and could breathe easily again.

Then she scrubbed her bathroom until the porcelain gleamed. When that was done, she attacked her bedroom. She vacuumed, dusted, changed the bedding and took the dirty sheets to the laundry room at the end of the upstairs hall. She pulled a forgotten load out of the dryer and carried it back to her room to fold. Unfortunately, she dropped a sock and managed to kick it under the bed.

"Fuck."

She knelt down and peered into the gloom. As much as she liked her modern conveniences, the dryer had a damned inconvenient way of eating her favorite socks. If she didn't retrieve this one, she'd forget it was there and that'd be another pair she couldn't use. If it weren't for humans having the same dryer problem, she'd suspect a god of bewitching the machine to play a prank on her.

"*What* are you doing?"

She jolted in surprise, popping her head up to see Erik standing directly beside her. It was unsettling for several reasons. First, it was odd to know someone could approach so silently even her advanced hearing didn't catch a whisper of sound. Second, her instincts usually screamed a warning long before anyone was close enough she needed to hear them. Her instincts hadn't warned her of anything, not so much as a peep that danger was but a handspan away. What message her psyche was trying to convey, she really didn't want to consider too deeply.

"Not that I'm complaining about the view, but..." His gaze fixed on her ass in her awkwardly bent position.

She cleared her throat and knelt up. "Looking for an errant sock."

He tugged at a lock of her still-damp hair, then trailed his fingertips down to stroke over that sensitive bit of skin beneath her ear. Tingles shivered down her neck and she shrugged away in reflex, covering up that vulnerable spot.

He was silent for a moment. "Bryn...we should discuss—"

No. Just no. That was the last thing she wanted to do, *discuss* anything. Time to evade and distract. Going for the one thing that had never failed them, she reached up and boldly cupped his cock through his jeans. His breath choked off, his gray eyes going wide in shock. But his erection thickened and strained against his zipper, and she rubbed a thumb over the bulbous crest.

His throat worked. "Bryn..."

"Mmm?" She flicked open the tab on his pants, easing down the zipper. Hooking her fingers in his belt loops, she pulled his jeans down around his ankles. The fabric was tight enough that it dragged his boxers down too. His dick popped free, curving in an arc to dance just below his navel. She blew a cool stream of air over his pulsing shaft, and a bead of precum slipped downward.

His hands knotted into fists at his sides, but he did nothing to stop her. "Are you sure you don't want to talk—"

"Erik, I don't really have any interest in *talking*. At all. I have other activities in mind." And then she took his cock in her mouth, all the way down until the head nudged the back of her throat.

His hoarse groan echoed in the bedroom. She formed her fingers in a ring around his erection, stroking him as she licked and sucked the head. The sounds he made were of ecstatic desperation, and they lit a fire deep within her. She'd started this as a way to sidetrack him, but his pleasure became hers. Her sex grew slick with juices, her breasts heavy and her nipples impossibly tight. Shivers of lust ran through her and every time she sucked him, her pussy contracted. She braced her free hand against his thigh, not wanting to stop, but needing the support as tremors ran through her legs.

"Fuck. That feels...Bryn, I...shit, I can't...*gods.*"

Humming deep in her throat made him inhale sharply, and she knew the noise vibrated along his dick. She continued to work him with her hand and her mouth, keeping the rhythm fast enough to bring him right to the edge, but not so fast he could go over unless she wanted him to.

Then a sprite of impishness sparked through her. Slipping her hand up his thigh, she massaged the soft sac between his legs. That was rewarded with another round of appreciative cursing and gasps of her name. Oh, but she wasn't done with him yet. She moved to stroke the sensitive strip of skin behind his balls. He seemed to freeze for a moment, then a harsh shudder quaked his body. His hand plunged into her hair, pulling the strands taut. She ignored the pressure on her scalp and instead slipped further back until she circled the pucker of his anus. He widened his stance to give her more access. His breathing became a ragged rasp, small groans breaking free. She pressed one finger into his ass, then two, then three, while his hips bucked, shoving his cock deeper down her throat.

"Please, Bryn! I need...I have to...Bryn, *please.*"

Oh, she liked that. Him, begging. Wasn't that just a nice little fantasy come true?

She was relentless and she was damn sure they both enjoyed it thoroughly. She fucked him with her mouth and her fingers, rubbing over that spot she knew would drive him mad with lust. A low shout ripped from him and he climaxed in long jets of come. Shudders wracked him and his hand in her hair yanked painfully tight. His knees buckled and he managed to land in front of her rather than on top of her. His palms set on the floor on either side of her knees. His forehead pressed to her belly, and they were both panting for air. Need still twisted within her, but she let her fingertips drift gently over his shaved head.

"Are you all right, Erik?"

"Yes," he rasped, another shudder quaking through him. "A moment, please."

"Take your time." She patted his shoulder.

A few more seconds, and then he moved with that lightning-fast speed, pulling her into his arms and standing.

"That was amazing, sweetheart. I think I should return the favor."

She arched her eyebrows, managing a sardonic tone, though her hormones were jangling for some relief. "Oral with a bit of anal fingering? I thought you did that the first day you got here."

"Hmm, no." He set her on the bed. "I meant I should fuck your ass."

Her breathing shallowed to nothingness, excitement wrenching through her. She loved ass play, had since the moment he'd introduced her to the sport. The one night they'd been together so long ago hand redefined *wild*. "There's lube in the top drawer of my dresser."

A rich chuckle issued from him after he'd opened the specified drawer. "That's not all that's in here."

"No," she agreed, propping herself on her elbows to watch him.

"We shouldn't let anything this entertaining go to waste." He pulled out the largest of her vibrating dildos, of course. Nipple clamps came next, and then a tiny spiked pinwheel.

She licked her lips, her heart pounding so loudly the rush of blood roared in her ears. "Most of that hasn't been touched in quite some time. I typically use those last two items on my lovers, not the other way around."

"Ah, but you've already blown my mind. You should get to lay back, relax, and have fun. What do you think?"

"Okay." At this point, there could be a gun to her head and she still wouldn't refuse what he was offering. Her body demanded release. Immediately, if not sooner. "Do you want me face up or face down?"

He considered her for a moment, flicking the pinwheel thoughtfully. "Up. I like to see your face when you come for me."

"Whatever floats your boat." She winked and stayed right where she was.

His chuckle was more sinful than dark chocolate. Glancing down, he waggled his eyebrows, and stroked his fingers up and down his renewed erection. "We're afloat."

The sight was enough to make her toes curl. His cock was perfect—long, thick, with just enough curve to hit her G-spot when he fucked her pussy. She throbbed with need that wouldn't quit, her nipples contracting into taut nubs.

His gaze zeroed in on her chest, and his smile promised all kinds of naughtiness. A promise she knew he could fulfill. Two long strides brought him to the bed, and he sat beside her. He lifted the clamps. "These first, I think."

His fingers curled around one breast, his thumb circling the tip. Impossibly, inevitably, her nipple beaded tighter, the ache between her legs so intense she had to squeeze her thighs together. He applied the first clamp. It bit into her flesh, shooting dual messages of pleasure and pain to her brain. The two sensations twined, became one, and she moaned, letting her head fall back.

"Too tight?"

She swallowed, trying to get her tongue to form words. "No."

"Good." Then his mouth closed over her other nipple, suckling the peak. His fingers toyed with the clip on the other breast, and moisture gushed into her pussy. Her arms gave out, and her shoulders collapsed to the mattress. Her nipple popped free of his mouth and he clamped it too.

Her hips bucked, her eyes slid closed, and her hands balled in the sheets. "More. Now."

"Anything you want, sweetheart." He pressed a hand between her thighs, spreading her. Cool air rushed against her hot flesh, and she shuddered. A low buzzing drew her attention to the dildo he held. He flashed the kind of grin a marauding Viking would wear on a raid. Teasing her clit with the vibration, he made her cry out. Pleasure jolted through her—almost too much to contain—and her fingers snapped around his wrist, forcing the phallus lower. He pushed it into her pussy in one quick thrust, and she came in a rush that had stars bursting behind her eyes.

"Erik!" Goose bumps exploded over her skin, her sex spasming around the dildo. Her body writhed against the sheets, sweat slipping down her temples. Gods, it felt so *good*.

"Ah, yeah." He groaned. "You, looking all flushed and well-fucked, screaming my name. My favorite wet dream just came to life."

An inelegant, snorting little laugh erupted from her. "Shut up and screw me, Erik."

"And a giggle, even. The night just gets better and better." He dropped a quick kiss on her lips, nipped at her neck, and then flicked a nipple clamp with his tongue.

She could only manage a mewl of pure want, and the dildo still vibrating inside her meant that one orgasm did very little to take the edge off her lust. She was far from satisfied. "More."

"Insatiable," he admonished, but spoiled it with a dimpled smile. "I like that in a woman."

She heard a creaking *pop* and knew he'd opened the top of the lube bottle. Excitement sent frissons of need coursing through her. Gods, yes. That was exactly what she craved. She eased her legs wider, giving him as much access as he wanted. She caught her lower lip in her teeth and watched him slip his hand between her thighs. He bumped the vibrator, and she stifled a moan as her sex clenched. "Hurry, Erik."

Two thick fingers pressed to her anus, the lube cool on her intimate flesh. He circled her entrance, then pushed both digits in. He pumped into her, working the lubricant deep. She couldn't hold back a shivery little moan. This was her favorite sex act, partially because it stripped you down to the raw, feral part of your soul, and partially because it was a little dark and forbidden. The illicitness made it so much better. Her breathing became erratic, her talons ripping through the sheets. He added a third finger to her ass, fucking her with them, but this wasn't what she wanted. She wanted everything he had to give tonight.

"Inside me. Now. Inside me." She was barely coherent, but somehow he understood her.

"Yes." He pulled his hand away, lifted her legs to drape her ankles against his shoulder, one arm holding her in place. The head of his cock nudged her ass, and she felt immense pressure as he bore down on her. The angle made it a tight fit as he slid into her one slow inch at a time, stretching her anus. The fact that she already had a thick dildo vibrating in her pussy meant she was almost too full. Almost. She skated along the razor's edge of agony and ecstasy. Moans broke from her throat, the feeling so damn amazing.

He pulled back until just the bulbous crest of his dick remained within her, then he pushed in, faster than before. Again and again and again. He picked up speed and force, and his pelvis slapped against her ass.

A metallic ping made her look at his hand. He held the small pinwheel aloft. "You didn't think I'd forgotten this, did you?"

She shook her head. "You assume I'm willing to think about anything but having another orgasm right now."

That made him laugh. Switching back and forth between legs, he ran the pinwheel up her pinioned thighs, the sides of her knees, her calves, the bottoms of her feet. The prickling tickle made her shriek and jerk against his hold, but he kept her in place, still plunging his dick into the tight ring of her anus.

"No tickling!" It was difficult to assume a threatening expression when a man was fucking your ass, but she managed.

"It's so tempting to ask *or else what*, but I have a better idea anyway." He tossed the pinwheel aside, then reached for the nipple clamps, slipping them off quickly. The sudden end to that pleasure-pain made her eyes pop wide, a new wave of sensation rocking her. He winked, curled his fingers around the dildo, and began pumping it in tandem with his cock. "Time to come, honey."

It was more than enough to launch her into orbit. Every inner muscle clenched at once, and he gave a choked groan. Her pussy flexed around the dildo, the vibrations just catapulting her higher. He continued to work her with his hand and his cock, dragging out her climax. She felt as if she would detonate like a firecracker, her skin too tight and hot to contain the heat. He pounded into her ruthlessly, and she came again, a harsh cry spilling from her throat. His claws dug into her thigh, his eyes going wolfish as he exploded inside her, hot come filling her.

He collapsed next to her on the mattress, and they both sobbed for breath. Reality faded away for a while, and she drifted in that lovely place where she wasn't quite asleep and wasn't quite awake. She was jolted abruptly back to alertness when he opened his mouth and ripped away whatever was left of her shattered defenses.

16

"I know the timing of this sucks, but there doesn't seem to *be* a good time. I need the truth, Bryn. Call me a sick fuck if you want, but I want the blow-by-blow." Erik leaned up on an elbow and stared down at her. "I get why you had your revenge on me. I deserved it. But...why would you kill Sigmund, *how* could you do it?"

She felt as if she'd been punched, crashing hard from such an amazing orgasmic high. "I already told you this. He would have grown up and tried to avenge you."

"I don't buy it." His gaze went darker than storm clouds, boring into her. "You would never have sat there and coldly thought that someday your little *skuggi* might possibly turn on the girl he thought was his cousin."

Her mouth worked, but she couldn't look away from his demanding gaze. "I killed him. I wasn't lying, but...it was Grimhild who decided he *had* to die. Not me."

"I don't understand." He shook his head. "He was her grandson."

Maybe he deserved the whole truth. Maybe it would push him out of her life for good, prophecies be damned. The gods knew she'd never been strong enough to resist the pull he had on her. It wasn't the only thing she hadn't been strong enough to stop. "She had a vision, that your death would twist his mind. He'd take *both* his sisters to his bed—Svanhild as his wife, Aslaug as his concubine. The children born of these unions would be hideous monsters that would warp the fabric of human history."

Air rushed out of his lungs as he pushed himself up to sit cross-legged on the bed. Utter rage suffused his face, and his fist slammed against the mattress. *"Grimhild."*

"Quite the psychotic bitch, that one. Every power she had, she twisted and abused."

The rage didn't lessen, but the ghost of a smile touched his lips. "For her sake, I'm glad she's dead."

She closed her eyes for a moment, and then focused on the ceiling. "I'd help you kill her if she was still around."

Taking in several slow, deep breaths, Erik finally spat, "Treachery like hers doesn't inspire the gods to bring her to Valhalla. She's rotting in Hel's realm now."

Turning her head, Bryn looked at him. "That's the only time I'm ever going to hope a giantess does her worst."

"Yes." He was quiet for a moment, though she still felt the heat of his anger. "How did she force you to kill him?"

"That's where things get…complicated." She swallowed, wishing she could tell the story without reliving the details of that awful day. "Right before your funeral, she and Gudrun brought Sigmund to my chambers. Grimhild said she'd given him *eitr* poison, and if I didn't want him to suffer, I'd—"

He twitched next to her. "It could have been a trick. She could have lied. It wouldn't have been the first time."

"Maybe, but I don't think so. He started convulsing, blood dripping from his nose and mouth." She cleared her throat, pushed herself up to sit against the headboard, and clutched a pillow to her chest. It was ridiculous, but she couldn't lay there completely naked while she stripped her soul bare. "Erik, he looked so scared."

"Bryn…"

She stared down at her lap, her hair falling in front of her face, offering at least a little cover from his penetrating silver gaze. "I didn't know if I should believe her about her vision, about Sigmund turning into a sick, perverted man, raping his own sisters. But I'd seen what *eitr* could do, how long a person would linger. It's a slow, awful death." She scrubbed a hand over her eyes. "And Gudrun just stood there like a half-wit while her kid cried for help."

Memories exploded through her mind, as crystal clear as if it had happened yesterday. Bryn remembered how she'd held the little boy close, kissed the top of his head, rocked him and sung to him. Trying to offer what scraps of comfort she could in those final moments while harsh spasms shook his tiny body. Then she'd pulled her sharpest dagger out of her boot, where she always kept it, careful not to let the child see. She'd made it quick, as painless as possible. But his blood was on *her* hands, just as Grimhild had wanted. No one would care about Bryn's intentions, nor would they ask if it was a mercy killing.

In the end, it didn't matter what anyone else thought, did it? Bryn had had to live with what happened. Immortality gave no rest and no peace, just a lot of ugly recollections to a keep her up at night.

If she closed her eyes, she could still see the dark red blood pooling on Sigmund's unnaturally pale skin, still feel the limpness of his body. Her husband's nephew. *Her* nephew. If things had gone differently, he might have been her son.

She'd carried him outside to Erik's funeral pyre, the blood soaking through her clothes, a stain she'd never been able to get out of her soul. She'd been so shell-shocked she hadn't even been able to shed a single tear. She hadn't cried since, not once in a thousand years. She had no right to tears after helping slaughter that sweet boy. Her *skuggi*.

Laying the boy beside his father, she'd stood over them and stared for long minutes. Numbed with grief and rage, she'd seen a flash of sunlight on stones and looked down at the ring on her finger—the cursed ring that had engendered so much greed and suffering—and she'd known a moment of cold, rational understanding. There was only one way to end all of this, to break the curse so it wouldn't fall on her daughter. A curse like this demanded a blood sacrifice to be broken, scoured clean by pure, purging elements. So she'd stretched out beside the man she'd loved and hated more than life itself, and called up the fire that had once surrounded her castle. She'd given the ultimate sacrifice, hoping her death would please the gods enough to end Andvaranaut's reign of destruction.

"I couldn't save him. I'm sorry." Her tone came out harsher than she meant it to, ripping through the silence of her bedroom. She hugged the pillow tighter, wishing it offered even an ounce of solace, but nothing ever did. Nothing ever would. "I wish I could have, but it was already too late by the time they brought him to me. Even knowing that, I still—" She jerked her chin to the side, cutting herself off. It was done and over with. There was nothing she could do about any of it.

Erik's hand closed over hers, his skin a blistering furnace against her chilled flesh. "I forgive you."

"What?" She couldn't have been more shocked if he'd slapped her. Actually, she might have been less shocked if he had.

He squeezed her fingers. "I forgive you for getting me killed. I forgive you for not being able to save my son."

Those simple statements rocked her down to the foundation. It couldn't be that easy. Hadn't he heard what she'd said? Didn't he understand what she'd done? "I—"

"Maybe you don't need or want my forgiveness, but you have it anyway. I just wanted you to know that." He stroked his thumb back and forth across her knuckles, his expression far kinder than she deserved.

Her throat closed and nothing but a strangled squeak emerged. She'd never realized how much she needed that forgiveness. Or that he was the only one left alive who could give it to her. Yes, she was a shieldmaiden; she was supposed to be fire and brimstone and revenge served on the cutting edge of a sword. At least, that was what she used to think, but time gives maturity and perspective. And guilt could eat away at a person. So could pain.

Erik had abandoned her—perhaps not purposefully, but he had—and then he'd betrayed her. Maybe he hadn't understood the true depths of his betrayal, but he'd known he was doing something wrong.

None of that absolved her of what she'd done. Or what she hadn't done.

A single tear tracked down her cheek. "Thank you."

He hauled her into his arms, pressing her face against his chest. She resisted, but he refused to let go, just crooned soft comfort into her hair. All her pent-up grief came exploding out. The dam burst inside her, and shuddering sobs wracked her body.

"I didn't want him to die." The words rose to an agonized cry, a truth she'd never confessed to anyone. Ever. Some people might have congratulated her on killing the boy who would one day harm her child, but she'd never think of it that way. Very un-Viking of her, but she'd have found another way to protect Aslaug. She would *never* have wished death on Sigmund. "I loved him like he was my own."

"I know, *hjartað mitt.*" He stroked her back, his voice rough with emotion. "I know."

And maybe he did. Maybe this man was the only person who could truly understand.

17

THE NEXT MORNING, BRYN took Rogue out for a joyride. She felt lighter than she had in her entire existence. Which was insane, because as far as she could tell, Earth might be destroyed at any second, and she might very well end up a giant's sex slave or midnight snack. The future wasn't looking so rosy, but the guilt that had plagued her for centuries was a little less awful today than it had been the day before.

She'd take it.

So she saddled up her favorite horse and let him do what he loved best—race the wind. Who knew when she'd get to do this again? With Greg and Tom back, her workload was much lower, and she took shameless advantage of being the boss. The guys were happy enough that she'd let them both bail on her at the same time to go see their mom that they didn't protest. Family was something Bryn had only had for a few short years, so she wanted them to enjoy that precious gift while they still had it.

Generally, she tried to look after the guys who worked for her. Since she didn't age like a mortal, she couldn't keep hands for more than a decade or so without it being really obvious that she wasn't *quite* human, but she did her best by them for as long as they stayed. Even if she wasn't all touchy-feely with her people, she did care.

And, when the time came, she *would* do everything in her power to stop those who wanted to bring on the apocalypse.

But this morning was all about cutting loose and having a bit of fun. She bent over Rogue's neck, stretching with him at each long stride, letting the wind whip past them. The scent of grass and cut hay filled her nose, Rogue's hooves churned up dirt as they pounded along the path. It was freeing, the closest she got to flying in her human form. She felt a grin tug at her lips. She was doing that more often in the last couple of days, and she had Erik to blame. Or thank.

The fence posts whipped past, small white markers that told her how far they'd gone. Miles, almost to the woods at the very edge of her property. She could press further, do a full lap around her farm, but Rogue's breathing had become labored. The horse was game to run, which was what had made him so successful on the track, but she leaned back and began pulling his speed down.

"Good boy!" She patted his neck firmly, while he whuffled a breath. "That's my good boy."

A breeze curled around her, and she didn't know why, but it sent icy fear sleeting down her spine. Rogue shook his head, dancing nervously on his delicate hooves, shimmying his hindquarters in a semicircle. Did he sense something was wrong, or was he just picking up her unease? Shading her eyes, she scanned the area. Was it one of the berserkers in wolf form? That would certainly freak out a horse, and the raven within her wasn't thrilled about being hunted either.

But that was the feeling. She was being hunted, eyes were on her, staring at her. The intent felt menacing, a threat.

She saw nothing, but she had too much experience to believe that meant there *was* nothing. Her instincts didn't play tricks.

Which told her it was definitely not the time to hop off her mount and go check out shadows in the dense woods. Nope, it was time to get the hell out of here. Wheeling Rogue around, she kicked him into a gallop, heading straight for the stables.

She never made it.

A flash of light blinded her. Time stretched, became elastic, and a single heartbeat lasted an eternity. She saw nothing, but her other senses sharpened. Searing agony up her right side, the hot metallic scent of blood, the ear-piercing sound of Rogue's scream.

Beyond all that, she heard something even more terrifying. Whooping, jackal-like, maniacal laughter. It echoed like a thousand deranged animals cackling in sync.

Oh, shit. She only knew one being who laughed like that.

Loki.

He'd escaped, and now he was *here*.

It was the last thought she had before unconsciousness sank its vicious claws into her, ripping her into the abyss.

18

A SHARP GUST OF wind blew across the stable yard, and an acrid scent hit Erik's nose. His head came up, his nostrils flaring as he tried to catch the smell. There was something familiar about it, but he couldn't immediately place it, just a nagging memory that tugged at the back of his mind. But he had a lot of years of memories to try to filter through. Whatever it was, he didn't think it was good. A prickle of unease sent urgency coursing through him.

"Val, Holm," he called. Only a screen door covered the entry to the kitchen, so they could easily hear him, but he was more interested in what they could smell. He wished Ivar were here too, but the man had left at the crack of dawn to track some lead. "Do you know what that scent is?"

Holm poked his head out, sucking in a deep breath. His brows snapped together. "Loki."

Yes, that was it. Odin had once taken Erik to see the chained giant. They'd kept their distance, but Odin liked to see for himself that Loki stayed put. That trip meant Erik knew the giant's unique scent. Gods help them all, Loki had escaped.

Someone pushed Holm from behind because he stumbled onto the back porch, and then Val stepped out too.

"Wind's coming from the southeast." Val squinted at the serene green fields.

Nauma edged outside behind the guys, concern in her voice. "Isn't that the direction—"

"Yeah." The direction Bryn had gone riding. Hours ago. Erik was already moving, heading for Bryn's beat-up farm truck.

"I have a bad feeling," Nauma said softly, but his enhanced hearing picked up her words. Val made a harsh noise, and Erik recalled what Nauma's *feelings* meant.

His blood went cold, and he started to run.

Ripping open the truck door, he was relieved to see the keys in the ignition. Thank the gods. He fired it up and shoved it into gear. Two jolting *thunks,* and he glanced over his shoulder to see Val and Holm had hopped in the back.

"Erik!"

Nauma's shriek snapped his head around. The woman pointed, and Erik saw a cloud of dust coming their way. The pounding of hooves made the air rush from his lungs. *Bryn.* He sent a grateful prayer up to Odin, sliding out of the truck to meet the horse.

But Bryn wasn't riding Rogue. Stirrups flapped like wings, and the stallion's coat was lathered with sweat, foam around his mouth.

Erik held up his hands. "Whoa," he soothed. "Whoa, boy. It's all right. Come to me."

Rogue stumbled to a stop and Erik grabbed the dangling reins. The stallion's ears flicked, his head bobbing, his hindquarters dancing in a circle. When he swung around, Erik saw a small gash on the horse's neck, and blood splattered over the saddle and down Rogue's long leg.

The stink of horse sweat almost covered the truth—most of that blood wasn't Rogue's, it was Bryn's.

He knew. He just knew that whatever they found wasn't going to be good. He looked at the other men. "You armed?"

Val patted his pockets. "I've got all Ivar's goodies with me."

"Don't so much as take a crap without them," Holm agreed.

"Good." Erik laid a calming hand on the stallion's nose. "I think we'll need them."

The farmhands came pelting out of the barn. "What's going on? What happened?"

"Rogue came back without Bryn," Erik replied as calmly as he could, though his fingers trembled and his belly roiled with unease. Something was very, very wrong. But spooking the mortals wouldn't help the situation. "The horse is injured. Take care of him. We'll go look for her."

"I'll come with you," Tom said sharply, the same suspicion on his face that he'd worn the night before during their introduction. "Greg can look after Rogue."

"Fine." Erik handed the reins over and returned to the truck. "I'm driving."

Val and Holm clamored into the bed, their backs against the cab. Nauma stood by, fingers balled in her caftan, her features pinched.

Erik met her gaze, conveying a wealth of information without putting it in words. "Would you be useful once we get to the scene?"

She swallowed. "I'm not sure. Maybe."

"Hop in." He held the door open for her.

Sliding to the middle of the bench seat, she folded her hands in her lap. Erik climbed in behind her and lit out of the yard with the kind of gravel-spitting speed reserved for times when someone was shooting at him. Rogue had left a fairly clear trail to follow—kicked-up clods of dirt and the lingering scent of blood.

Within ten minutes, he was pulling to a stop along the path. Val and Holm got out, and Holm went right for the flattened spot of grass Erik had noticed. While the man was terrible with words, he had the kind of tracking ability that was so accurate it was eerie. He wandered the area for a few minutes, his keen gaze taking in everything.

Tom opened his mouth. "What's he—"

"Quiet," Erik ordered. "Let him concentrate."

"This is where she landed." Holm knelt and skimmed his palm over the crushed grass. "I think she was unconscious by the time she hit the ground."

"How can you tell?" Tom demanded.

"No signs of struggle." Holm's fingers fanned out to encompass the area. "She didn't try to crawl. No footprints to show her walking or running anywhere."

Nauma pointed. "Those are footprints."

"Too big to be hers." He brushed his hands down his thighs, rising to his feet. "Looking at everything, I think she was hit with something, maybe a bullet, maybe just a thrown rock. Both she and the horse were injured. She fell off—either before or after she passed out—and someone grabbed her and carried her off."

"It would probably have to be a man, then. It'd take a bodybuilder of a woman to lift Ms. Ravencrest." The mortal shook his head. "If there were trespassers, she would have called us before she approached them. She always had her cell phone with her when she rode."

That was when Erik realized he *didn't* have his phone with him. He'd left it on the nightstand in Bryn's room. Shit.

Val slid his hands in his pockets. "Might have been a long-range rifle. Maybe she didn't approach them. Maybe she never saw it coming."

Tom strode forward, his gaze on the ground as if he could read the same signs Holm had seen. Pointless. Tracking like that was as much a gift as it was years of training. Holm was the very best.

"More than one person, do you think? Or just Loki?" Erik turned to Holm.

The other berserker considered for a moment. "Loki alone. I think he teleported her or we'd see tracks leading *away* as well. There's only the set that approached her after she went down."

Erik switched his focus to the *völva*. "Nauma?"

"I'm not getting anything," she whispered. "Just a very bad feeling. Like...doomsday bad."

Doomsday. *Ragnarök.* "Shit."

Tom came back to the group. "We need to call the police."

"Right." Erik nodded. What else could he say? Trying to dissuade the man from alerting the authorities when his boss had gone missing was a good way to make him ask questions that couldn't be answered. "I don't have my cell phone with me."

Holm blinked. "Me neither."

"Nor me, mate." Val patted his pockets again.

"I don't even own a cell phone." Nauma winced. "Though I'm guessing Ivar's going to change that when he finds out."

"No question." Erik returned to the truck. It was time to call Ivar and see if he had any way of tracking a person that had been teleported.

"I'll call." Tom pulled out his phone and dialed. He relayed the pertinent information, and Erik began to pace the length of the pickup. Every little delay to keep up appearances for humans was one more minute where Loki and his allies had Bryn. An unconscious, wounded Bryn.

Unfortunately, Erik had been around long enough to know the possibilities of what they could do to her were as endless as they were horrific. His stomach turned and he had to clench his jaw to keep the wolf inside him from howling with rage, with pain, with the suffering of its mate having been stolen. Every instinct within him screamed to hunt the bastards down and rip their throats out. It took conscious effort to keep his fangs and claws retracted.

The moment Tom had hung up, Erik hopped into the truck. "I'm heading back to the house to wait for the cops. One of us can bring them out here when they arrive. You guys can stay put or come with me, but I'm leaving now."

His deadly mood must have shown through the veneer of civilized calm because everyone piled in without a word of protest, including good old Tom. At the main compound, Tom went to check on the horse, the other immortals stayed at the truck to talk, but Erik needed a moment alone. He headed into the kitchen and looked around, more lost than he'd ever been in his life. Two days ago, he'd barged into Bryn's world. They'd made love here on this floor. Last night, he'd thought they'd made a real breakthrough, and there'd been a glimmer of hope, a single glimpse of a second chance for them.

To have it snatched away so soon...*gods*. Emotion threatened to drown him, but he couldn't let himself get dragged under now. Bryn was counting on him.

How long had they had her? An hour? More? How long had it taken the horse to get back to the house? Had the stallion taken a direct route or wandered before he'd come back? The scents had been fairly fresh, but that meant within the last few hours.

Hours.

It only took half a second to end a person's life. The things that could be done in minutes...

A hard hand clamped on his shoulder, solid support from Holm. "I will track these sons of bitches to the end of every realm, if that's what it takes to find her. This just got personal, and I don't take that lightly."

"Thanks, man." Erik slapped his friend on the back, telling himself to get a grip.

"I hear Ivar's van. I'll go meet him in the driveway, get him up to speed quietly, so the humans won't hear." Holm gave his shoulder a final squeeze. "Take a minute to pull yourself together, if you need."

As the other man disappeared, Erik drew in a breath, but it only brought him the scent of Bryn. A red haze filled his vision, the precursor to a berserker's rage, where man and beast merged into a killing machine. The man held onto control by the thinnest thread. The moment he had a target for his rage, the beast would be unleashed and may the gods have mercy on whoever had taken his mate.

"I get why you keep him around now," Nauma said, and he glanced up to see her watching him through the screen door. "He came off as a complete jerk at first, but he's really just...the proverbial bull in a china closet and overly blunt, isn't he? Sometimes that bluntness is a good thing. Like now."

Erik had to clear his throat twice before he could get words out. "He's got his faults, but he's a good friend."

"Leave the man in peace for a moment, love." Val's hand reached out to tug at Nauma's elbow, though it was the only part of him that Erik could see from where he stood.

She jerked away. "I am not your *love,* and I don't answer to you."

The woman stomped off, and Erik stepped out on the porch to see Val looking annoyed and frustrated. Erik couldn't manage a smile, but he offered a commiserating glance. "Women."

"Can't kill them, can't imagine life without them." Val slung an arm around Erik's neck. "Come on, mate. Chin up. We'll get your bird back. And kill the bloody bastards who snatched her. Slow and painful, like in the old days."

His inner wolf growled in agreement, but the man felt flayed open. If he hadn't been here, would Loki have taken her? Had *he* brought this on her by being unable to resist the temptation to see her again?

Ivar fishtailed into the driveway, his van spitting gravel. Within seconds, his chair was bulleting down the ramp, his arms bulging as he controlled the speed of descent. He looked furious. "Why the hell hasn't anyone been picking up their cell phones?"

Holm was already there, bending to speak to Ivar, and Erik's sensitive ears picked up Holm's harsh hiss of, "Loki escaped!"

Ivar drew back, blinked. "I know, that's why I've been calling you. How do *you* know?"

Erik was across the yard in a few strides, words spilling from his mouth. Anything to speed this up. They needed to *do* something now. "He took Bryn. I know it was him, that stench is unmistakable. Her horse came back without her, covered in blood, so we went out to track her. The horse's neck was cut, but some of the blood was hers. She's injured, but how badly, I'm not sure. He teleported her away, so they could be anywhere now. Earth, Jötunheim, maybe even Asgard if Frey really is involved. There's no tracking them to other realms since *we* can't get there. Only gods and giants can jump between realms."

"You're assuming they didn't come back to Earth. If they did, their asses are mine." Reaching back, Ivar grabbed a laptop out of the backpack slung across the back of his chair.

Val appeared at Erik's elbow. "What do you mean?"

Tapping furiously at his keyboard, Ivar didn't bother glancing up. "I put a tracking device in all of Bryn's boots."

Disbelief expanded inside Erik, both at Ivar's audacity as well as a small bloom of fragile hope that Bryn might be found so easily. "You—"

"Yes, there's one in yours too." Ivar waved one hand. "All of yours. No, I'm not sorry if it invades your privacy."

"Just tell me where she is," Erik demanded.

"Gladly." There was a short pause, then Ivar sighed. "You're not going to like it though."

"Why?" It was all Erik could do not to snatch Ivar up by his shirtfront and shake the information from him. "Tell me, damn it."

Ivar's expression flashed from frustration to helplessness to grief. "Because gods and giants can zap up and down anywhere on Earth they want. We can't."

Oh, gods. "Where are they?"

"Still in the U.S., but in the middle of fucking nowhere. Even if we hijack a plane to get as close as we can, it'll take another day to get there." Ivar slammed a fist against his chair. "Assuming they don't move her."

"Maybe I can help," a mellifluous female voice called.

They turned as a unit. Erik already had his gun out.

19

"Sif," Ivar rasped, incredulity coloring his tone.

She inclined her head. Her wheat-gold hair fell in shining waves to her waist, but her famed beauty was marred by the lines of stress at the corners of her eyes and mouth. She was dressed as a regular woman—sneakers, jeans, and T-shirt. "I can take you anywhere you want to go."

"Why should we trust you? How did you even know to come to us?" Holm voiced the same questions racing through Erik's mind. "You're a goddess, and we know Frey's in league with the giants."

Actually, they didn't know it, they just strongly suspected it, but Holm said it like it was hard fact.

A smile twitched across her face. "Isn't it obvious? Sure, all the prophecies talk about the heroic battle and deaths of specific gods, including my husband, but do you think the men are the only ones who will perish? No. I'm fundamentally connected to earth. If it's destroyed by fire and water, what do you think will happen to me? I die too." She tugged at the hem of her very modern top. "What do they call it nowadays? Ah, yes. I'll be a...civilian casualty of this war. It helps me to help you."

Nauma stepped forward and bowed. "We thank you for your offer. We're grateful for the assistance."

The golden earth goddess looked mildly amused. "So you've Seen that I won't betray you, *völva*?"

"Yes." Nauma beckoned to the men. "You should get going. Now."

Sif held out her hands. "Just tell me where. I know every centimeter of this realm—I can get us there without going to Asgard first." She glanced at Holm. "And to answer your other question, I didn't know to come to you. *Loki* came to you, and I followed him. I felt him defile the earth by setting foot off that mountain we had him chained to, and I wanted to know why he came to this tiny corner of the world before he returned to Jötunheim."

If Bryn was somewhere in the U.S. and Loki was in Jötunheim, then who had Bryn? Frey, or some other ally of Loki's? There was only one way to find out.

"We'll take the transportation offer." Erik stepped forward and clasped Sif's forearm. "Thank you."

"Don't thank me." She shook her head. "It's mostly self-serving—I won't lie. Thor and I will live or die based on what happens now. I'd rather we live."

"Understood." Ivar reached into his backpack and pulled out a small box. He flicked it open and held it out to the team. "Comm units. They'll work anywhere on the planet."

Val, Holm, Erik, and Nauma each took one tiny earbud, and Ivar slipped another into his ear.

With a quick jerk of his chin, Erik summoned his men, and Val and Holm formed a small circle with him and Sif.

"Longitude and latitude coordinates work for you?" Ivar gave her a smile that was so bright with relief and gratitude it hurt Erik to look at him. He wasn't sure there was much to be grateful for yet. He needed Bryn in his arms, alive and in one piece, before he'd feel anything except sick with rage.

The goddess nodded. "Coordinates are fine."

Ivar rattled off a string of numbers and directions that meant little to Erik, but he felt heat and magic surge up his arm from Sif. Then it felt as if he'd been jerked forward into utter darkness, a cool breeze brushed his skin, and finally brilliant, blinding light exploded before his eyes. He blinked to bring the world into focus, flinching from the glare of sunshine, and saw they were in the middle of a rocky desert, a compound of old Quonset huts before them.

"Looks abandoned," Val said quietly.

Ivar's voice sounded in Erik's ear. "It was, until recently. An old research facility they haven't used since they stopped testing nukes on U.S. soil. You're in Nevada."

"Which one is Bryn in?" The howl of hot, sandy air stung his nostrils and ears, rendering his enhanced scent and hearing useless.

A moment of static and then Ivar spoke. "Her shoe's currently in the third hut from the right, second row in. Hopefully, she's still wearing it."

As if Erik had needed that reminder. "Yeah. Thanks."

"I'll be going now." Sif flipped something coin-like through the air, and Erik's hand snapped out to catch the spinning disc. A small rune stone carved with the symbol for rowan—the tree associated with Sif. "You can use this to call me if you need me, but I'm no use in a fight, as my husband has pointed out many times."

"Thank y—"

A blood-curdling scream ripped through the air. A battle cry, thank all the gods. Bryn was alive and awake and able to *fight*.

Erik spun toward the noise as the goddess disappeared with a *whoosh* of displaced air.

20

Bryn pried her eyes open during teleportation, though her entire body throbbed as if she'd been beaten with a baseball bat. She was wrapped in something—a blanket? Too tight to really move, but the end of the cloth flapped around her head, enough so that she could peek out at her surroundings without giving away that she was awake. They went to Jötunheim first—she recognized the symbols carved into the walls of the giant king's great hall. They walked a long way with her bobbing against Loki's back, and it was all she could do not to vomit. She heard the rush of water—a river? She never found out for sure because he shoved her into the arms of another man. Then another teleportation to a place so hot she felt her mouth dry in seconds. Were they in the land of the fire giants? The dark flames they wielded made her little fire-conjuring spells of old seem like child's play. Her heart hammered, fear coating her tongue. The fire giants were some of the most vicious, with an insatiable appetite for human flesh. No wonder they were helping Loki jump-start *Ragnarök*. Earth would become their buffet.

She was dumped headfirst onto the floor and got a mouthful of dirt. A reflexive cough erupted from her, no matter how she tried to repress it.

"Ah, she's coming to. Good."

The baritone voice was smooth and pleasantly well-modulated. She knew that voice.

"Frey," she hissed. This was one of the few times she was sorry to be right.

Someone jerked the end of the blanket, and Bryn went rolling until she slammed hard into a wall. She got her hands up in time to cover her head, but the impact made the breath wheeze out of her lungs. Refusing to give in to the dazed shock, she rocked up on her hands and knees, spitting the grime out of her mouth.

She forced herself to her feet, though icy tingles shot up her legs from having been in a cramped position so long. Bracing herself against the wall, she took stock. Her head hurt from whatever Loki had hit her with, and she could feel dried blood crusting her left eyebrow. The room swayed before her, nausea gripping her gut. She blinked hard, breathing in through her nose and out through her mouth.

"Head hurting?" Frey asked solicitously. He'd always been well-liked, seen as one of the more amiable gods. There was something…off…about him now, a gleam in his gaze that reminded her of a rabid animal. Dangerous. Very, very dangerous.

She licked dry lips. "You helped Loki get loose."

"Very astute." His smile was so genial it made her skin crawl. She glanced around the room. It was more of a bunker than a room, a long space with corrugated metal walls that curved up into a rounded ceiling. It stank of age and ill-use. The floor wasn't actually dirt, but was coated in over an inch of filth and sandy soil.

Some kind of old military facility? It looked like something from the Cold War-era. They definitely weren't in the land of fire giants, but that didn't tell her where they *were*. She saw a few swarthy-skinned fire giants speaking to an icy pale frost giant at the far end of the bunker. They'd shifted sizes down so they looked like basketball player-sized humans, but she knew them for what they were. Plus, the frost giant had two heads.

A few facts about Frey clicked into place, especially his unusual marriage. She returned her focus to him. "Your giantess wife flipped you to the *jötunn* side."

That cheerful grin turned wicked. "She can be very persuasive."

She nodded as if that made perfect sense. In a way, it did. Of course he'd have been susceptible to his wife's influence. The fact that he was mild-mannered *and* Freya's twin brother had probably made other gods turn a blind eye to his obvious vulnerability. "So why kidnap me? I've had nothing to do with Asgard politics in centuries."

"You think this is just about politics? Perhaps you're not that astute, after all." That maniacal gleam entered his gaze again, more intense this time. "I took you because of *him*."

"Erik?" She shook her head, and that was the wrong thing to do because her skull gave a sickening throb. "Until two days ago, I hadn't had any involvement with him since the day he died and ascended to Valhalla."

"Ah, the World's Chosen. The prophecy always seems to focus on him, but it's going to be very hard to repopulate the planet without his woman, won't it?" He ran his tongue along his teeth. "I'm sure you'll be very entertaining before I feed you to my new friends. Valkyries are always fun. Such fighters—it's delicious. I've had several of them lately."

The way his gaze raked over her body left her with no illusions about what he intended. Her gorge rose, memories flashing of battles where men had raped and pillaged their way through villages. Women sold as sex slaves, whored out to whomever paid their masters the most silver. She'd witnessed it, helped those she could, but there was only so much she could do about an entire culture. Contemporary times were much kinder to her gender.

Frey, however, was not from contemporary times. And kindness wasn't what he had in mind.

A door opened near the giants, letting in a shaft of piercing light and whipping wind. Kata stepped inside. One of the giants grunted and reached out to touch her. She went for the knife strapped to her belt, but Frey called, "Leave her be, Surtr. Kata, come here."

Surtr. The *king* of the fire giants. Shit. The *jötunn* grunted, his gaze following Kata as she walked down the long bunker. When she reached them, Surtr turned his gaze on Bryn. His thick lips peeled back in a grotesque smile that promised an experience night terrors were made of. Her heart pounded with sickening dread. She was alone, unarmed, and outnumbered five-to-one by beings more powerful than her. Only Kata would offer an even fight, and Bryn doubted Frey would let her tear his little pet apart.

She gave the other valkyrie a look of pure disgust.

"Traitor," she hissed. "You're supposed to be my sister, supposed to fight *with* me. If he's had several valkyries lately, then you've betrayed us all. I hope this is worth it, knowing what will happen when Odin and Freya get hold of you."

Kata went deathly pale, but her chin rose. "There are more forces at play than you know."

"Every backstabbing bitch has an excuse." Bryn watched Frey take a menacing step toward her, his genial expression dropping to reveal a look that would freeze the blood.

Guilt and shame shone in Kata's brilliant blue eyes. "You, of all people, should know that nothing is ever as black and white as it looks on the outside."

True, but Bryn didn't give a damn at the moment. She saw no reason to be fair when she was about to become a meal. "Yeah, and those shades of gray will haunt you for all eternity. Been there, done that. What he wants to do to me is gonna keep you up at night. Have fun with that."

Kata actually heaved as if she was going to puke, but then she squared her shoulders. "May I go now, Frey?"

"Oh, that's right," Bryn taunted. Because, hey, what more did she have to lose? Playing on the other valkyrie's obvious remorse couldn't hurt. It at least delayed the inevitable. "Running away like the spineless coward you are is going to make it all better. If you don't have to *watch* what your treachery unleashes, it won't give you nightmares."

"Shut your mouth!" Frey swung out to backhand her, but Bryn managed to sidestep the blow.

Fury lit his gaze, and he launched himself at her.

He was a god, and he had backup, which meant her chances of survival were slim to none. Her chances of victory were nonexistent, but if she was going to go down, she was going down fighting. Maybe that gave him what he wanted, the sick fuck, but she could do nothing else. She was a valkyrie and it wasn't in her nature to stand there and take it. This asshole wanted to murder her just so he could screw up some ancient prophecy. Well, she hadn't asked to be part of any prophecy, so fuck that.

He caught her around the waist and dragged her to the floor. Instead of resisting, she went with the momentum, using it to hit the ground at a roll. She managed to get out from under him and crawled away. He caught her ankle, trying to yank her back. With a quick glance over her shoulder, she slammed her heel into his nose.

It gave a very satisfying snap and blood poured down his face. He screamed, his hand loosening and she got her feet under her, scurrying away, deeper into the bunker. Her gaze shot around, trying to find another exit. A window, a skylight, *anything*.

All she found was old office furniture, coated in grime. She had only a few seconds before the god caught up with her. He moved almost soundlessly, but the busted nose meant she could hear the wheeze of his breathing. Her heart slammed against her ribs, and the sensation of being hunted sent adrenaline coursing through her veins. Fight or flight. The raven in her voted flight, but she resisted the urge to shift. Being a bird would let her fly, but it also meant she couldn't fight. She needed an exit strategy first or she'd just be flapping around in a dingy cage. She reached the end of the bunker. No escape, but she found the next best thing: a weapon. An old chair with a leg broken off. She picked up the leg to use as a club, already swinging it as she turned.

With a deep-throated battle cry, she connected hard with his stomach, doubling him over. She brought the metal bar down on his back and he hit his knees.

A ball of ice slammed into her, knocking her back into a filing cabinet. Her head connected hard, and stars burst before her eyes. Long enough for the frost giant to be on her. He rammed both fists into her sides, crushing her between them, and she felt ribs give way. Grabbing the front of her shirt, he lifted her with one arm until she was level with both of his heads. She kicked and punched, but only managed glancing blows. He pulled her in close, and she gouged her thumb into one of his eyes. He bellowed, the sound half-rage and half-pain.

He flipped her over his head, launching her across the bunker. She hit a heavy metal desk, her leg twisting badly beneath her, and her ankle snapped. The air rushed out of her lungs so that her scream emerged a soundless gasp. She tried to roll away from the desk, but massive hands pinned her. Two albino-pale heads stared at her upside down, both mouths smiling in obscene delight. He bent and bit her collarbones, cracking them like twigs, and tearing into her flesh. A shriek of sheer agony ripped from her.

"Enough of that! She's mine first!" The giant was wrenched away, and Frey stood over her.

He spun her around, shoving her legs apart and ripping at her clothes. She struggled, slicing at him with her talons, though moving her arms at all was excruciating and her energy levels were in the toilet. Fear and pure adrenaline kept her fighting. She slammed the heel of her unbroken leg into Frey's thigh, but missed his groin.

Shit.

"I hear something!" Kata's shout echoed through the bunker. "Frey, someone's outside."

Two small, percussive booms rocked the building, and Bryn curled in on herself, arms thrown over her head. Acrid smoke hit her nose. The grinding squeal of metal rending pierced her ears, and then she heard nothing but a high-pitched whine. She shook her head, trying to clear the noise so she could hear what was going on. Sunlight poured into the space, scouring wind and sand whipping into her eyes. People seemed to be scrambling in every direction, some pouring in, others fighting them off.

The first sound that came through was Holm's roar. His battle-axe gleamed as it swung at a fire giant. She'd never been so happy to see that pain-in-the-ass berserker before.

The cavalry had arrived.

Unfortunately, as she lay there bleeding and broken, she thought they might be too late to save her. But maybe they could stop the traitors from ending the world. She could hope for that because she had no hope left for herself. The injuries were catastrophic. It felt as if half of her ribcage had caved in, and she struggled to breathe.

Frey balled his hand in the front of her shirt and lifted her bodily, using her as a shield as Erik pelted toward them, sword in one hand, chain in the other.

"Kata! Come to me *now* or you know what happens!" Frey shouted, the threat in his tone unmistakable, and Bryn managed to turn her head to look.

"Coming," the other valkyrie rasped. She picked herself up off the ground, blood pouring down her arm, a piece of the metal wall protruding from her shoulder. She was white-faced and wide-eyed with terror. Whatever "what happens" was had scared the living shit out of her.

When Kata raised her palms, magic tingled over Bryn's skin. That was when she realized why Frey had brought Kata along for this ride and *hadn't* turned her over to his giant friends. Because, as a valkyrie, she could decide the outcome of fights between warriors.

If she was around, she could make Frey the winner in all of his battles. Including the one with Erik.

21

Holm had had C-4 in his pocket. How he got it or why he had it, Erik didn't care. The other man had managed to blow a couple of neat holes in the side of the Quonset hut, which meant they could get in without using the door and without risking injury to Bryn.

His first look at her made his stomach sour. Frey had his hand around her neck, hiding behind her like a gutless coward. Her face was contorted with anger, but she was covered with dark crimson. The way she held herself told him how badly she was injured. She needed medical attention, right now.

Fuck. *Fuck.*

Tension vibrated through every inch of him, his hackles rising as he locked gazes with Frey. He was going to rip the motherfucker limb from limb. He didn't give a shit if Frey was a god. Bloodlust rose high and hot within Erik, the berserker's rage merging man and beast until there was one focus, one purpose. Dealing death to his enemy.

The asshole actually *smiled* at him. "Siegfried. I knew you'd come, but you were faster than I expected."

"I had help." He flexed his hands around the hilts of his chain-swords. He couldn't attack while Frey had Bryn in a chokehold. "I've got friends in high places."

Something odd flashed through the god's eyes, gone too fast to name. "Odin?"

Erik just bared his fangs. If Frey didn't know where Odin was, then that meant

Odin might not be dead yet. Erik saw no need to give away the fact that he had no idea where their ruler was either.

A sneer formed on Frey's face. "Odin's favorite child, always the one called first, always asked for advice, even though you're not a god."

Erik snorted. "You're jealous. Of me."

"The one who gets to survive? To repopulate the planet, remake an entire race in your image?" The glitter in Frey's eyes was eerie. The god was unhinged. His grip tightened on Bryn's throat, and she gurgled, her fingers locking around his wrist. "Not if I have anything to say about it."

Time to distract him before he snapped her neck right before Erik's eyes. Fear slicked his gut, cold sweat breaking out on his skin. "I didn't ask to fulfill the World's Chosen prophecy. I didn't even know about it, and I had no idea I had a few molecules of Odin's blood in my lineage."

"Poor, perfect boy." Frey tsked in mock sympathy.

"Hardly perfect," Erik replied as reasonably as he could. "Bryn could tell you all about how dishonorable I can really be."

"Dishonorable, and yet you were favored above others far superior to you. That should *never* have happened."

Holm went tumbling past, wrestling with a two-headed frost *jötunn*. Erik saw Val shoot another giant at point-blank range. The giant went down with a resounding crash. Well, that was one less worry. Erik refocused on Frey. "Why are you doing this? Just to try and save your own skin in *Ragnarök?* Or because you want to be the most powerful god left standing, the new king of the gods, instead of one of Odin and Freya's sons?"

"It's been eons since that prophecy was laid out. Gives a man time to think." He fondled Bryn's breast, and it took every ounce of Erik's control not to leap at him. The god continued as if there was nothing out of the ordinary. "I could unite giants and gods. My children have both bloodlines, all the power of our combined races."

"Right." Erik sidled to the side, trying to get a better angle on the god so if he launched a sword, it wouldn't hit Bryn.

Frey's gaze sharpened, and he shifted to keep her firmly between them. "Jötunheim is behind Gerda and me."

Asgard wouldn't be, but Erik didn't say that. "Why involve Bryn? She's got nothing to do with any of this. She's not supposed to be involved in *Ragnarök*. The final battle prophecy doesn't even mention her."

"True, but it occurs to me that if you don't have this sweet piece of tail..." Frey slid his tongue along her neck, leaving a gleaming line of spittle. Fury flashed in Bryn's midnight gaze. "Ah, I can see why you've never been able to resist her. She's delicious." He ground himself into her ass, his fingers tightening around her throat again. Her nails dug into his hand until bloody weals were left behind, but Frey didn't seem to notice. "Where was I? Yes. If you don't have her, it doesn't matter if you survive the final battle. There's no repopulating the world. Kill her and I'll take your precious future with me, Chosen One. I will rip the heart out of you, and I don't even have to touch you. It's perfect."

It *was* perfect, revenge for a crime Erik hadn't even committed, and he wanted to vomit. He'd never imagined so much hate was festering inside of the jovial god. He could understand not wanting to die, could see how that prophecy had hung over Frey's head for ages, but blaming Erik for *not* being slated for death was madness.

The worst realization was that the apocalypse was being instigated by something as stupid and juvenile as envy.

Maybe an equal measure of pettiness would spare Bryn. Erik shrugged casually. "So kill her. It looks like the prophecy is changing with you switching sides anyway, so I'm sure fate will provide me with someone else to help repopulate the world. I haven't given a shit about Bryn since I found out she murdered my son." Her head came up, and what little blood remained in her face drained away. She couldn't *believe* that line of shit, could she? He forced his attention back to Frey. *Get her out of this and explain later, Erik.* "I didn't even go near the bitch until two days ago, and only because a *völva* told me to."

That truth seemed to catch his attention, and Frey blinked. "You came after her now."

Erik snorted. "I came after *you*, the bottom-feeding traitor, the wannabe-*jötunn* so scared to die he's willing to sell out his entire race." Frey's face flushed purple with rage, veins bulging in his neck. Erik flashed a befanged, challenging smile and held out his sword, using it to beckon the god to fight. "Come on, coward. Let's see who survives *Ragnarök*. Or are you afraid of taking on a mere berserker? As you said, I'm not even a god."

Frey hesitated, and Erik feared he'd refuse the challenge. Or kill Bryn first, just for sport.

"Hey, Erik?" Bryn spoke for the first time, her voice a mere croak.

He didn't look at her, kept his gaze locked on his prey. "Yeah?"

"I forgive you. For everything."

Every inch of his body froze in response to her words, and he did look at her then. She met his gaze, winked, and then went utterly limp. She caught Frey off-guard and slipped through his arms to hit the ground on her side. A strangled, pained cry burst from her, and it made Erik's heart seize, but he reacted as he knew she'd want him to. He hurtled himself forward and slammed the god back, tumbling him through the opening they'd blasted through the side of the building, carrying them both away from Bryn.

He hoped she would be safe, but the thought was fleeting. He had to give all his attention to Frey. If Erik lost, he didn't want to consider what would happen to Bryn. He'd be kicking his own ass for all eternity if he failed her now. Again.

The impact as they hit the ground was bone-jarring, but Erik came out on top and sliced his chain across Frey's face. His cheek sliced open, the flesh peeling back to reveal the god's teeth and jawbone. He screamed, slammed a fist into Erik's chest and bucked hard enough to send Erik flying. He landed against the outer wall of the Quonset hut, a shard of metal slicing into his back as he slid to the sand and hit his knees.

The roar of rage as Frey came off the ground was chilling, and he grabbed Erik's wrist to try to get the chain away. While Erik had superhuman strength, he was no match for a god in sheer power. The choice was lose the chain or get his arm broken, so he let go, but rammed the hilt of his sword into the god's temple. Frey rocked back for a moment, giving Erik the chance to spring to his feet and put some distance between them.

He heard the battle cries and the sound of skin hitting skin. He didn't have to look to know his team was still fighting, so that was good news. This day could use some good news. The valkyrie Nauma and Bryn had identified on the newsfeed slithered out of the Quonset hut, her eyes on Frey and him. She didn't try to interfere, just watched, but he'd have to keep an eye on her in case she leapt to the god's defense.

Frey charged, swinging the chain over his head. It was an awkward swing, and he managed to accidentally snap the chain into a solid sword. The change surprised him enough that Erik was able to pivot out of his way and bring his blade across the back of Frey's thigh, slicing the muscle open, but not as deeply as he'd have liked. The god stumbled, but whipped his sword around to leave a shallow furrow along Erik's pec up to his shoulder. It burned like a son of a bitch, but was superficial.

They circled each other, looking for an opening, any weakness they could exploit. *There.* The god dropped one shoulder just a bit, and Erik knew his hold on the blade wasn't as strong as it should be. A rookie mistake. He brought his sword down, and Frey's wrist gave out, leaving his torso unprotected. Erik used his wolf's claws to slash across the god's stomach, hoping to gut him like a gaping fish.

Another glancing wound. Painful, but not life-threatening. *Shit.*

Letting his sword arm go lax, Frey made Erik stumble. Swinging his free hand, the god drove three quick punches into Erik's side. Kidney shots. He'd be pissing blood for a week if he survived this. Pain shuddered up his ribs, and he wheezed in a breath. Frey grabbed for Erik's head, aiming for his eyes. Ducking, Erik sank his fangs into the god's arm, ripping a large chunk of flesh out with a vicious shake of his head.

With a pained cry, Frey fell back a few steps. "Fucking animal!"

Erik spat the chunk out as if it were foul and smirked at Frey. "That was for Bryn. I saw the marks on her neck from your *jötunn* scum."

"I knew you loved her." Gloating rang in his tone.

Erik swiped at his mouth. "Congratulations. I'm going to kill you for ever daring to touch her, you worthless piece of shit."

Their swords clashed again, sparks flying every time the metal met. Erik kept his extra senses open, in case Kata or a giant approached. Moving in the loose sand made the fight more exhausting, sucking his feet down if he stayed in one place a moment too long.

They jumped back, separating again to circle. The god was panting hard, blood and sweat pouring down his face. It was clear he hadn't fought anyone in quite some time, but he was a god of fertility, fair weather, and sunshine. Not much warring needed for that. But he had the strength of a god and that was a definite advantage, while Erik had his centuries of battle-hardened experience and training behind him.

How much stamina did the god have? More than Erik, or less? Who could outlast the other might be the deciding factor on who won.

22

Bryn couldn't even begin to count how many broken bones she had. Every breath was a struggle, and she could only manage a shallow panting. Pain was a living, writhing beast inside her, threatening to wrench her back into unconsciousness. A part of her would welcome the oblivion, the cessation of agony, the peace, but she couldn't give in. Not now. Not yet.

Soon.

She was the only one still left in the bunker, except for the stiffening corpses of two fire giants with a bullet holes in their foreheads. Kata had followed Erik and Frey outside, so Bryn knew if the other valkyrie had the opportunity, she'd make sure Erik lost. That thought alone was enough to have Bryn crawling toward an overturned desk and using it to haul herself to her feet. The broken ankle throbbed as if someone were stabbing a hot poker into her joint. Her vision went black for a moment, and she had to lean heavily against the desk to remain upright. She gritted her teeth to keep in a scream. It hurt. Every fucking part of her *hurt*.

One of the desk legs was loose, and she yanked at it until it came free. She used it as a cane as she made her way through the debris to the opening Erik had shoved Frey through. The light and blowing sand stung her eyes, and she turned her face away for a moment, shielded her gaze with her free hand and looked again.

Chaos reigned.

To her right, Val was in a sword fight with Surtr, though the berserker appeared to be losing. Not far from them, Holm lodged his battle-axe in the back of the two-headed frost giant. He went down with a great spray of sand, the axe still wedged between his shoulders, but Holm had already turned to sprint toward Val. Good. Two against one. They might stand a chance against the fire king.

A rough shout drew her gaze to the left, where Erik battled Frey. Though Frey was a god, he wasn't much of a warrior. He'd given up his sword when he'd married his giantess. The match was more even than it would normally be. But Frey had Kata on his side. The valkyrie's gaze was fixed intently on the combatants, which made it easy for Bryn to get behind her.

Hefting the desk leg like a baseball bat, she swung as hard as she could, put every ounce of her lagging strength behind the hit. A dull *thud* and blood poured from the gash in the back of Kata's skull. She went down like a ton of bricks.

Bryn felt the air waver and change, magic flooding her being, enervating her until her skin was too hot and too tight.

The victory judgment had shifted to her.

Bracing her feet apart, she dropped the makeshift cane. It wasn't much use in shifting sand, and it was getting harder and harder to move her swelling fingers. Sweat slid down her face, her hands shaking, muscles in her legs cramping with pain. She wasn't going to remain conscious for much longer—the beating had taken too much out of her. But she had to stay on her feet long enough to render judgment, which came only at the end of the fight and she couldn't force it forward. All power had its limits. Locking her gaze on the combatants, she waited for a moment when Erik had the upper hand, when the magic coursing through her would let her make that final decision. It coiled, waiting like a snake ready to strike. She clenched her jaw, ignoring the agony screaming through her, the darkness that edged at the corners of her eyes.

Stay awake, Bryn. Just stay awake. A few minutes more, that's all.

Shifting her weight made her catch her breath. The ankle throbbed sickeningly, the wounds on her collarbones still oozed blood, and fiery pins and needles prickled her arms and hands. Nausea roiled within her, and she wanted nothing more than to bend over and heave her guts up. Tremors ran through her and her palms went clammy. Even in the desert heat, cold sweat slicked her skin.

A wolf's howl wrenched from Erik's throat, and he charged the god, his sword hammering down again and again, taking advantage of the god's flagging endurance. He used martial arts moves the god clearly didn't know how to counter. Even exhausted, they fought with speed almost too fast for her to track, but she stayed with them. A single slip of the foot on this sand could spell Erik's doom—even if he *looked* better than his opponent, there were no guarantees.

A roar sounded to her right, and she flicked her gaze in that direction. The frost giant wasn't dead and bellows issued from both of his mouths. He carried Holm's battle-axe and came at her, each stride seeming to eat up a mile. He'd be on her in seconds. She knew she was going to die. Her immortality was over.

She could have tried to run, tried to shift forms, but that would have left Erik to a fate she couldn't bear. Having even a small part in his death—again—would shred what little remained of her blackened heart. She couldn't do it, *wouldn't* do it. Maybe Nauma was right, and love was what would end this thing. Bryn loved him too much to let him die. So she stood her ground, praying to Freya that judgment would come before she died.

Erik dropped down and swiped out a leg, toppling Frey. Rearing up, he used both hands to drive his sword deep into the god's chest. Even then, Frey struggled, tried to slash at Erik with his blade.

"Now," she whispered and managed to hold up her palms, throwing every ounce of magic and willpower she had behind Erik's victory.

A harsh cry, and the two combatants went still.

The berserker had beaten a god.

She turned her head, knowing that the giant would be on her in the next split-second, and she braced for impact. His arm raised, the battle-axe clutched in his meaty fist.

Here it came.

A short crack sounded in the distance, and then the giant's elbow exploded into shards of bone and bloody flesh that splattered across her face. The axe fell to the ground and deafening screams rent the air. Bryn swayed, staring dumbly. She blinked and he was gone, teleporting away—probably back to Jötunheim.

On a rock outcropping above her, Nauma slowly stood. Beside her, Ivar heaved himself into a sitting position and lifted his massive rifle so it laid across his lap.

He'd shot the giant and saved her life.

"Bryn?" Erik shoved the prone form of the god off of him and used his sword as a crutch to heave himself to his feet. He was covered in gore, blood seeping from several cuts she could see. None looked too deep.

"Here," she whispered.

"Good." He lifted the long blade high and brought it down on Frey's neck, severing the god's head.

The battle was over.

The magic that had flooded her evaporated, leaving her empty and cold. Exhaustion finally won, and she hit her knees hard. Pain shafted up her legs, but it was just one more agony on top of all the others shrieking within her.

"Bryn!"

There was panic in Erik's voice, and she wanted to respond but couldn't find the energy. She couldn't even lift her hands to catch herself before she toppled over into the burning sand. It filled her mouth and scorched her cheek.

The world spun in a sickening whirl when she was flipped over, and Erik hauled her into his arms. She blinked hard, but couldn't bring his beloved face into focus.

Please, Freya. Let me see him. One last time.

But the goddess didn't answer her prayers. Perhaps a fitting punishment for one who'd been so lax in her service.

She blinked again, and his hand had risen into the air. When had he moved? He shouted words, but there was something wrong with her hearing, because sounds kept fading in and out.

Then a woman peered down at her, the sun reflecting off her golden hair so brightly it made Bryn flinch. Sif? What was a peaceful earth goddess doing on a battlefield?

Erik's voice demanded, "Take us to Eir."

23

Erik paced in a tight circle at the end of Bryn's bed. His hands clenched and unclenched at his sides as he watched her still body for even a hint of movement. "Why doesn't she waken?"

Breath easing out in a quiet sigh, Nauma answered the question he'd already asked a dozen times. "Eir gave her a healing potion and said Bryn would sleep until she was fully healed. Apparently, she's not fully healed yet."

"It's been three fucking days," he snapped. "How long will it take?"

He knew it wasn't reasonable to take his frustration out on the *völva*, but he'd left reasonable behind long ago. Three. Fucking. *Days*.

"Eir is the goddess of healing, Erik." Nauma folded her arms over her breasts and gave him a look that said her patience was wearing thin. "If you think the human doctors can do better, feel free to take her to a hospital. Good luck explaining how she ended up in a coma."

He growled, the wolf barely leashed. He'd already had to call in favors from some of his old contacts in law enforcement to get the local cops to drop Bryn's kidnapping case. Bringing doctors in would just start that problem over again. Though if he thought for even a moment the mortals might help her, he'd do it, problems be damned.

Nauma's expression softened. "I know you're worried—"

"I'm not worried. She's going to wake up. She'll be fine." His voice gave a humiliating crack on the last word, and he cleared his throat. "She *will* be fine."

"Of course she will."

He rounded on her, desperate for even a tiny scrap of reassurance. "Did you See that? That'd she'd be all right?"

She shook her head. "No, but I have faith in Eir's abilities. She said Bryn would heal, and I believe her."

"Right." He paced another circle at the end of the bed. A bed they'd shared. But his Bryn was fire and passion, and the woman who lay there was still as death, pale as a winter moon, and cold to the touch.

What he wouldn't give to have her dark eyes open. Her sharp tongue would be a welcome respite from this deafening silence. He hated it. He was going to start crawling the walls soon. Every second that passed killed him a little more, but he couldn't bear to leave her. The moment he turned his back, she'd awaken just to spite him. Or die. He needed to be near, needed to see her chest rise and fall with every breath, proof that some life still flowed through her veins.

Gods help him if that stopped.

He might actually lose his mind. The wolf inside him struggled for dominance, luring him over to the bestial side. Give in to that, become the wolf and disappear, never look back.

It was tempting. So very tempting.

But the man couldn't let go yet. Not while she still lived. If she died…

He shook his head, trying to banish that thought. She had to live. She *had* to.

He'd never quite realized how much comfort he'd taken in knowing that, no matter what happened, she would survive to see the new world with him. That they would find each other again, at the end of all things, and even when the worst had come to pass, she would be by his side. He would spend his days in her arms, finding endless pleasure in her body, coaxing her into that rare smile that lit his soul, having the life that *should* have been theirs so long ago.

But there was no comfort now, no solace as he watched her, helpless to do anything. Powerless to stop fate from ripping her away from him again.

The wolf within whined, and it was all Erik could do not to throw his head back and keen with the same agony. Man and beast both wanted their mate.

"She's going to wake up, Erik," Nauma said softly.

"When?" The word emerged as half-groan, half-sob. He didn't give a shit that it was a noise a warrior shouldn't make. Nauma could think whatever the hell she wanted of him.

"Now," a rusty voice said from the bed.

"What?" He jerked around to face her, and found himself pinned in place by uncanny midnight eyes. Then he did sob, covering his face with one hand and setting the other against the wall to keep himself upright. "Gods."

"What happened?" Bryn asked, her voice like gravel in a blender, but it sounded perfect to him. She was *alive*. She was awake. Finally.

Nauma answered her because Erik was still swiping tears from his face. "Our guys are all fine. Eir patched them up, and you too. Surtr and the two-headed frost giant escaped. Frey's dead. That's all we know at the moment."

Nodding, Bryn rasped, "Water."

"Right here." Nauma aimed a straw at her mouth. "Eir said to give you this when you woke up. You've been in a coma for three days."

Bryn sucked down whatever was in the glass, but Erik waited, tense. Eir had given the other berserkers and him similar healing draughts, but he no longer quite trusted the drinks that magic-wielders offered. Potions had stolen her from him before. Would losing her be his punishment for killing Frey? Such a move would be divisive amongst those who dwelled in Valhalla.

Bryn licked her lips and pushed herself upright.

"Should you be moving so soon?" His question cracked with more harshness than he'd meant, and both women glared. His wounds had healed in seconds after he'd drunk the stuff, but he'd had nothing bad enough to kill him. Bryn had.

"I feel fine, actually." Bryn nodded to the empty glass. "Eir's potion did its work. I could use a shower though."

"I'll carry you." He took a step forward, but she flinched back, and he froze.

"I can walk." She swung her legs over the side of the mattress, her movements as fluid as ever. Her hair swung forward and covered her expression. She wore one of his T-shirts—the closest thing at hand when they'd returned—and it slipped off one shoulder. "I feel fine, I told you. Don't concern yourself."

Her eyes didn't meet his, and that was wrong. Except for that first moment when she'd woken, she hadn't looked *at* him. Why? Did she blame him for what Frey and the *jötunn* had done to her? What she'd gone through had been an act of revenge against Erik. If she'd never met him, she'd have been spared so much pain and suffering. He swallowed, willing her to face him, to say something.

Nauma seemed to sense the tension and pushed to her feet. "I'll leave you two alone, but...you realize events have unfolded in ways not called for in the great prophecy. It's a whole new ballgame now, kiddies."

Looking at the *völva*, Erik asked, "What's going to happen next?"

"I have no idea." She smiled ruefully. "I'll meditate on it—maybe I can See something. No promises though. This mess has been murky from the day you approached Bryn."

He spread his hands. "You told me to."

"I said you'd need a shieldmaiden. I never said which one and you know it." She shook a finger at him. "Kata would have been another useful one to track down, wouldn't she?"

Bryn rose easily, the hem of his shirt dancing around the tops of her thighs, just barely keeping her decently covered. A pity, that.

"If Erik hadn't come to me, Frey might have killed me in my sleep. My farmhands would have been easy prey—lambs to the slaughter. Even if Frey had just kidnapped me, if other immortals hadn't been here to *do* something about it... Well, we all know what would have become of me."

He'd held the guilt at bay during the time she'd been comatose, but now it bit him hard. "If I hadn't led him to you—"

"He'd have found me anyway," she insisted, cutting him off. "It's not like I was in deep hiding. I had no idea I needed to be, that I was a real target for anyone."

"Would you have been a target if it weren't for my love for you?" he snapped back. "If you had no connection to me, if I hadn't come straight to you the second Nauma even *nudged* me in your direction, would Frey have come after you? How far in advance was his vengeance planned? We'll never know, but..."

"Love?" Bryn's eyes were wider and more vulnerable than he'd ever seen them. Utter shock molded her lovely features.

"And that's my cue. I'm off to meditate and focus my Sight. Good night, you two. Have fun—you've earned it." Nauma disappeared through the door, the knob clicking softly as she shut it behind her.

24

Bryn was dreaming. She had to be. Only once had Erik ever said he loved her, right before he left her forever.

Or maybe she was dead.

Was this what Niflheim was like, what Hel did to the departed? Mocking phantasms that reminded you of all you'd never achieved in life? Shattered hopes turned to nightmares? Bryn doubted she'd be in much favor with Hel, so perhaps this was a special form of torment reserved just for the damned.

She pinched her arm hard, and it hurt...but maybe that didn't mean anything.

"What are you doing?" he demanded, grabbing her wrist. "I didn't drag your ass to Asgard and back *right after I'd killed one of the most popular gods* just so you could injure yourself. What the fuck?"

"Just...making sure I was awake." And wasn't that a stupid thing to say? She sounded half-cracked. Clearing her throat, she yanked her arm away from him. "How did you get me to Asgard?"

"Sif helped us."

"Ah." Now that he mentioned it, she recalled seeing the golden goddess before she'd blacked out.

"Ah? You have no other questions than that?" He prowled around her room like a caged animal. The wolf was unhappy about something.

From the corner of her eye, she watched as he went back and forth. "The goddess helped you because she doesn't want the Earth to be consumed during

Ragnarök, and because—despite their marital estrangement—she doesn't want her husband to die during the apocalypse. Then she helped you because you were on a mission to throw a wrench in Loki and Frey's plans, which also benefits her. How close am I?"

"Spot on," he barked.

She tilted her head, a tiny bit of amusement filtering through her. "Why are you pissed off at me?"

"Because you almost died, damn you! Because you're not even looking at me!" He scrubbed a hand over the back of his neck. "Because...because I just fucking said I loved you and your response was to start pinching yourself."

Love. Gods, he'd said it again. A sense of unreality swamped her, and she drew in a calming breath. "Erik, I..."

"You? What?"

How could he love her after all she'd done to him? Yes, he'd said he forgave her, but there was a pretty big distance between forgiveness and love. Then again, hadn't she always loved him, even when she hated him? She pushed her hair back, wincing as she hit a tangled snarl. "You just surprised me."

His mouth opened, then shut so quickly his teeth clacked together. He folded his arms and stared at her. "How could that surprise you?"

"Aren't you the man who said you hadn't given a shit about me since I murdered your son? Aren't you the one who encouraged Frey to murder me?" She tilted her head. "Call me crazy, but that doesn't scream undying love to me. That screams hate with the fire of a thousand suns."

His dark expression eased a bit. "You had to know I didn't mean it."

"I hoped you didn't." But it had still hurt to hear the words, and admitting that would make her feel like an idiot so she kept it to herself. "I knew you'd try to come after me and you'd do what you could to save me, but...you're supposed to stop *Ragnarök*. I got caught in the crossfire. That doesn't have anything to do with love."

He rubbed a spot between his eyebrows as if she'd given him a headache. "I didn't come after you just because you got caught in the crossfire."

Impatience radiated off of him, and maybe she deserved that. Maybe she should just take this perfect, beautiful thing he offered and not question it too much, but…she couldn't. "Ah."

He shook his head. "Ah?"

"You surprised me."

Pinching the bridge of his nose, he groaned quietly. "You said that already."

"Yes, I did, didn't I?" She glanced away. This wasn't really going well, was it? She'd always been better with swords and horses than with people and emotions. Maybe it was time to beat a retreat. "I think I'm going to take that shower now."

But his words brought her up short. "You said you forgave me for everything. Was that just a heat of the moment thing?"

"No, it wasn't," she answered softly. She *had* forgiven him for the pain he'd caused her, both inadvertent and deliberate. His apologies had eased the bitterness, and his understanding of her actions had made all the difference in the world. They weren't the people they had been back then, and she was glad for that. She loved the man he'd grown into more than she'd imagined possible.

His voice went dull and flat. "You forgive me, but you don't love me."

"I don't know how to trust love." She worried the hem of the shirt between her fingers. "That doesn't mean I don't feel it, it just means I know how quickly it can evaporate into nothing. It's fickle."

"My love isn't."

She just gave him a look and didn't respond.

"I have always loved you, Brynhild. My Bryn. I will love you until the end of time. Not even death could stop it." He shook his head. "As soon as that vile, evil potion wore off and my memories came back, I loved you. Still, always. The one truth that makes up the utter core of my soul, Bryn, is that I love you."

Oh. The sincerity that rang in his tone made moisture burn the backs of her eyes. Her lips trembled and she pressed them together to stop the shaking.

He caught her shoulders in his hands, forcing her to meet his gaze. "I need you. I pretended I didn't for so long, but I'm only half-alive without you. Being with you again made that so clear. *I need you.* Maybe if we stick with each other this time, you'll find a way to trust in me, in *us*. It seems to me the worst stuff happens when we're apart."

"I…I could try that." She blinked back the tears that threatened. "I don't want to lose you again. I need you too."

"You love me too?" He shook her a little.

She arched her eyebrows. "I said so."

"You said you feel it, but don't trust it. Say it directly," he demanded.

"I love you. Even when I wanted to kill you, I loved you." She didn't mention that she'd hated herself for that weakness. He knew her well enough to have figured that out by himself.

He closed his eyes, his throat working as he swallowed. "Thank you."

He wrapped an arm around her waist, drew her in, and buried his face in the crook of her neck. It felt so good to be close to him again, to feel the warmth of his big body, the resilience of his skin. She cupped the back of his head, stroking down to the nape of his neck. A bit of stubble prickled her palms—he hadn't bothered to shave it smooth for at least a couple of days. Not while he was watching over her. Her heart squeezed at that realization. She wouldn't have wanted to leave his side for very long either, if their roles had been reversed.

"Erik…I love you," she whispered.

"I love you more." He turned his head and caught the ultrasensitive flesh just below her ear between his teeth. Her body quivered in response, her eyes rolling back. Desire was a hot glow in her belly that spread and consumed her like fire. She'd never thought to feel it again, when that giant came at her. The lush beauty of it made the pleasure that much sharper.

He tried to capture her mouth with his and she chuckled, evading him. "I really do need to shower. And brush my teeth. I think something died in my mouth."

He laughed outright at that, holding her tight and rocking her in his arms. "Back in the day, that wouldn't have been such an issue."

"Welcome to the New World, my friend." She tugged on his earlobe. "Hygiene is a fabulous thing."

"You won't mind if I help you in the shower, will you?" He squeezed her bare buttocks, sending a teasing finger gliding along the midline. "You have been convalescing for a while."

She grinned, unable to help a shiver of need. "I wouldn't want to overexert myself, you mean?"

"Exactly." He nipped at that sweet spot again.

Her breath stopped, her nipples going tight. "I might be convinced to let you wash my back."

"I'll be very thorough," he promised, his voice taking on that dark, sinful note that he used in bed.

A little humming noise escaped her. Slipping away, she turned for the bathroom and tugged the shirt over her head as she went. She glanced back when she dropped it and—oh, yeah—his glittering gaze was glued to her ass, a flush of lust already highlighting his cheekbones. Nice.

She crooked a finger at him. "You haven't moved, lover. Come to me."

His lip curling up to bare his fangs, he growled, "I am resisting the urge to drag you to the floor and mount you."

That mental image made hot fluids slick her sex. His nostrils flared and she knew he could smell how wet she was. His gray eyes turned an incandescent silver, and a muscle ticked in his jaw.

"I suggest you hurry, Bryn."

Normally, that would prompt her to go slower, just for the sheer joy of teasing him. But she found she couldn't wait either. Picking up the pace, she strode into the bathroom, and made quick work with the toothbrush. Then she moved to the bathtub and bent to turn on the shower. She knew the position would be too much temptation for him, and she grinned when his palms curved over her butt.

She laughed quietly. "Are you naked yet, Erik?"

"Stripped on my way to the bathroom." His fangs nipped at the top of one buttock, and she couldn't help an inelegant yelp. He licked the spot he'd bitten. "You just didn't look back."

"You suggested I hurry," she pointed out, glancing over her shoulder. "That means I don't stop and ogle. One or the other, sweetheart."

Instead of replying, he scooped her up in his arms and stepped under the stream of warm water. It sluiced down their bodies, slipping over her breasts and making her shudder. He set her on her feet, making sure every inch of her slid against him as he let her down. His chest hair stimulated her nipples and they beaded tighter. The steam curled around them, dewing their skin further. Somehow that made the moment even more intimate, the mist shutting the rest of the world away, dampening the sounds even her sensitive ears could pick up. Everything turned soft and sensual.

She tilted her head back and shut her eyes, savoring the feel of his hard body against hers. The shower spray hit her hair, sleeking the locks into a wet sheet down her back.

The noise he made was one of pure need. "You are the most beautiful woman I have ever known."

Opening her eyes, she shook her head, ran a fingertip down his nose, and tapped the tip. "I'm pretty enough, but you've met women who were more beautiful. Your wife was. Kata is."

"None can match you in my eyes." His expression was reverent.

Her heart cinched, but she didn't know how to respond to that, so she drew his head down and kissed him, telling him with actions how his words moved her. She loved him so much. Always had, always would, no matter how she might have fought it or denied it.

He tasted like coffee and sugar and Erik. She slipped her tongue into his mouth, wanting more of that addicting flavor. She couldn't get enough, didn't want to. His lips played over hers, hot possession and slow seduction. She strained against him, wanting nearer, wanting everything he had to give. His thick cock rode into the curve of her lower belly, close to where she needed it, but not close enough. He pressed her against the slippery tile wall, and she curled a leg around his hip, opening herself for him. She tilted her hips in blatant invitation, but he continued to kiss her leisurely, even though she could feel the hard urgency of his need.

Why was he suddenly hesitating?

Extending her talons, she pricked them into his shoulders. She felt him smile against her lips, and she chuckled into his mouth, smacking her palm lightly against the back of his skull. He lifted his head and grinned down at her. "I love making you laugh and smile."

"You've mentioned that," she answered dryly. Then she slipped a hand between them and twirled a finger around the flat disc of his nipple. His breath caught and he groaned. She pinched and twisted, using the same slow precision with which he'd kissed her. "I love making you want me so much you lose control."

A muscle twitched in his cheek and she could see the pounding of his pulse at the base of his throat. His voice was a wolfish rumble when he spoke, "You've always been able to drive me wild, Bryn."

"Good," she purred, flicking her thumbnail against his nipple. "But if you were really wild, Erik, you'd be inside me now, fucking me so hard my eyes rolled back."

"You've been in a coma." He swallowed, but his burning quicksilver eyes betrayed how much he struggled to maintain his restraint. "I love you. I don't want to hurt you."

"I'm perfectly fine," she whispered. "Magical healing is miraculous that way."

Curving her hands over his broad shoulders, she used him as leverage to wrap both legs around his waist. A quick arch of her back and she'd taken his cock deep inside her. He gasped and she let loose a throaty moan. The fit was as perfect as always, the way he stretched her was beyond amazing. Still she managed a small grin. "See? Not hurt. Just wanting you to take me exactly the way I like." She brushed little kisses over his chin, the corner of his mouth. "Fast...hard...deep..."

The sound that issued from his chest was like a human volcano erupting. His hands gripped her ass with bruising force and he began to piston in and out of her pussy. The shower poured over them, hot beads of water streaking down their skin. It was like being caressed over every inch of her body, the silky feel of liquid plus the rough satin of his flesh.

But it was his expression that made her burn for more. He was flushed with heat and lust, his fangs bared in feral display, but his gaze was more open and tender than she'd ever seen it. So much love was there—an ocean of it, enough to last a million lifetimes. Her heart tripped and hammered against her ribs. Emotion and sensation swept through her as he pounded into her sex. Orgasm beckoned, her pussy contracting every time he filled into her. They moved together, breaths mingling, hearts pounding. Tingles swept over her skin, excitement and need twining within her.

She let him see what she felt, didn't try to hide it from him or herself. No other man had ever suited her as well as him, no other man had ever challenged her the way he had. They would never be perfect people, but they were as perfect for each other now as they had been the day they'd met.

"It really does get better every time." He grinned at her, flashing his dimple as he ground his pelvis into her clit.

"*Yes,*" she gasped. In response to his statement or his actions, even she didn't know, but she tumbled over into climax just the same. Her channel clenched around him, and still she looked at him, let him see it all. How he turned her inside out with pleasure, how he made her *feel*. His chest hair rasped against her nipples, and the way he kept thrusting into her made orgasm build again, hot and swift, until she careened over that edge again. Her nails dug into his shoulders, a sob ripping out of her. "Erik!"

"I love you," he groaned, shuddered, and then jetted come inside her. His gaze remained locked with hers, and she saw ecstasy sharpen his features. Low groans spilled from him as he continued rocking into her pussy.

They stayed that way for a long time, their heart rates and breathing slowing, just looking at each other, savoring the chance to be together. She'd come so close to never having this opportunity again. It wasn't until the shower grew chilly and her legs began to cramp that she slipped her feet to the tub floor.

"My Erik." She pulled him down for a kiss, trailing her fingers down his cheek, his jaw, the back of his neck. When they broke apart, his lips formed a soft smile. She tweaked his chin and winked at him. "Damn, the water's freezing."

She reached over and twisted the knob to turn off the shower, then stepped out to towel off. He followed her, and they went through their grooming routines. It was odd to have someone else's toiletries next to hers, to share her personal space with another human being. Odd, yes, but still good. She could definitely get used to this. It was a little scary to consider getting used to having him and then losing him again, but she'd already come far too close to never seeing him again. He'd have been here or in Valhalla, and she'd have been locked in with Hel. Forever. Maybe Bryn would have died valorously in battle, but with Odin and Freya missing in action, Bryn had no doubts about Hel using Bryn's death as a way to imprison her in Niflheim. Frey wanted to stop Erik and her from repopulating the planet after *Ragnarök*, and his allies would probably have happily kept that plan on track whether the god was dead or not.

But it was Frey who'd be stuck in Niflheim for all eternity. His treachery wouldn't go unnoticed in Asgard, and he wouldn't be welcomed back. Good riddance.

Erik's gaze met hers in the mirror. "What are you thinking about?"

"You. Frey. Everything." She leaned in and kissed his shoulder. "But mostly you."

"We lost a lot of time we could have spent together, you and I." He didn't say that the minutes they had left might be limited, but she saw in his expression that he was thinking it.

She hesitated. "It took a long while to get to a place where I could cope with what had happened. Acceptance takes time, and it can't be rushed."

"A thousand years?" His eyebrows went up.

"Maybe not quite that long," she conceded. "But I don't think either of us wanted to approach the other, given the circumstances of our last meeting. Fate in the form of Nauma had to give us a push. Or you, rather."

Even with a *völva* pushing, Bryn wasn't sure she'd have been convinced to go near him. Not unless Freya forced her to. It was probably best he'd been the one Nauma prodded. Stubbornness had served Bryn well through her long life, though she usually knew when to bend. But for good or ill, she'd always had a blind spot where Erik was concerned. Just by existing, he made her react, made her feel. That meant she lost some of her control, but it also meant there was one person who could make sure that she never turned into to a cold, empty shell. Some immortals did, and as uncomfortable as emotions could be, she wanted to feel them.

Especially when it came to him.

Turning away from the vanity, she held out her hand to him and they walked hand-in-hand to the bed. She lay on her side, and he dropped onto his back next to her. He turned his head and met her gaze, something troubled in those silver depths. "Bryn..."

She ran a fingertip along his brow. "Yes?"

"I almost lost you," he croaked. His fingers tangled in her damp hair, and he scowled. "Don't ever scare me like that again. You're not allowed to die on me, do you hear? I forbid it."

She smiled then, a huge, brilliant smile. The one she knew he liked best. "I love you, too."

The sound that escaped him was a sob tangled with a laugh. "I love you so fucking much, Bryn. Never leave me again."

"Never willingly," she agreed, resting her chin on his chest. "If you promise the same."

He cupped her cheek. "I swear it."

Because she was a realist, and happiness was so often an ephemeral thing, she said, "Death continues to nip at our heels, Erik. *Ragnarök* still threatens."

"I know, *hjartað mitt*, but we stand together now." He brought her hand to his mouth and kissed her palm. "It's only when we've been turned against each other that we've ever fallen."

"True." They'd be a hell of a lot harder to pit against each other ever again. That was one lesson she knew they'd both learned well.

They'd made a lot mistakes—they'd hurt each other and hurt themselves and they would likely do so again. Hopefully not as deeply as they once had, but love wasn't easy. It was hard, it was painful, it was beautiful, it was sweet.

She might not be ready to put her faith in love, but she trusted *him*. It had taken close to forever, but she finally trusted him not to hurt her deliberately. Gods help anyone who ever doped him up with a forgetting potion again. She'd kill the bitch in a hot second. Maybe that was too bloodthirsty for modern sensibilities, but she *was* a Viking after all. Her people weren't exactly known for their peaceful solutions to problems.

His expression turned fierce, the grip of his fingers painfully tight. "Stay with me, in life and in death, if that's what comes for us."

"Until death and beyond," she vowed. "I love you."

THE END

Reclaimed by the Immortal Viking Bear

Crystal Jordan

CJ Books

1

Valhalla, Odin's Hall, Asgard

"Sif."

She froze at the sound of her name, one foot inside the door to the guest chambers she used whenever she stayed in her father-in-law's home. No one should be here when she wasn't, but her estranged spouse liked to think he was above such rules. "Thor."

Arms folded over his brawny chest, he leaned back against the footboard, which was carved with ravens and falcons—symbols of his parents, Odin and Freya. The armoire, dressing table, and several tapestries on the walls featured the same animals. But Freya had designated this room for Sif, so the bed's gold-and-bronze silk canopy and duvet were embroidered with her standard, a rowan tree.

The elegant furnishings only made Thor look that much more rugged and dangerous, the calm before a brewing storm. He was the picture of casual, yet his laser-blue gaze seared into her. One hand rose, his thumbnail rasping over his bearded jaw. "I understand you went over to Earth today."

Her heart skipped a beat at the leashed rage in his tone, but she raised her chin and stepped into the suite. How he always knew where she was and when, despite the fact that they rarely spoke anymore, was a source of constant annoyance for her. Why he bothered keeping tabs on her was a mystery she'd never solve.

"I go quite frequently. In fact, I practically live there." She arched her eyebrows and shut the door. "This may have escaped your notice in the last few millennia, husband, but I'm an earth goddess."

The sarcasm did nothing to appease his temper, but she had no real interest in appeasing him. As far as anyone in Asgard knew, they had a good marriage, were cordial when together in public, never spoke ill of each other, and had diverse interests that often kept them away from their home at Bilskirnir hall. In reality, they'd had a love-hate relationship for centuries and tried never to be at Bilskirnir at the same time, which was why she was currently "visiting" Valhalla.

Since they'd broken up, they'd mostly just gone about their lives as if they weren't married—traveling where and when they pleased, spending time in their separate vacation homes, sleeping with whomever they wanted—and it had worked out well enough. They stayed out of each other's way, but when push came to shove, they were *technically* still wed.

However, if the ancient prophecies were correct, their marriage was about to come to an end with his death in *Ragnarök*—the Twilight of the Gods—the apocalyptic battle between gods and giants that would destroy Earth. She'd gone to help those who wanted to stop it, but she doubted Thor would thank her for it.

For all she knew, he was now on the *jötunn* side, the giants she loathed with every fiber of her being. He wouldn't be the first major god to switch sides—to decide he could change the prophecy through treachery, thus avoiding his death. Another of the major Viking gods, Frey, had done so, and there was no telling who else would make the same choice.

The bottom line was, she had no idea who she could trust anymore, including her husband.

It was just a shame she still loved him.

Not that she'd ever tell him but, hoping he'd remain loyal to the gods, she'd done what she could to make sure there were warriors to fight beside him when the time came—a group of berserkers lead by Erik Siegfried, the one man the prophecy said would survive the coming battle. The World's Chosen.

Though if she were completely honest, she'd admit she wanted the giants to lose the fight because one of their kind had murdered Thor's and her daughter,

Thura. Centuries ago, and yet the wound still felt fresh. Not to mention the one giant who'd felt free to put his hands on Sif while she was blitzed out of her mind—the memories of that incident still gave her nightmares. Since both of those events combined had made her marriage implode...why, yes, she'd like every single oversized bastard wiped from the known realms. Maybe a peaceful earth goddess shouldn't think that way, but she *was* a Viking. Taking a breath, she tucked her fury away. The future was what she needed to focus on, not the past.

Thor's nostrils flared and his gaze dropped to her midsection. "Is that blood?"

"Probably." She tugged at the hem of her T-shirt, seeing a dried, dark smear across the fabric. "There was a battle, as I'm sure your terrifyingly efficient informants have told you. Frey and his giant friends kidnapped a valkyrie—Bryn, Siegfried's lover—and nearly killed her. Siegfried wasn't exactly happy about that, and Frey's dead now. Most of the giants with him too." *Good riddance*, but she kept that thought to herself and just provided a bare-bones report of events. "I brought Bryn here to be healed and then took her to the farm she owns in Virginia. Some of her blood must have gotten on me while we teleported."

A low snarl issued from his throat, the sound more animal than man, the bear inside him coming to the fore. Vikings had often called him Björn or Björn-Thor when he appeared as a massive brown bear before them. Most never saw him shift between forms, but they knew him for who he was—a god, a warrior, a ferocious beast. One whose enemies quaked before him.

Maybe she should have been scared, but she wasn't. Mostly, she was wired from having witnessed a bloody skirmish, stressed about the end being nigh, and just didn't have the patience to deal with her irate, possibly treacherous spouse. Rubbing her forehead, she sighed. "I've had a long day, Thor. What do you actually want?"

The question seemed to make him even angrier, and his cheeks flushed red. He dropped the casual pose and was across the room in three long strides, backing her against the wall beside the thick wooden door. He loomed over her, his nose a hairsbreadth from hers as he got right in her face. "I want you to stay out of this. You're no soldier—don't act like you have any place in a battle."

Did he want her out of the way because he was worried about her safety, or because he was worried she'd help the gods win? Which side was he on? Either way, her answer was the same. The end of the world was coming, and no one had the luxury of standing on the sidelines. Inaction meant annihilation.

She glared up at him. "I won't stay out of it and you can't make me."

A bit of fang showed when he curled his lip in disgust. "You sound like a petulant child."

Spank me, then. Another thought she kept to herself. He'd actually take her over his knee, and she'd no doubt enjoy it far more than she should. No matter how crappy their relationship became, the sex was amazing. Chemistry was a bitch that way.

Shoving aside the carnal awareness that filtered through her whenever he was near, she tilted her head toward the door. "If that's all you have to say, you can go now."

"Damn you, Sif." And then his mouth slammed down on hers, an act of possession and dominance that wouldn't change her mind.

But her body didn't care about logic. No, her hormones went wild the moment he touched her, just as they always had. Two thousand years, and she still craved this man like an addiction. No matter how she'd fought it, the need was never ending, uncontrollable, consuming. His hard angles fitted to her softer curves, and fire danced over her skin everywhere their bodies met. Her pussy clenched, going hot and slick in moments. She set her hands against his shoulders, not sure if she wanted to push him away or pull him closer.

His palm wedged between them, his fingers zeroing in on her nipple, pinching and twisting. Oh, *gods*. She couldn't manage to strangle a whimper as a lightning bolt of lust shot from breast to loin. All the adrenaline and tension of the day exploded into something far more dangerous and greedy. Using him to burn off her excess energy suddenly sounded like a damn good plan. He was here, he wanted to be demanding and rough—she could give as good as she got. She shoved her hands into his long hair, twisted the strands tight, and raked her teeth over his lower lip.

But the small violence only called to the animalistic side of him.

He growled, the sound approving. He nipped and sucked his way down her neck, and she felt the prick of his fangs against her skin. She shivered, arching into him. His beard prickled, both soft and rough at the same time, adding another layer of sensation to those already swamping her system. His thick cock dug into her lower belly, so close and yet so far from where it could do the most good. Her breathing sped until she panted, her pussy fisting on emptiness that needed to be filled. *More.* That was all she could think. She wanted his wildness now, wanted to lose herself until all her worries and fears melted to nothing. He bit the base of her throat and those sharp fangs sent wicked pleasure-pain zinging through her.

He teased her nipples, plucking and twisting until she wanted to sob with frustrated need. She curled her leg around his thigh, opening herself to him. He rocked his erection into her sex, the hard ridge riding over her clit. Gods, that felt good. Pressing herself forward, she increased the friction and moans spilled from her mouth. She let her head fall back against the wall, and every time he ground himself against her, a wave of tingles coursed down her limbs. She could feel herself building toward an orgasm, her inner muscles quivering as she drew closer and closer to the edge.

She dug her nails into his scalp. "I want you inside me. Now."

"Yes." His expression was feral when he drew back, the line between man and animal blurring. His control was slipping, and she shivered in anticipation.

Extending his claws, he sliced the front of her shirt from neckline to hem. Cool air rushed over her skin, making her nipples pucker even tighter and chafe against the lace of her bra. Since she'd been on Earth, she wore the clothes of a modern human. He had on the leather and wool typical of Asgard.

"Strip," he ordered. He ran his tongue down a long fang as his gaze slid over every centimeter of her body, pausing at her breasts and the juncture of her thighs. Her skin tingled as if his look had been a physical touch.

"I will if you will." She tugged at the laces on the front of his pants, untying them. "Take these off."

His hand went to the bottom of his tunic and pulled it over his head. The hard slab of his abs came into view, followed by his muscular pecs and arms. Gods, he was a beautiful man. One palm drifted down his stomach to his fly. He pulled the loosened laces open, then pushed the leather down his lean hips. He bent to tug his boots and pants off. When he straightened, he was nude, his cock a hard arc, wet with precum.

Biting her lip, she stared. Sucking him off sounded like fun, but the way her pussy ached told her that would have to wait for another time. Full penetration sex was on the menu today. Shrugging, she let the shredded shirt fall off her shoulders. Reaching back, she unhooked her bra and it went the way of her shirt. His eyes burned with blue fire, lust flushing the sharp angles of his face. His cock twitched and he took a step toward her, as if he couldn't hold himself back. She liked that—it made her feel powerful, sexy. She unsnapped the button on her jeans and unzipped them. Kicking her shoes aside, she shimmied out of the denim. The tight pants pulled her underwear down with them and then she was as naked as he was.

A low sound of utter need burst out of him, and he was on her in the blink of an eye. He buried his fingers in her hair and kissed her again. His tongue mated with hers and she met him willingly, fighting for control of the kiss. His unique Thor flavor filled her mouth as his hot, masculine scent filled her nose. Her arms went around his neck, the feel of his rougher skin and crisp curls revving her up even more. The hair on his chest rasped over her nipples, sending gooseflesh down her limbs. A moan spilled out of her, her heart raced and her breathing sped. She was so hot, so slick and ready. Nothing had ever been as exciting as touching him and having him touch her. The man just did it for her, and she wanted him pounding into her. Right now.

He jerked away and whipped her around to face the wall. "Brace yourself."

"Inside me," she demanded. Setting her palms on the uneven surface, the stone cooled her heated skin. "Inside me. *Please.*"

He buried one hand in her hair, wrapping the waist-length strands around his wrist. Her golden locks were her signature, and every man she'd ever met loved them. Thor was one of her few lovers who had ever figured out how much she liked having her hair pulled. Hard. He gave a sharp tug and she moaned, her pussy fisting tight and growing damper.

He kicked her feet apart, spreading her wide. The head of his dick rubbed over the lips of her sex. A shudder ran through him. "So wet for me."

"Yes. Fuck me hard."

He groaned. "Sif."

After pulling her head back so far she felt almost bent in half, he drove deep in one swift plunge. She hissed in a breath. He was so huge within her, stretching her to the limit. If she hadn't been so slick and ready, it would have hurt. As it was, it just made her burn for more. She reached one hand back and raked her nails across his heavy thigh, silently communicating her urgency.

"Greedy girl," he rumbled. He withdrew more slowly than he'd entered her, the drag of his flesh in hers making her moan.

"*Thor.*"

She gripped his leg, digging her fingers in to bring him back to her. He obliged, entering her in another breathtaking thrust that buried him to the hilt. Her sex contracted around him, making them both gasp. Sweat beaded at her temples, slipping down in slow beads. The pace he set was swift and punishing, his stomach slapping her ass, the sound loud and obscene. He drove her toward the wall, and for a heart-stopping moment she thought she'd go face-first into the stone. She had to release his thigh and set both palms on the wall. Despite the scare, she couldn't stop, didn't want to. She *needed* the surcease only he could grant her.

"More." She squeezed her pussy around his thick shaft each time he penetrated her. "I want to come. Make me scream."

Snorting, he yanked her hair again. "Yes, my goddess."

Agony twisted with ecstasy until there was no difference between the two, and she shivered. The fingers of his free hand clamped on her ass, his talons pressing into her sensitive flesh. Then he drew back his palm and slapped her upper thigh. She jolted in shock, a small cry wrenching from her. Her sex fisted on his dick, the first shimmer of climax sweeping through her. She was so close, and she thought she might die before she went over the edge.

"You wanted me to make you scream, didn't you?" There was a lilt of male satisfaction in his voice. "We can do better though."

She felt his claws retract as he glided his finger across her backside and dipped between her cheeks. Oh, gods. He stopped thrusting, but excitement writhed like a living thing inside her anyway. She *loved* ass play. He circled the pucker of her anus, letting her tension build for a moment before he slipped a fingertip into her. She wriggled, forcing him deeper. He added another digit and then another. He began to rock his hips slowly and pushed his fingers into her anus in a tandem rhythm, so she was always filled by him.

Her nails scrabbled against the wall. "Oh, oh, *oh*."

Having him stretch her front and back was incredibly erotic, and every few thrusts was accompanied by a jerk on her hair. The combination quickly took her to the pinnacle of madness. It was too much. It was perfect. Each time he entered her, the tip of his dick hit her in just the right spot, and little mewls broke from her throat. *Yes*. A few more thrusts and she was going to implode.

She arched into him, meeting his swift strokes. His fingers rubbed the head of his cock through the thin membrane that separated her two channels. So good. So fucking good. When he released her hair and swatted her ass hard, it catapulted her straight into orgasm. Her pussy contracted around his shaft, goose bumps breaking over her flesh. Every muscle in her body tensed as her sex pulsed repeatedly, ecstasy making her skin feel too hot and too tight. He spanked her again and again, each time sending another wave of climax crashing over her.

"*Thor!*" she screamed.

"There it was." Satisfaction oozed from his tone, but then he shuddered against her, as helpless in the grip of lust as she was. He jetted come into her pussy, hoarse groans spilling from his throat.

He bent forward, his hands braced on the stone next to hers, quaking as he rested his forehead between her shoulder blades. His breath rushed over her sweat-dampened skin and made her shiver. It took a long time for her heart to stop galloping and for her mind to drift down from euphoria. This was exactly what she'd wanted, a complete escape.

A quiet moan issued from him. "Fuck, Sif."

She hummed, a smile curling her lips. "Yes, that was the idea."

"Actually, it wasn't. I didn't come here for this." He sighed and shook his head, the tips of his hair brushing her back. "But you make me insane. Always have, always will."

And there was the harsh intrusion of reality, bursting her bubble of quiet calm. Always, he'd said. But *always* might not last very long. The signs were all pointing toward the end times. High-magnitude earthquakes, super storms, monster hurricanes, the hottest summers in memory—and her memory went back a long, long time. She knew her Earth, her element. Mortals could call it climate change, but Sif knew better. They were all precursors for *Ragnarök*, where the god-giant war would result in Earth being consumed by fire and submerged by the rising sea, ending all life except for two human survivors, and then a new and supposedly golden era would begin.

Thor wasn't supposed to live through it, and she had serious doubts if Earth died and was reborn, that she wouldn't die right along with it. Without the resurrection part.

They both might be dead soon. She'd understood that for a long time, but somehow it hit her harder than it ever had before. Dead, finished, gone. Their dysfunctional marriage where they hated each other one moment and fucked each other's brains out the next would be done.

What she didn't expect was the rush of grief that swamped her at the prospect.

She didn't want him to see her cry, so she gritted her teeth and made herself respond to what he'd told her. "I make you *insane*? That's sweet, Thor. Just what every woman wants to hear right after she gets off."

She pushed herself upright, forcing him to do the same. He stepped away, and she had to bite back a groan as his flesh slid free of hers. When she turned around and met his gaze, his expression was wary. Even after what they'd just done, even completely naked, they still wore armor around each other. Emotional, yes, but a shield was a shield.

Sex didn't equal trust, and even great sex wouldn't alter the course she'd set.

2

HE WANTED TO SHAKE some sense into her, but it wouldn't help. He'd known her for more years than he could remember, even before they'd wed. She was remarkably stubborn when she made up her mind.

She sighed, shaking her head. "The sex doesn't change anything."

The corner of his mouth kicked up in a small smile. "It never does."

The little fool was going to get herself killed. Giants weren't enemies to make or take lightly—when crossed, they were wily as jackals and twice as vicious. They'd eviscerate someone as soft as Sif. Not that he thought her weak. Far from it. His wife had a will of steel, but it was no battle of wills the giants were after. Didn't she see the danger she'd put herself in by so openly declaring her loyalties? Right now, the giants thought every god's and goddess's honor was as flexible as Frey's, which meant they could be turned...or bought. By aiding Erik Siegfried and his cronies, she'd made herself a target. Didn't she know the sorts of things a *jötunn* would do to her before he killed her? Death would be a blessing after that.

When Thor died in the apocalypse, who would protect her? The thought had tortured him for millennia, but never more than now, with the end so near. They'd been politely estranged for most of their marriage, and the situation wasn't likely to improve, but that didn't change his duty to watch over her.

Whether she liked it or not.

She swept over to her wardrobe and pulled on a dressing gown, belting it tight around her slim waist. A pity. Her body was a work of art, all snowy skin, wheat-gold curls, and amber eyes. She was, quite simply, the most beautiful woman he'd ever known. When he'd first pursued her, he'd seen her as a prize to be won, but he'd quickly learned how stupid that attitude was—and it was unlikely to gain her favors. She was lovely, yes, but it was what she hid beneath the surface that mattered. She was quick-witted, kind-hearted, and while most people thought she was as sweet as she appeared, she was incredibly *earthy* in her sexual appetites. He loved the dichotomy.

Her chin firmed, her eyes narrowing. "You can't keep me from helping the humans."

"I could tie you to the bed and keep you here." The idea appealed to him on several levels, his mind supplying a number of delightful and devious things he could do to her while she was at his mercy. He thrust those thoughts aside. *Focus, Thor. Now's not the time to be led around by your cock.*

Clearing her throat, she pointed out, "I can teleport."

His gaze went from her to the large, carved bedframe and back again. "You'd have to take the bed with you if you're tied to it."

She fought a grin. Making her laugh always took the anger out of her argument, which made it a tactic he'd used to his advantage often. No such luck today. She wrinkled her nose. "True, it would be awkward to explain, but you can't keep me where I don't want to be kept."

He wished that were true. "There are ways to bind anyone, even a goddess."

"Even a giant," she retorted, and he winced.

There was a direct hit. They both knew which giant she was talking about: Loki. It took strong magic to keep an immortal captive. For centuries, Loki had been chained to a rock on Earth using the ironized entrails of his murdered son. He'd pissed the gods off one too many times, and that had been his punishment. His vengeance was going to be apocalyptic. A Viking prophetess—a *völva*—had foretold that when that giant got loose, it was a sign of the end times.

Thor gave her a hard look. "I know Loki escaped."

"And you know what that means." She pulled the belt around her waist tighter. "So, tell me again how I should stay out of this when the apocalypse could kill us all."

He shook his head. "You aren't destined to die during *Ragnarök*."

That was his fate, not hers. It had been hanging over his head for half of his life, but he'd always taken some comfort in knowing the same misfortune wouldn't befall her.

What comfort was there now, when she'd thrown herself into the middle of the deadliest battle of all time? The fucking apocalypse was coming and she'd suddenly decided to get reckless. Was she hoping to be killed? The mere idea curdled his insides.

No. He refused to let that happen. If there was one thing he could get right in his life, it was to make sure his wife wasn't slaughtered by a *jötunn* the way their daughter had been. He refused to fail so miserably twice.

She huffed. "We both know *anyone* can become a casualty of war, and prophecies never tell the whole story."

"Damn it." What argument did he have against that? She was right, but that didn't mean he had to like it. He wanted her as far away from any action as possible. He *needed* her to be safe with a desperation she wouldn't understand if he tried to explain it. Even if she understood, he doubted she would care. He shoved a hand through his hair and gripped the strands tight, as if that might force this entire interaction to make sense. Couldn't she see she had no place in a war zone? "Why can't you be reasonable?"

Some emotion flashed across her expression, gone too fast for him to recognize it. "This argument is pointless. Neither of us is going to change our mind."

The bear in him growled at the idea of its mate being endangered. He stabbed a clawed fingertip at her chest. "You're going to end up dead if you continue on this path, Sif. I'm warning you. Stay out of this."

"That sounds remarkably like a threat," she returned mildly.

He shook his head. "When have I ever bothered with threats? I'm speaking plain truth."

"Then here's more plain truth." She stepped over to the door and held it open. "Go away, Thor. You have nothing to say that I haven't already considered. I'll stay the course, no matter where it leads. If I die, I go with a clear conscience about the choices I've made today." She gestured for him to leave. "I may not be a warrior like you, but I'm also not so spineless that I hide my loyalties. Can you say the same?"

"Are you calling me a coward?" Now his fangs extended, deadly points that matched his talons. "I've killed men for lesser insults."

Rage slammed through him, as much at himself as at her. He'd hated playing political games, but in order to survive, he had to know his enemies. His parents had gone missing more than a year ago, and he didn't know where they were. They might have been kidnapped by a *jötunn* but, if so, he'd found no evidence of it. Wherever they were, they didn't want to be found. Looking surreptitiously for Odin and Freya had meant being friendlier with certain giants than he'd liked.

"More veiled threats." Sif folded her arms. "Make good on them, or get out. This conversation is over."

Make good on them? Had she lost her mind? Other than a bit of rough bedsport, he'd never laid a finger on her in violence. Not once in two thousand years. Not even when she'd cheated on him with his worst enemy. With *Loki*.

An incoherent noise erupted from his throat—anger, frustration, and agony stealing any ability he had to continue the discussion. "This isn't over, Sif."

He needed to get out of the room before he did or said something he couldn't take back. Not bothering to dress, he shifted into his bear form, letting the beast take over. His body warped and twisted, skin and bones reshaping. He hit his front paws, shaking from head to tail as he settled into the massive predatory body. He lumbered out the door without a backward glance.

She slammed the door behind him, barely missing his rump.

He stormed into his rooms, his paw smashing the door open so hard, the iron handle scored into the stone wall. He had his own hall, Bilskirnir, but his childhood rooms were kept in Valhalla for his use when he visited. Loosing a low roar, he had to restrain the need to tear the place apart. Some outlet for his ire and fear would be welcome. His gaze caught on his sword and his war-hammer, Mjölnir. He'd left them here before he'd gone to see his wife. Probably for the best, or Mjölnir might have been used to vent his frustration and put a hole in her wall—or level that wing of Valhalla. Not a dignified use for so legendary a weapon, and not something he'd want to explain if his father should return.

Perhaps he should unleash his energy on the training field. Some of Odin's berserkers or Freya's valkyries could surely use the practice. Though there were very few of them left that his parents hadn't sent over to Earth to walk the world and get a feel for modern human culture. They usually rotated the number they sent, but now the place felt deserted. Perhaps they'd emptied Valhalla for reasons they'd never shared with their son. Perhaps they'd known how the giants would infiltrate the ranks of the gods before *Ragnarök*, turning them against each other.

Thor had no idea. He'd spent most of the last decade on Earth, only returning permanently when his parents vanished. It had been a year rife with annoyance. Too many questions and far too few answers.

And now he had a kamikaze wife to deal with.

Fuck.

Shifting back to human form, he dragged on some clothes and snatched up his weapons. Yes, a good hard training session would do a world of good. He smiled, though only a fool would call the expression friendly. Stalking into the main hall, he glanced around and found the place almost empty. A goddess or two, a few handmaidens, and an elderly servant.

He looked to the servant. "Where is everyone?"

The man bowed. "All the warriors have gone hunting, my lord. They should return shortly for the evening meal."

Fuck.

He strode over to a table, set Mjölnir down, hooked his finger through the handle on a jug of mead and took a swig straight from the bottle. Shit-faced wasn't his preferred method of dealing with his problem, but it was the sort of day his mortal friends called a clusterfuck. Bloodshed or booze were his options, and bloodshed seemed out of the question. Dropping onto the bench, he drank deeply. The sweet, honeyed liquor flooded his taste buds. He sat for a moment, but couldn't relax. Awareness made his shoulders twitch.

He was being watched.

The bear's hackles rose, and Thor's hand tightened on the jug. He glanced around, keeping his body language casual. One of the goddesses stared at him, then turned to whisper to a handmaiden. Gossip was nothing new, though he had no doubt these tales were centered around Frey's recent death. Killed by Erik and his band of merry berserkers.

A part of Thor wished he'd been there for the fight. He'd have liked to rip Frey's perfidious heart from his chest. Instead, it was Sif who'd been there. She'd helped teleport the berserkers to the giants' stronghold. Teleporting was the purview of gods and giants—berserkers and valkyries were made immortal by Odin or Freya and had their own set of supernatural skills, but those skills were paltry when compared to the abilities of a born immortal.

Thor made a mental note of the goddess who'd been staring. Zisa. She was Tyr's lover. Like Thor, Tyr was slated to die during the apocalypse. So, what was her sudden interest in Thor? Was she—or Tyr—wondering about his godly fidelity the same way Sif was? For that matter, Thor had no idea where Zisa or Tyr's loyalties lay. There was no one he could depend on implicitly.

Except Sif.

A humorless laugh escaped him. By making herself a *jötunn* target, she'd also let the faithful residents of Asgard know she could be trusted.

He hadn't a clue which of them had the better survival strategy at this point. Only time would tell, and time was a commodity of which they had precious little left.

A gong reverberated through the hall, calling everyone to the evening meal. He cocked his head, the bear's enhanced hearing picking up the faint sound of horses returning to the stables. The remaining berserkers and valkyries were back from their hunt just in time to stuff their faces. Good. Maybe he could do a bit more investigation of where *everyone's* loyalties lay. Their reactions to Frey's death would be telling.

Sudden alertness flooded him, the beast within him sensing danger. Another glance around revealed nothing, but the feeling intensified. He listened for anything new. Just people going about their usual business. He pulled a breath in through his nose, sorting through the myriad aromas. Food, wine, perfume, sweat, body odor, horses, dogs...giants. His head came up. Any visiting giants usually stayed in the main hall. A few giants were married to gods or goddesses, but he knew their scents. These were different. These giants shouldn't be wandering Valhalla unescorted. Something was off. Perhaps it was overreaction, but he'd been a warrior too long to ignore his instincts.

The bear sensed a threat, and that was enough for Thor.

He rose from the bench, picked up his weapons, and followed the scents. It didn't bode well that they all wafted from the same direction.

The wing that housed Sif's rooms.

Icy fear skittered down his back. The bear had sensed a threat to *her*. He quickened his pace until he was running, pelting down hallways, careening around corners. Someone slammed into him going the opposite direction, and he ricocheted off the wall, but didn't bother to stop or offer an apology or explanation. The smell of blood had reached his nose, and he pushed his speed to the limit.

He had to get to Sif before it was too late.

3

After Thor left, Sif sat on the side of her bed, staring into space. Too many thoughts chased each other in circles through her mind. She didn't know how long she'd sat there when a low gong tolled in the distance, calling everyone in Valhalla to dinner. She debated whether or not to go. While this was Odin's hall, neither he nor Freya had been present for a long time. The gods were heading into a war without their leaders. Sif winced. Then again, Freya's twin brother had switched over to the giants' side and been killed for his duplicity. There were rumors that Odin and Freya's absence meant they were dead too. Why else would they hide?

Sif wasn't inclined to believe rumors, not without some evidence to back them up. Right now, no one knew anything for sure. The original *Ragnarök* prophecy claimed that all the major deities—Odin, Thor, Frey, Tyr, Heimdall—would die and take most of the major giants with them.

But the prophecy had already gone awry with Frey's death before the final battle even began. Odin was missing and Heimdall had most likely been kidnapped by giants. So, when the end came—and it would—who would stop the giants from taking over Earth? Giants liked to eat humans and they liked to play with their food before they consumed it. Gang rape and cannibalism, that was what would become of humanity if those monsters won *Ragnarök*.

With so many of the gods' greatest warriors missing in action, the future looked grim from where Sif stood. She'd do what she could, but she feared she was grasping at straws.

She discarded her robe and reached into her wardrobe for a gown, quickly changing. Hiding in her rooms wouldn't help her figure out who her allies were. Going to the evening meal meant she'd be dining with a group of people she should be able to trust—gods, goddesses, valkyries, berserkers—but there was no telling who had been turned by the giants. Their strategy with Frey had been simple but effective: if he changed sides, he'd break the prophecy, and therefore have the chance to live. He'd been so afraid to die that he'd betrayed his entire race. It hadn't hurt that he'd been married to a giantess, and she'd been very persuasive.

Thor had had his fair share of giantess lovers. He'd even had a couple of sons with them. Immortal women had the power to control certain aspects of their fertility, so accidental pregnancies were almost unheard of. Which meant at least the giantesses had wanted to get knocked up—whether or not Thor had been on board with that plan was unknown. He'd certainly helped raise the boys, as attentive to them as he'd ever been to Thura. Sif pushed aside a twinge of pain, and forced herself to face hard facts. Her husband had a number of *jötunn* and half-*jötunn* influences in his life. She wanted to believe he would never turn traitor, but she'd lived too long and seen too much to put much faith in *nevers*. Everything was possible, be it good or bad.

A knock came at her door. Thor again? She smoothed her gown and went to see who was there. Not her husband. She sensed a feminine presence on the other side of the thick wooden panel, but that was all she could tell. Which meant it could be any number of handmaidens, goddesses, or valkyries, though she was surprised anyone would seek her out after her public act of defiance today.

"Yes?" She unlatched the door and it exploded inward, the handle wrenching from her grip. She screamed and stumbled back, panic scrambling her wits.

Giants!

It was a giantess who came through the opening first, a wicked-looking knife gripped in her hand. "Hello, little goddess."

Two giants followed her, one of whom Sif recognized. Gymir, Frey's *jötunn* father-in-law. They shouldn't have been able to cross into Asgard or enter Valhalla so easily.

They'd had help. There was another traitor.

Her moment of hesitation to realize that cost her the chance to escape. The dagger shot across the room, pinning Sif's dress to the ground. Being pinioned that way meant she couldn't teleport. *Shit.* She grabbed fistfuls of her skirt and yanked, ripping the fabric away from the blade. The giantess was on her inside of the next heartbeat, slamming her into the footboard. The impact robbed Sif of breath. The woodcarvings jabbed into her back and sent pain shooting straight to her brain.

The other woman was twice her size, and clearly warrior-trained. Everything Sif wasn't. She kicked out, catching the giantess in the chest. It was like shoving a brick wall, so she pushed harder, using the leverage to go over the footboard backward. She sprawled across the mattress in an ungainly heap, scrambling to get away long enough to teleport. It took a moment of complete concentration to make the jump from one place to another. She needed to get a grip on her panic, but her mind gibbered with it, pinging in too many directions.

"What are you going to do, Gymir? Make an example of me?" Talk, think, be reasonable—that's what she had to do now. Get space and calm down.

"Of course." His smile was an ugly sneer as he approached the bed. "Asgard needs to know what happens to those who get in our way. Thank you for volunteering."

The third giant closed in on the other side, leaving Sif backed up against the headboard. This one's swarthy complexion marked him as a fire giant, and that did nothing to soothe her. They were the most vicious of the giant races, with a voracious appetite for human flesh. Her heart raced, sweat sliding down her face and back, leaving her palms sticky.

He ran a hand over his bald pate. No—he had scales instead of hair. Some giants were very humanoid, some utterly monstrous. He was somewhere in between. "She looks tasty. Not as tender as a mortal, but I'm hungry enough to make do." He drew in a breath, lust and bloodlust merging in his expression. "I can smell the sex on her."

Her stomach revolted and she fought a gag. She closed her eyes, trying to focus on somewhere to go. A safe place. Her hidden cabin in the middle of Patagonia. She'd been staying there before all this started. Away from everyone and everything. *Away.* She locked on the visualization, the Earth coordinates. She could do this.

Gymir's meaty fingers clamped onto her wrist, breaking her concentration. He tsked. "You're not thinking of leaving the party so soon, are you?"

"Enough talk," the giantess said. "Let's get this done before someone comes."

"No one came running when she screamed." Gymir patted the thick stone wall affectionately. "I doubt anyone will hear anything. We can savor this a little."

Sif clamped her free hand over her mouth, her gorge rising. Was this how it had been for her daughter? Three against one, *savoring* her death? Sif wanted to howl in pain at the questions she'd forced herself to never ask. Not once in a thousand years. She didn't really want the answers—her sanity might not survive.

But Thura had been trained by her father and a slew of valkyries. She knew how to protect herself. Not that it had saved her, but she would have gone down fighting.

And so would her mother, even if it wasn't much of a contest. Sif was caught. There was no escape. So she'd make her end one that Thura would be proud of. Sif's rioting emotions settled into cold, hard, ruthless resolve.

With a shriek, she turned on Gymir, slamming her fist into his nose. She felt her fingers pop, the bones breaking, but Gymir's head snapped to the side and blood gushed from his nose. He staggered back and she leapt on him, kicking and biting, tearing at every piece of his skin she could reach. If she had to die, she was taking her pound of flesh with her. She latched onto his ear with her teeth, ripping the lobe off while he roared.

He shoved her away, launching her across the room. She hit the ground hard, sliding across the slick marble until she hit a heavy rug. She spat out the earlobe and tried to roll, but her skirts twisted around her legs. Damn it. What she wouldn't give for her jeans now. The giantess landed on top of her, a crushing weight that made Sif struggle to breathe. She shoved up, but there was no dislodging someone double her size.

The dagger drove deep into her shoulder, and it was all she could do to hold on to consciousness. She slapped, punched, and clawed with her other hand. It was a futile effort. The giantess got her hands around Sif's throat, and she bucked and writhed like a wild thing. She stabbed at the giantess's eyes, which got her to rear away long enough to let Sif suck in air. Her throat and lungs burned, involuntary tears sliding down her cheeks. Something hard connected with her side, knocking what little breath she had out of her. She sobbed for oxygen, still fighting with every last ounce of strength she possessed.

"Just tenderizing the meat." The fire giant grinned down at her, drew back his boot and kicked her again. This time, she felt her ribs give way. Dark spots swam before her eyes, reality fading in and out for a few moments. Pain such as she'd never known pummeled her, so intense she couldn't even cry out. The giantess reared over her, swung a fist, and connected hard with Sif's jaw. Her head whipped back and bounced against the marble floor.

The marble.

Realization exploded through her brain, a last spurt of sanity, of survival instinct. Freya had had the stone specially imported from Earth, and Sif could manipulate any natural earthen element. The thought sped through her mind and her powers reacted automatically. The marble around her liquefied, boiling and turning into red-hot lava.

The echoing, animalistic screams of the giantess and fire giant were sounds that would haunt Sif for the rest of her days. The marble under one of the giantess's knees gave way and she toppled sideways into the magma. She screeched as she was consumed in seconds, going under and never resurfacing. The fire giant tried to use his power over flames to save himself. The heat was incredible, but it didn't burn Sif. She pulled the knife from her shoulder, curled into a fetal position, and floated on a tiny patch of solid marble. He tried to scrabble onto the little island with her, his hands clutching the edge in a death grip. She twitched her fingers and sent a plume of molten lava over his head. He shrieked, his skin and scales blistering, melting until there was nothing left of him but the hand on her island. The stench of cooking flesh made her retch, the vomit hissing as it ran off the edge of the stone and hit the magma.

She could feel her energy sapping, pain and the power it took to hold the lava in place draining her quickly. Shudders wracked her, sweat pouring down her face to sting her eyes. She blinked hard and turned her head to see Gymir bolt out the door before she could send the lava his way.

Dragging in air made her ribs ache, but she couldn't guarantee he wouldn't come back with reinforcements. She needed to get out of Asgard. Her cabin.

Patagonia. Yes, escape. Now.

The last thing she saw before she teleported was Thor standing in her doorway, weapons ready. Was *he* the giant's reinforcements? His gaze dropped to the liquid fire on the floor, eyes going wide in shock. Then she snapped into the utter blackness of teleportation as she transitioned between realms. It took every scrap of concentration she had to push away her agony and focus on her destination.

She landed on the ground outside her cabin with a bone-jarring thud, a silent scream wrenching from her swollen throat. Her cabin was built next to a healing spring, and she half-crawled, half-dragged herself to the edge, sobbing the whole way. If she could get to it, the waters would take care of her wounds.

Earth would heal her.

Reaching the side of the spring, she lay for a moment panting and shaking from exertion, her body covered in cold sweat. One last heave and she'd be in the water. She gathered her strength, gritted her teeth, planted her hands in the muddy shore, and shoved herself forward.

She overshot, plunging into the middle of the warm water. She gagged as her head went under, and her sodden skirts pulled her down. Clawing at the fabric, she tried to rip it, but she didn't have the strength. She scissored her legs and stroked with her arms, but with one injured limb, she barely managed to break the surface. *Air*. She sucked in a lungful of sweet oxygen and water that burned her lungs. Coughing and choking and trying to stay afloat, her skirts hampered her ability to kick.

She was going down, and she knew she'd never make it up again.

Roaring filled her ears, and she felt something tear at her scalp, a white-hot pain that only added to the agony gripping her body.

Then she felt nothing at all.

4

Sif was alive. She'd survived. He'd gotten there in time.

Thor had to remind himself of that a million times, the words becoming the mantra he lived and breathed by as he waited for her to regain consciousness. He'd managed to haul her out of the water by her hair—not the most elegant way to do it, but the golden tresses had been the only part of her left floating when he'd arrived. Terror still sat like a lead weight in his belly. She'd been so close to death. A few more seconds and he might not have been able to save her.

He paced in circuits through her cabin, guarding her as she slept. He needed to move or the rage might make his head implode. Someone had attacked her, put their hands on *his wife*. If he hadn't followed her to Earth, she would have drowned. As far as he knew, she had no idea that he was even aware her little mountain sanctuary existed.

The place was so isolated, he couldn't sense another being for miles. A few birds and foraging rodents, a small herd of llamas, but that was it. Her cabin was a timbered structure, simple and built to blend in with the surroundings. The most modern convenience was the solar panels that gave her electricity, but there wasn't even a road nearby, so she had to have teleported the panels in. Tall grasses filled the clearing around her cabin and spring, quickly turning into dense forest and high, rugged mountains even taller than the one they occupied. He might have thought it beautiful, if he wasn't so pissed.

She'd been a hairsbreadth from death and hadn't called for his help. Bitter bile burned his mouth at that realization.

Gods were immortal, but that meant old age would never conquer them, it didn't mean they couldn't be killed. Sure, they were *hard* to kill, but it could be done, and was easier with those who weren't warriors. Like Sif.

He'd stripped the sodden dress off her and left her to heal in the spring for as long as he dared, but she'd started thrashing in her sleep and submerged herself again. Holding her had only made her struggle harder, so he'd brought her inside and found a set of scarves to tie her to the bedposts. He could only hope she didn't try to teleport in her sleep, because she *would* take the bed with her. Then again, he also hoped she didn't try to defend herself by turning the floor to lava. He could teleport away, but he'd probably get burned first. He couldn't afford to be injured now, but he couldn't leave her either.

So he paced. And waited. And died a little every moment until she opened her golden eyes and looked at him.

"Thor." Her voice was its usual mellifluous tone, so her throat had healed. The bruises there when he'd found her told him that one of the giants had nearly crushed her larynx. Her brow puckered as she took in her surroundings. "What are you doing here?"

Really? *That* was her question? His hands balled into fists at his sides. "Saving your skin. How are you feeling?"

"Fine, I think. Nothing hurts anymore. The healing spring did its job." She blinked slowly. "How did you find me?"

"You're still my wife. It's my duty to know where you are and ensure that you're safe." It was that simple, and that complicated. Just like their marriage. "Why didn't you call for me?"

"I don't wear your rune stone anymore, Thor." The small stones allowed gods and goddesses to communicate with anyone who had one marked with their symbol. She shook her head, her long hair rustling against the pillow and sheets. "When was the last time I called you for anything?"

He knew the exact day, the day his life had unraveled around him. The day the worst year of his life had gotten even shittier. The day he'd learned she'd cheated on him with Loki. The giant who would lead the army that killed the ruling gods—including Thor. Of all the men she could have fucked around with, Loki was the one Thor couldn't forgive. Was that why she'd done it? That was the one thing he'd never been able to figure out. *Why?*

She seemed to realize she was tied up and tugged at her wrists. "Even if I could have called you, I didn't know if I could trust you. Maybe you were the one who sent the giants to attack me."

"That's not..." He blew out a breath. "If I wanted you dead, woman, I would have left you there to drown."

"Untie me," she insisted. "Right now."

"Calm down." He extended his claws and sliced through the silk that bound her ankles. "You were fighting phantoms in your sleep. I was trying to make sure you didn't hurt yourself."

"I believe we talked about binding an immortal." Her eyes narrowed, and she held out her hands as far as she could. "It would take more than scarves to imprison me, Thor."

He stared at her. "I've never tried to harm you *or* cage you."

"No?" She snorted. "I saw you."

"What?" Had the beating she'd taken addled her brain?

"I *saw* you," she bit out. "Standing in my doorway, looking shocked that I wasn't dead yet. Your friends didn't get the job done. Sorry-not-sorry."

"I wasn't *standing there*. I was running to help you." He shook his head, unsure how the conversation had taken this turn. Retracting his talons, he worked at the knots on her wrists. Best not to slash at anything near her face.

As soon as he freed her, she sat up and yanked the sheet to her breasts to cover her nudity. At least she didn't try to run away. That had to count for something.

Her expression was dubious, one eyebrow arching. "How would you know I needed help if you had nothing to do with the giants coming in the first place? You did warn me I was going to be killed if I didn't behave the way you wanted."

Valid questions, but he hated that she couldn't give him the benefit of the doubt. He'd never once acted as if her security didn't matter to him. Even when he'd found out she'd slept with Loki, he'd just walked away from the relationship. He hadn't hurt her, hadn't wished her ill, then or now. He may have gotten everything else wrong, but not that. "It was an instinct that told me you were in danger."

Both eyebrows rose this time and her arms crossed over her chest. "You're no *völva*. You can't See anything."

It had been a difficult day for her, so he checked his annoyance and sat on the side of the bed. "It wasn't the man whose instincts were aroused. It was the bear side of me."

That seemed to throw her and she blinked. "I've always assumed there was no distinction between the beast's instincts and the man's."

"There is. Somewhat." He cleared his throat. "The bear sensed a threat to its mate. I responded. Its instincts have never failed me."

Glancing away, her cheeks reddened. "I wouldn't have thought any part of you considered me a mate anymore."

"We're still married." A situation she could remedy if she wanted. They both could. Divorce was rare in their culture. It was socially stigmatized, but it *was* possible. So, they'd had ample opportunity to renounce each other if they wanted to do so. Neither of them had. He rolled his shoulders, not wanting to admit any vulnerabilities to a woman who'd crushed his heart, but knowing the truth might allay some of her suspicions. "I...suspect the bear would consider you a mate for life, whether we divorced or not."

Her lips twisted. "That's sad."

Sad? The last thing any man wanted was his woman calling him sad. Stiffening, he retorted, "Spare me your pity."

Her nostrils flared in annoyance. "It was empathy, not pity."

Yeah, as if he was going to dive into the touchy-feely differences between those emotions. Best to get the conversation back on track. "Tell me why you think I want you killed. We may be separated, but I've never done anything to make you believe I'd hurt you or allow anyone else to do so. Yet you doubt my loyalty."

"I doubt everyone's loyalty," she shot back.

He poked a finger at her. "That's the smartest thing you've said all day."

Her gaze turned to molten gold, fury tightening her expression. "Go fuck yourself."

"My hand has never been my favorite way of getting off, but that's beside the point."

He could all but hear her teeth grind, and he half expected the floor to open up and swallow him. She snarled, "I did it to save you."

"I think *I'm* the one who saved *you*."

More teeth grinding, and her fingers curled into fists, bunching in the sheet. "I'm talking about Erik. The berserkers. Helping them while they took down Frey and a few of his giant friends. If I hadn't gone to their aid, it would have gutted their group."

"Only Bryn would have died. Everyone else made it out of there relatively unscathed." His informants had looked into the matter thoroughly, but he'd seen red the moment they explained his wife's involvement.

"I'm not even going to ask how you know that." She sighed and met his gaze. "Someone once told me that if you rip the heart out of a man, it doesn't matter what else is left of him. He has no reason to live."

He'd said that to her, right before he'd walked out on their relationship. He didn't know what it meant that she remembered that. He nodded, encouraging her to continue.

"Bryn has always been Erik's heart, no matter how much they professed to hate each other. Any fool could see that." Her shoulder hunched in a shrug. "He's the World's Chosen, the leader of that berserker team. We need him—it's that simple. So I made sure he has a reason to live, to *win*."

"Thus declaring which side you're on," he pointed out. "Not very cagey of you."

"Politics has never been my forte. *Ragnarök* is coming, the lines are being drawn in this final battle, and I know where I stand. I don't care if everyone else knows too, even though it puts me in danger. I knew the risks and I made the choice I could live with." She lifted her brows. "You, on the other hand, have played the political games very well. No one knows if you've sold out your people."

"Do you *really* think I would do that? I'm not talking knee-jerk reactions to seeing me in your doorway while someone tries to kill you—that would fuck with anyone's mind. I'm talking about what you truly believe about me." He tensed, waiting for her answer. What she thought of him mattered far more than it should. He shouldn't give a damn but, at least to himself, he had to confess he cared a great deal.

"I want to say no, but…" She let out a slow breath. "We all do things we never thought we would, and there are always consequences. Frey paid with his life. Maybe I will too."

"No." Everything in him rejected that idea, even though he knew his own death was looming large, and there was no one to protect her as vigilantly as he did after he was gone.

"There's no way to save everyone, Thor. You of all people should know that." A sad, crooked smile formed on her lips. "If this war doesn't go well…you can't save me any more than you could save Thura."

That was a punch to the gut. "You would throw our daughter's death in my face?"

Pain and shame twisted within him. Of all the failings of his long, long life, that was one of the few he still struggled to make peace with. His only daughter, dead and gone long before her time. She was only twenty-three when she died, a mere babe in immortal terms. And he hadn't been able to do shit to prevent it. Thor, the famed warrior, powerless and pathetic when it really counted.

"Our daughter's kidnapping and murder by a *jötunn*, you mean? I hate how everyone sidesteps who was responsible. Like she perished in some horrible accident." Fire blazed in her eyes, all the helpless rage he felt reflected in her gaze. "Could you imagine I would want anything to do with giants after that? No, never. I wouldn't trust any of them, but you were just as happy to fuck your way through Jötunheim and have two sons with two different giantesses."

Who he'd slept with after they'd separated was none of her business. *She* had cheated first, and he'd considered their union basically over after that. Neither of them was required to act as if they had any need for faithfulness. But then, fidelity wasn't expected of Viking gods anyway. Sif and he *had* had an exclusive relationship after they'd wed—from his perspective, no other woman would do. Why would he accept a poor substitute when he already had the perfect woman? After the break up, they'd both gone on to other lovers but, for him, none before or since had ever compared to Sif. He sighed, wishing it wasn't true, but knowing there was nothing he could do to change the way he felt. "I think the subject of who we have or haven't fucked and why is a conversation for another time. Whether you like it or not, I don't share your hatred of *all* giants. Some are evil, some are not. For Thura's death, I blame only the one who killed her, and I ended him myself."

"Now who's being naïve?" she asked. "They're the enemies of the gods. Open warfare could erupt at any moment, and some of them probably think they can count you an ally. So the question is: are they right?"

No one else had had the courage to ask him outright. A wry smile curved his mouth. Of course, it was she who dared. Her softness hid a core of pure steel. He cupped her chin in his hand, forcing her to hold his gaze and see the truth of his words. "I swear to you that I haven't betrayed my people and that I never will."

Her lips pursed. "You have half-*jötunn* sons. What about your loyalty to them?"

"As I said, I would never betray Asgard. For my sons...I grieve for the choices Magni and Modi will have to make soon." Something else that had tormented him of late.

"You don't know—"

"Which side they'll be on? No, and I'm not going to demand they take my side over their mothers'." He stroked his thumb along her jaw, savoring the silky feel of her skin. "I doubt they could avoid this war even if they wanted to, which I also doubt. They aren't the kind of men who'd run from conflict when their family is in peril. So they'll have to make an impossible choice. My poor boys."

She scrunched up her face. "I don't want to feel sympathetic."

"It's terrible when facts get in the way of blind prejudice, isn't it?" Tapping the tip of her nose, he smiled.

She jerked her head to the side to dodge his touch. "Asshat."

"Well, that's a form of anal play we haven't tried yet," he drawled. "And we've gotten pretty creative over the years."

Though she flushed pink, she heaved a deep sigh. "You can make anything perverse, can't you?"

"It's a gift." He reached for the discarded scarves, draping them over his palm and waggling his eyebrows suggestively. "Speaking of pervertibles, these could be put to better use. Maybe they can help you decide if you trust me."

She huffed. "I don't need to let you fuck me tied up to prove I trust you. Put those away."

"Can't blame a man for trying," he replied, cheerfully unrepentant. Though he sobered quickly. "So you believe me when I say I'm not a traitor? I'm on your side. I would never hurt you."

Closing her eyes, she pressed her lips together. "Yes. I believe you. Maybe that's not wise, but...I believe you."

"Thank you." Relief bloomed within him. Her suspicion had stung far more than it should. They'd never get back to the loving relationship they'd shared before Thura died and Sif made him a cuckold, but Thor would soon need all the allies he could muster. Even if he wanted her nowhere near the actual fighting, she might become a touchstone for those true to Asgard. That could be incredibly useful.

If that justification for needing her rang a bit hollow, he ignored it. They'd maintained their status quo for centuries, and now wasn't the time to rock that particular boat.

She shifted position and her thigh brushed his, sending a zing of awareness through him. He'd done his level best to ignore the fact that only a thin layer of cotton separated him from her incredible body, but now that they'd tackled a few important matters, it might be time for less business and more pleasure.

He ran the scarves through his fingers. "Are you *sure* you want me to put these away? I was under the impression you enjoyed it when I tied you to the bed."

"Usually." She swallowed, and her pupils dilated slightly. "This time it wasn't for sex though."

"Not earlier, but it could be now." Being this near her, smelling her sweet scent, was having a predictable effect on him. And he'd learned long ago that no matter how pissed he was at her—even at their worst, when he'd come close to hating her—he always wanted her. There was nothing he could do to control his visceral response to her. Now, he no longer wanted to. He was a dying man, and he wouldn't mind going out with the taste of her on his tongue.

She licked her lips and his body tightened, his cock swelling against his fly.

Reaching out, he let the tips of the scarves slide from her elbow to her shoulder. She shivered and he could see her nipples bead. She was tempted, he could tell. He brought one of her hands to his mouth and bit the base of her thumb. She jolted, and he grinned when her breathing hitched. "Sif?"

"Okay, but under one condition." Her look was pure challenge. "If I'm going to let you truss me up like a chicken, you'd better make it worth my while."

He'd never been one to back down from a dare. "How many orgasms would make it worth your while?"

"Two," she answered promptly, then tilted her head. "Maybe three."

"I think I can manage that." He jerked the sheet away from her and had her wrists manacled in under thirty seconds. Ah, yeah. That was amazing. He let himself drink in the view for a moment. Her gorgeous body, all gold and cream, laid out across white sheets. His fingers drifted down her arm, across her collarbone, into the valley of her cleavage, and over so he could cup her breast. The soft mound filled his hand to overflowing, the stiff tip stabbing into his palm. Sweeping his thumb over her nipple made her squirm, and he could smell her rising arousal, which only made his cock twitch and harden painfully. He winced and adjusted the fit of his pants.

Her gaze followed his hand and she whispered, "I want to suck you."

A groan was his answer to that. If there'd been any blood left in his brain, it immediately rushed south. He rose, stripped out of his clothes, and was naked within moments.

Running her tongue along her bottom lip, she eyed his dick. "Come here."

"Yes, my goddess." As if he was going to resist that demand. He wasn't an idiot.

Crawling onto the bed, he straddled her torso, his cock bobbing above her face, and she lifted her head to lick the crown. *Gods.* He gasped and braced a hand on the wall behind the headboard. Reaching down, he aimed his dick at her mouth and she drew him deep. The feel of her lips closing around his shaft was so fucking amazing, his eyes damn near rolled back.

He slipped his fingers into her hair, supporting her head. He gripped the strands tight enough he knew it had to hurt, but he also knew that would make it better for her. She hummed in delight, the sound vibrating up his dick. Damn, but he loved the prurient side of her.

Using his hold on her hair, he forced her to take more of him, driving in until her throat contracted on the tip of his cock. He wasn't gentle, but she wouldn't want him to be. She rarely did. He fucked her face with ruthless precision, shoving his dick deep, deeper with each thrust.

Sweat slid down his skin and his muscles quaked. He was so close to pumping his come down her throat, he held onto his control by the tips of his claws. He closed his eyes, dragging in a lungful of air. It did nothing to calm his racing heart, especially since she was still sucking him, her tongue working along the length of his shaft.

He jerked away from her before he exploded, shuddering in near-pain at denying himself.

Lips shiny, she pouted. "I wasn't done."

"I almost was, and I owe you a few orgasms first."

She chuckled. "Yes, you do. Get to it."

"Don't mind if I do." Moving down the bed until he was even with her pussy, he settled between her legs and forced them wide with his shoulders.

The ripe core of her was bared for his gaze, slick and swollen with desire. He drew a deep breath, taking in the heady scent of her excitement. Ah, yeah. That was perfect. Dipping his head, he licked her slit from one end to the other. The rich, musky flavor of her rolled over his taste buds. She moaned, her hips lifting to push nearer his mouth. Closing his lips around her hard little clit, he suckled her, batting the nub with his tongue. Her knees closed around his ears, which blocked out everything but what he was doing.

Somehow, the sensory deprivation made it more stimulating for him. His cock throbbed against the sheets, and it was all he could do not to rub himself into them. Slipping his hand up the inside of her thigh, he pushed two fingers into her and continued to torment her clitoris with his mouth. She squirmed on the bed, her bare feet pressing to his back. He nipped at her sensitive flesh, and she jolted. Pistoning his digits in and out of her, he worked her channel at a speed swift enough to drive her wild. Her toes curled against his back, and he knew she was close. Time to push her over the edge. He grinned, bit her clit, and rubbed across just the right spot inside her. She arched and twisted, shuddering while her pussy squeezed around his fingers. Her juices flooded his tongue as she came against his mouth.

He lifted his head. "That's one."

Catapulting up the bed, he planted his hands on either side of her shoulders, and buried his dick in her pussy in one smooth motion. They both groaned, and her slim legs encircled his waist. Her slick warmth wrapping around his cock made his skull feel as if it was going to explode. Gods, yes. That was the good stuff. There was nothing—absolutely nothing—as amazing as sliding snug into this woman. He'd once thought he could happily spend his existence with some part of his body inserted into her. But that was long ago, and it was best to focus on now. He smiled down at her and she grinned back, her amber gaze alight with pleasure. He worked his cock in and out of her slowly, building up speed until he was powering into her pussy.

"*Thor.*" She writhed underneath him, increasing the already intense friction. "Please, I need...I'm so...*please*, Thor!"

He loved it when she said his name that way, all breathless and pleading. "I intend to please you, sweetheart."

Shifting his weight to one arm, he reached between them to fondle her breast. Pinching her nipple hard, he twisted the tight tip. She cried out, her pussy fisting on his cock as she climaxed. He gritted his teeth and made himself think of anything else—fighting maneuvers, his favorite horses, the various benefits of modern versus magical weapons. It only ratcheted his need down slightly, but he'd take what he could get.

He settled onto his elbows above her, driving his dick deeper. "And that's two."

"Yes." She giggled, the sound giddy. "Well done."

Her face was dewy and flushed, her golden hair spilling in a silken cloud across the pillow. With her hands bound, she looked like something straight out of his most erotic wet dreams. "We still have one more to go, sweetheart."

She cinched her legs tighter around him, rocking her hips upward. "Yes, please."

"Insatiable little witch."

"Goddess," she corrected, tone prim. "Witches get burned at stakes. Goddesses turn stone into lava."

"True, you're an impressive woman, and that was quick thinking." He ground his pelvis into her clit. "Let me reward you."

She bit her lip. "Ooooh."

Changing his angle of penetration made her sob and arch into him, jerking the scarves around her wrists taut. He loosened his grip on his self-restraint and felt his fangs slide forth. A growl ripped out of him, and he pounded forward as if his life depended on it. She moved with him as best she could while bound, her gaze glazing with renewed passion. It was like a storm brewing between them, and they rode it out together. Harder and harder, faster and faster. With each downward stroke, he circled his hips against her, and she whimpered and quaked.

"Oh. *Gods*." She closed her eyes. "*Yes*."

Her sex clenching rhythmically on his cock was more than enough to shatter what was left of his control. He spurted into her, coming in hard jets, emptying himself into her sweet warmth. "Sif!"

He sank down on top of her, sighing. Their damp skin stuck together, but he was too relaxed to care. His heart rate and breathing slowed gradually, the shaking in his muscles subsiding.

"My fingers are tingling." The words emerged on a yawn.

"Sorry, one second." He heaved himself up onto his knees, unknotted the scarves, and rubbed her reddened wrists. She sighed, the sound utterly satiated, and he couldn't help a flicker of pride at having satisfied her so fully. He settled beside her, leaning his back against her headboard.

"It was for me, you said. Helping Erik and Bryn." He brought up a knee and propped his arm across the bony plateau.

Something closed in her expression, shutting him out. Her words were careful, guarded. "You're the champion of the gods—we have no chance without you and you have no chance without help. I...hoped...that you'd stay on the right side of this war. I wasn't sure, I doubted, but I hoped." Sitting up, she emphasized, "You're our best warrior, but you can't win alone. It's simple logic."

Logical, yes, but it didn't sit well with him. He wanted more from her, though he had no right to anything. It was a damnable position to be in. "Is it only because I'm the best warrior? Because I'm a weapon to be wielded?"

For a moment, he'd swear he saw tears swim in her eyes, but she blinked and they were gone. "No. I don't want you to die. We've had our ups and downs, but I wouldn't wish harm upon you. If the prophecy can be changed...I don't want my Earth to be destroyed, I don't want humanity to be wiped out, and I don't want you to be killed by a giant dragon."

"One of Loki's sons." He couldn't help a shudder, disgust curdling in his belly.

"I hate reptiles. *Hate*."

Her lips formed a moue. "Anyone who's supposed to be bitten to death by Jörmungand deserves to have a problem with scaled beasties."

"Loki escaped, but thank all the gods he hasn't managed to awaken Jörmungand."

"He sleeps in the middle of the Earth, and Loki can cause massive earthquakes. A high-magnitude quake could definitely disturb his son's slumber. It's only a matter of time," she observed, her tone fatalistic. She finger-combed her mussed hair, the golden locks pooling in her lap.

"If that happens, I don't think there's any way to turn back the tide of *Ragnarök*." He gave her a tight smile. "For many reasons, I'd prefer to let sleeping dragons lie."

"Agreed." She nodded. "I'd like to confirm if he's going to be woken soon. I need to contact Nauma—she's a *völva*."

"I remember her." He scratched his beard. "My mother made her an immortal handmaiden, used her for prophetic readings. Brown hair, rather plain looking, but a voice like a phone sex operator?"

"That's her, though I always just thought she had a *nice* voice." She rolled her eyes. "Nauma is staying on Bryn's farm with Erik and his team. When I last spoke to the *völva*, she was planning to focus her Sight, check if she could get a bead on what might happen now that at least part of the *Ragnarök* prophecy is toast." Her headed tipped. "I think I should give them a couple of days before I bother them. Bryn was still in a healing coma when I left, and my feeling is they'll be sitting vigil until she wakes up."

"Should we just visit them together?" It was a major reversal of his neutral stance the last year, but he was hardly going to infiltrate the enemy without offering them assurances he refused to give. So he'd leave spy-craft to someone else. Neutrality had never been natural to him anyway.

She stood and stretched. "You don't think the giants will notice if you fraternize with the World's Chosen?"

"I have to go public at some point." He rose, scooped his clothes up from the floor, and draped them across the footboard. His weapons sat on a wooden trunk at the end of the bed, within easy reach if anyone came near the cabin. He took a breath, widening his senses to confirm that, yes, they were still alone in the wilderness.

"I need a quick shower and then I want some food. I'm famished." She flipped her hair over her shoulder, and the curls danced around her lovely, heart-shaped ass.

There were a variety of hungers they could sate. "I'll join you."

Glancing back, she lifted an eyebrow. "In the shower?"

"Absolutely."

She grinned and led the way.

5

The problem with fucking Thor was that the man was addictive. The more often Sif had him, the more often she wanted him. That hadn't been a problem when they were happily married because he would scratch whatever carnal itches she had, frequently and with great enthusiasm. After they'd separated…well, they'd hook up for a quickie or hate-fuck every now and then. Definitely not often enough to develop a habit.

Now? They were neither together nor separated. They'd spent three days in her cabin, and they'd taken advantage of every available room or surface for sexcapades: the shower, the bathroom counter, the kitchen table, the healing spring, the floor, several walls. It was seventy-two hours of unrelenting closeness, and she didn't know how to handle it emotionally. She had no defenses against him when he was being caring and concerned for her safety *without* being demanding and dictatorial. The longer she was with him, the more convinced she was that he truly hadn't and wouldn't betray the gods.

They'd both quietly contacted their sources of information—his much more extensive than hers—and it was clear her absence had been noted. Whether or not the giants were bothering to search for her was another story. Not knowing was frustrating, but neither she nor Thor thought it was wise for her to return to Asgard just yet.

So here she was, stuck in the middle of nowhere with her not-quite-ex hovering nearby to remind her of how good things used to be before it all went to shit. She stood in her kitchen, cooking breakfast, reviewing everyone in Valhalla who might have let the giants in to attack her. Was it someone who had *jötunn* sympathies, or someone who had a grudge against her? Either one might be willing to turn a blind eye to certain uninvited visitors, and help make sure there wasn't a single berserker or valkyrie around to help even if Sif had managed to call for aid.

"Have you tried contacting Erik yet?"

She glanced up and saw Thor standing in the doorway, his broad shoulder propped on the jamb.

"Not yet." She turned back to the omelet on the stove, adding bits of ham and cheese. "He was barely holding himself together when I last saw him. If Bryn recovers as predicted, he'll be fine. I did intend to contact Nauma today. She'd be in a more reasonable frame of mind." She smiled wanly. "Plus, her prophetic powers told her I was trustworthy, so I know she'll talk to me."

"That is a handy skill to have." He crossed the kitchen and popped an extra bit of ham in his mouth.

"Prophecy or trustworthiness?"

"Both." He bent and nipped at her ass through her yoga pants. She yelped and swatted at him, but he came up with a pirate's grin anyway and snagged another piece of ham before he stepped out of her reach. He went to the sink and began washing the dishes she'd dirtied while preparing the meal. Her heart squeezed. Having him around to work with her on mundane tasks was...nice. Too nice.

"Nauma has one of my runes. I'll try to call her after we eat." She flipped the omelet onto a plate and set it on the counter next to him. She focused on cracking a couple of eggs for her own omelet as if the act required her full concentration. Thor was, at best, a fuck-buddy she happened to still be married to. There was no getting mushy over domesticity. He'd hate that.

"This looks delicious." He kissed the side of her neck, his beard tickling her skin. "Thank you."

"You're welcome." The words emerged more gruffly than she'd intended, but she didn't bother apologizing. She felt his gaze on her for a moment, but then he grabbed some silverware and went to the small table tucked against the wall. Letting out a sigh of relief, she quickly finished cooking and sat down in silence.

"What's wrong?"

Balls. It had been a temporary reprieve, not a pass on talking. How much should she say? It would be easier to blow him off, but why bother? "It's strange having you here. I'm not used to anyone else in my space, and we haven't shared a home in a very long time."

"You've had other men in your space."

"Not here."

"Never?" His tone was far too mild, and his features were devoid of emotion.

"No."

What looked like satisfaction crossed his face. "You seem to prefer human lovers. I assumed you'd have brought them to your place on Earth."

"How—" She held up a hand. "No, I truly don't want to know how or why you've kept track of my lovers." It had been more than a hundred years after he'd left her—long enough that it was pretty clear they were never reuniting—before she'd chosen another lover. Sometimes a woman needed more than her dildo for company at night, and for all intents and purposes, they had no longer been married. She doubted he wanted that explanation. "Suffice to say, I don't bring them here. I have two other homes on Earth that I use, when needed. We're a little far outside of civilization here, and I come to this little corner of Argentina when I want to get away from everyone. Plus, the fastest way to get here is teleportation. Humans tend to ask questions when you can jump across thousands of miles. It kills the mood."

She kept her voice light, and gave him a sunny smile. But talking to her husband about her paramours made her insides twist, and she set her fork down, no longer hungry. Thor knew nothing about *why* she preferred mortal lovers, and she felt no need to enlighten him. He might have ferreted out the truth—that he was the *only* immortal she'd had sexual relations with since Loki—but her reasons weren't something her husband's spies could uncover.

Memories assaulted her, a night where she hadn't been in control of herself or anything else. It had been only a few weeks after Thura was murdered—

No. Sif stomped down on those nightmares. That was the past and it couldn't hurt her anymore. Cold sweat broke out along her hairline, and she swiped her damp palms against her thighs. She rarely thought about it anymore, and had never spoken of it to anyone. Maybe she *should* have told Thor, but she hadn't known how back then, and didn't really care to now. She pushed back from the table and picked up her plate, heading for the sink.

"You didn't finish."

She shrugged, attempting to appear nonchalant. "I wasn't as hungry as I thought I was."

He made an exasperated noise. "What aren't you telling me?"

So many things, husband. So many, many things. Glancing back, she met his gaze and gave him part of the truth. "I don't like being in hiding or having my movements restricted. I don't like not knowing what's going on, if I'm being hunted or not. Can you blame me for being antsy?"

"No." He shoved a hand through his shoulder-length hair, the sunlight streaming through the window turning the red locks to pure fire. "But that's not what has you upset. Or at least it's not the only thing. Tell me."

"Hm. Are those your bear instincts rearing their head again, telling you what's up with me?" She dumped the uneaten food into a bin destined for composting—her little part in saving the environment. She was an earth goddess, after all.

A gusty sigh sounded behind her. "There are times when taking you over my knee and spanking your ass sounds like my best option."

Her sex clenched at the very thought, and she couldn't prevent a quiver or the way her heart skipped a beat. That sort of deviance was something else she only did with Thor. He brought out all the little kinks in her soul.

"I can smell how that turned you on."

She made a noncommittal noise, finished washing her plate, and tucked it into the drying rack. "I'm going to call Nauma. Maybe she's been able to See something."

His chair scraped across the floor as he rose to follow her out of the kitchen. She went to an old steamer chest tucked against the wall in the living room. Opening it, she rifled through its contents until she came up with a small, carved wooden box. Flicking the latch with her thumb, she pulled out one of the rune stones she kept inside.

Thor reached over her shoulder to touch one carved with a stylized Mjölnir. "You said you didn't have my rune anymore."

She pulled out a stone with a rowan tree on it—her symbol—and snapped the box closed. "No, I said I didn't wear it anymore. I never said I got rid of it."

There was a beat of silence before he said, "I want one of your runes."

"Really? You're going to walk around wearing my emblem?" It was much more common for a wife to wear her husband's stone. She cocked her head. "How very progressive."

"Shut up." He rubbed a knuckle into his temple as if she'd given him a headache.

After slipping the box back into its space, she shut the trunk and went to a long mirror on an adjacent wall. She could just do a voice call, but she wanted to look at the other woman. The clearest way to do that was through a reflective surface, and while she knew it wasn't possible for anyone to spy on her using a mirror, she still refused to keep one in any of her bedrooms.

She faced the mirror and cupped the small stone in her palm, feeling it heat as the magic embedded in it awakened. She could contact any person who carried her rune, but it was easier if she held a stone as well. "Nauma."

The word echoed a bit, as if she was at the end of a long tunnel. She said the *völva's* name several times before there was a response. Sif's reflection wavered, and then another woman peered back at her through the looking glass. Brunette with even, unremarkable features.

"Sif?" Her eyebrows rose as she leaned closer. Her form was crisp and clear, but the room behind her was blurred. Sif thought she might be standing in a bathroom.

"You were expecting Freya?" That was the goddess Nauma was sworn to, possibly the only other person the *völva* had ever spoken to this way.

But she shook her head, her dark eyes reflecting regret. "After all this time of not hearing from her, not really. I hope she's safe, wherever she is."

Thor stepped up behind Sif, cupping his hand around hers. "You've tried to use your visions to locate her?"

Nauma squinted, as if Thor was out of focus. Which made sense, considering the rune wasn't marked with his symbol. The *völva* shrugged, her expression helpless. "Yes, but I've had no luck. I...don't think she's dead, but that's more an instinct than any real vision. I'm sorry, my lord, I wish I had more to tell you about your mother."

Disappointing, but Sif nodded to encourage the other woman. "Do you have news about anything else?"

"Bryn is well." Nauma suppressed a grin. "She and Erik are…ah…reuniting as we speak. I doubt they'll come up for air for a few days. We made need to throw some food at them soon though."

"I'm glad to hear it." Sif didn't bother hiding her smile. Good. Her efforts hadn't been in vain. "Anything else?"

Nauma rocked her hand back and forth through the air. "My Sight is still cloudy, but I've been meditating. The *Ragnarök* prophecy is null and void—events definitely won't play out as anticipated. However, certain wheels have been set into motion that can't be stopped. Loki escaped, and we can be damn sure he's going to raise whatever forces he can to try to take over the human and godly realms. Revenge against the gods, plus using Earth as a playground. Humans—the other white meat. Yum."

Sif's stomach turned. Hearing the fire giant's clear relish at the prospect of making a meal of her, she didn't think it was a joking matter. "What else can you tell us?"

Propping her hands on her hips, Nauma made a sympathetic face, as if she'd Seen what revolted Sif and why. *Völva* had an uncanny ability to know where all your vulnerabilities were and had little compunction about pressing on those emotional bruises.

Nauma stated bluntly, "Gods will die and so will giants, but not the way the prophecy said. I don't know who and I don't know when, but I'm trying to figure that out." Her gaze went to Thor. "Some slated to die will live, and some who were supposed to survive will perish."

"Not Sif." His fingers tightened painfully on hers.

"I can't say for sure. Both of you are in grave danger, and many obstacles lie in your path. Your destinies are still in flux. Be careful, trust few, choose your allies well." She tucked her hair behind her ear. "When I know more, I'll call you."

The *völva's* image wavered and faded, leaving a reflection of Thor holding Sif's hand, his expression stricken.

"Well." She fought the urge to squeeze his fingers and comfort him. They were no longer a couple, and acting like it would only confuse her already battered heart. Being in love with your husband was incredibly inconvenient at times. "I'm not sure we know anything more than we did before. Our suspicions were confirmed, but that's about it."

"Yeah." His voice was little more than a guttural rasp. His hand dropped away from hers and he stepped back.

"The good news is, you might survive after all." Thank the gods. Hearing that had given her real hope for the first time, which was both a beautiful and dangerous thing. Hope was so easily shattered and took your heart with it in the process.

His gaze blazed brilliant blue. "And you might not. How the fuck is that good news?"

"There was never any guarantee I'd survive anyway, Thor. You had to have realized that."

But looking in his eyes told her that he'd been living on hope for a long time. Maybe his hope had solidified into certainty, and Nauma had yanked the rug out from under him. Perhaps Sif's actions of late had started the process of killing his optimism, but the *völva's* words had ended it.

Apparently, Sif's survival meant as much to Thor as his did to her.

Her chest tightened at the implications of that, both good and bad. She tried to offer him a smile, but doubted she succeeded. "I'll do my best not to die if you do the same."

"Deal." But he paced in circles around the room, something he did when he wanted to settle himself and think. Thor was not a man who sat still for very long. She'd often thought his fighting practice was almost a form of meditation for him. She didn't understand it, but there were any number of things that didn't make sense about the male mind.

She returned the rune stone to its place and closed the trunk again. When she straightened, she watched him circumnavigate the furniture. Clearly, he was upset, but she had to ask herself, why did it matter to him so much that she lived through this? Just because she was under his protection? He could have ejected her from that long ago. "Can I ask you something?"

"Of course." He didn't stop moving, barely glanced at her.

"Why didn't you divorce me?" She watched him freeze at the question, but there was no taking it back. When he faced her, she raised her chin and braved his stony stare. "Loki made a public announcement about fucking me. Even if divorce is frowned up, no one would have blamed you for ending our marriage after that."

Why she felt the need to bring this up now, she didn't know. But...even after Thor had left her and started shacking up with anyone with a vagina, he'd made it clear that keeping her safe was his sworn duty. He'd said he loathed her and she was the bane of his existence, but he *never* shirked his duty. At the time, she'd pointed out he'd also had a duty to protect their daughter and hadn't managed to man-up on that one.

Those conversations had gone well, naturally.

Instead of latching on to the opening to discuss his worst enemy, he countered with, "Why didn't *you* divorce *me?* I doubt anyone would have been shocked if you'd repudiated me."

Because I never stopped loving you was the truth, but she'd rather cut her tongue out than tell him. Emotional armor was all she had, and she needed to stay strong or he'd know just how much power he had over her. She folded her arms. "I asked first."

He shrugged. "Never met anyone else I wanted to marry, so why bother? Also...I'll admit I didn't want to make it easy for you to wed someone else."

Figured. Dealing with her was part duty, part petty revenge, and part sexual chemistry. It wasn't because he still cared, and it was stupid that she felt even a twinge of disappointment. "So, I'd basically have to make a public decree if I wanted to throw you over for some other man on a permanent basis."

It wasn't a question, but he answered anyway. "That's about the size of it, yeah. Now your turn."

She headed for the kitchen, throwing a half-truth over her shoulder. She was better at lying if she didn't have to look him in the eyes. "At first, I assumed you'd do it. Plus, I couldn't stand to be around you long enough to go through the ceremony to divorce you. After a while, it didn't seem that urgent and I didn't fall for anyone else, so...as you said, why bother?"

He grunted, and she glanced back to see him looming in the doorway. His eyes were narrowed, but she couldn't tell what he was thinking.

"Was that not the answer you expected?" She grabbed the omelet pan and scrubbed it, then did the same for his breakfast plate.

Instead of addressing her question, he asked one of his own. "Why did you bring it up?"

Yes, Sif. Why did you do that? Her nerves jangled, feeling his gaze on her. "You watch over me because I'm still technically a member of your household, which doesn't have to be the case, and clearly it matters to you that I live through the apocalypse. Why? We're no more than fuck-buddies now, so my fate shouldn't mean anything to you."

He glowered. "Us not being together anymore means I have to wish you dead?"

And he'd sidestepped that question too. Okay, then. Discomfort twisted through her, and she was more than ready to let the subject drop. "No, of course not. Why don't we just assume neither of us wishes the other dead and let it go at that?"

"Fine." The word was clipped, and his dour expression didn't ease.

"Let's discuss something else." Anything else would be better than this. Shutting off the faucet, she dried her hands with a dishtowel and decided practical logistics was a non-awkward place to focus. "If we're hiding out here long-term, we're going to need to figure out food delivery. There's not a town within a hundred kilometers, so I always teleported supplies in. Plus, Spanish isn't my best language."

The sigh that escaped him said he was merely humoring her by engaging in this new subject. "I speak Spanish well enough, though I think we'll need to sort out a more secure way of resupplying."

"Röskva?" she asked, referring to a servant who—along with her brother, Alfi—had been with Thor for a thousand years.

He nodded. "I believe her trustworthy."

"And she's devoted to you." Which was the more important issue to Sif's mind. Blind devotion had its perks.

"To you as well," he pointed out. "She worships you. Literally."

Her lips quirked up. "Occupational hazard."

"She was born mortal, so she can't teleport." He rocked back on his heels. "Not necessarily a disadvantage. I'd rather no one come to our location."

Sounded reasonable to her, and she'd prefer to keep this place private. She'd never brought a guest before. It had always been her secret escape. Having Thor here felt both right and wrong.

She turned to lean back against the edge of the sink and brushed a fingertip over her lower lip, trying to consider how they might pick up supplies without being seen. Maybe he had a system in place already, but she had rarely needed to use stealth for anything. She bought what she wanted and teleported here. No one ever asked her why or where she was going.

Glancing over at her unlikely roommate, she found him staring intently at her mouth, his gaze following the glide of her finger. A shiver passed through her at the heat in his eyes. She hadn't intended to be provocative, but apparently she'd succeeded anyway. He reached out and set a hand on her waist, sliding her down the counter until she was in front of him. Crowding her against the cabinets, his body pressed into hers. Having his heavy muscles molded to her curves made her heart trip and race. She had to tilt her head back to look at him, he was so much taller than her.

His gaze locked with hers, held her captive.

Those eyes were so blue she could drown in them. He bent his head so his lips almost touched hers. Almost. Anticipation made her breathing accelerate, and she felt his chest rise and fall just as fast as hers. Still he didn't kiss her. She tried to rise on tiptoe to close the distance between their lips, but his weight pinned her in place. The message was clear—he was in control, and they'd proceed at his pace. That just ratcheted up her need, made it a game where she wasn't quite sure what would happen. It only intensified her craving that this was the one man she had ever—would ever—trust to take command of her sexual play. In this arena, if nowhere else, she'd never doubted him. Her hands lifted to touch him, but he captured her wrists, keeping her trapped and at his mercy.

She drew in a shuddery little breath. "Oh, gods."

"Now, this is my kind of discussion." A tiny smile creased his handsome face when she whimpered. Excitement sliced through her, painful in its intensity. He kept a hairsbreadth of space between their mouths. Waiting, waiting. The sexual tension between them hummed like a live wire. She couldn't move, but she could speak.

"Kiss me. Take me hard. Fuck me until I can't even remember my own name." She arched into him as best she could. He liked when she begged, and she had no compunction about using that to make him give her what she needed. "Please, Thor. *Please*."

He made a rough, guttural noise, and seized her lips in a swift rush. Shoving his tongue into her mouth made her moan, and she wriggled against him, trying to get closer, wanting more. Her body ached with emptiness, wetness flooding her core until she thought she might die if he didn't fuck her soon. Releasing her wrists, he set both hands on her waist, lifting her off her feet to sit on the countertop. The contrast of cold stone against her heated skin made her gasp.

She twined her legs around his waist, keeping him pressed to her. He shoved his fingers into her hair, jerking her head back to catch the sensitive spot where neck met shoulder between his teeth. Her scalp burned, pleasure pulsed through her, and her sex fisted tight. A precursor to orgasm. She was close to combusting and he wasn't even inside her yet. She undulated against him, trying to convey what she desired while she chanted his name. He groaned and leaned away from her.

"No," she sobbed.

But he didn't listen, of course. He stripped out of his shirt, and then discarded hers. Her bra snapped under his rough treatment and he tossed the flimsy scrap of lace over his shoulder. His claws shredded her yoga pants, and he ripped them and her underwear away. He retracted his talons and reached for something behind her. "Let's make this more interesting."

"If it gets any more interesting, I might have heart failure."

"Luckily for us, that's a human condition." He held up a bottle of olive oil. "*Extra* virgin, huh? Poor thing. Let's pop its cherry, shall we?"

A surprised chortle burst from her. "I can't believe you just said that."

He winked, set the oil down, and reached for his fly. The hiss of laces whipping out of their holes as he unfastened his leather pants made her shiver. *Finally*. He freed his dick, and the thick column of his erection brushed her inner thighs. She picked up the bottle, twisted off the cap, and handed it to him.

"Thank you." He took the offer and poured some of the slick liquid into his palm. He stroked it up and down his shaft, a shudder wracking him. Watching his long fingers work his cock made her burn. She wanted him thrusting that hard dick inside her, filling her to the limit.

When he was done rubbing oil onto his skin, she knew it was her turn, and her heart pounded so loudly in her ears, it drowned out the rest of the world. He lifted her legs to brace her ankles against his shoulders. Palming her hips, he pulled her ass to the very edge of the countertop. "You know what I'm going to do to you now, don't you, Sif?"

"Yes." She nodded, leaning back on her hands. "Yes. Please."

He dribbled a good amount of oil onto his fingers and slipped them between her legs. He tweaked her clit, making the muscles in her thighs jerk and additional wetness flood her sex. A single fingertip circled her anus, then pushed inside. He sank his finger deep, withdrew, and added another digit on the next thrust. He stretched her and worked the oil deep, leaving her ass as slick as her pussy. She bit her lip to try to keep from screaming, so turned on she was shaking with it. He shoved his thumb into her pussy, rocking his hand to pump his digits back and forth between her channels. Ecstasy built higher and higher within her, and her sex began to spasm in time with his movements.

Fire flashed through her veins, sweat slipped in beads down her temples, and all she could do was let her head fall back as she moaned. "Ah, gods. Thor."

"I can't wait." His fingers jerked away from her, and she felt him position his cock at the entrance of her ass.

A little keening noise spilled from her throat, and his thick cock pressed her rear channel wider than his hand had. The tight ring of her anus clamped down on him, and she had to concentrate to make her muscles relax and accept the hot invasion. He worked his cock deeper with every roll of his hips, forcing her to take all of him. The agony of how he stretched her sent ecstasy arcing like lightning along her nerve endings.

Oh. Gods.

He began plunging into her ass with excruciating slowness, but quickly picked up speed until he fucked her just the way she'd asked, rough and hard. Taking her. Possessing her. Her back bowed, her heels pushed against his shoulders, and her legs shook with the force of his thrusts.

"Look at me," he demanded, and she obeyed. His fangs were fully extended, his eyes had gone bear-feral, and the carnal hunger in his gaze made her quiver.

She loved it when he went wild for her.

His gaze dropped, watching his dick piston in and out of her anus. He held her ass, keeping her from falling off the counter, but that also kept him from touching her in other ways. "Play with yourself."

The command made her inner muscles clench, and they both groaned at the resulting sensation. Almost too intense, and still more than perfect. She shifted her weight to one hand and used the other to reach between her thighs. She stroked alongside her clit, stimulating the hard little bundle of nerves. He growled his approval, and she began to flick her fingers in time with his pounding thrusts. Ah, that was so right, driving her to the brink of madness. Climax building high and fast, ready to launch her into the stars at any moment.

"Pinch your clit. Hard."

She did as he bid, and it was more than enough to hurl her into orgasm. Her eyes rolled back, and every ounce of her focus was on the exquisite sensations rocketing through her body. The feel of his dick stretching her anus, the way his skin slapped against hers, the clench and release of her pussy as wave after wave of completion rolled through her. He fucked her through her climax, driving her up and over the edge again, and sobs ripped from her throat. Too much. It was too much to handle, but she didn't want him to stop.

A few more minutes and his come pumped into her ass, filling her with his hot fluids. He roared, the sound more bear than man. He shuddered against her and slowed to a halt. Their muscles quaked and their choppy breathing was the only noise in the room. The scent of lingering sex perfumed the air as her body finally began to drift down from the high.

"What's your name?" he asked.

She opened bleary eyes. "Huh?"

"Mission accomplished." His grin was all kinds of cocky.

Snorting, she swatted his shoulder. "Smug bastard."

"Sex that delicious is worth getting smug over." He picked her up from the counter. "Time for a shower. You're a very dirty girl right now, so we'll need to be very, very thorough."

Seemed like a stellar idea to her.

6

THE FRUSTRATING THING ABOUT being in the back end of nowhere was Thor felt cut off from his usual forms of communication. He could only check in with his informants when he felt it was secure, and there were a lot fewer opportunities when he was hiding out. The beautiful thing about being here was, besides patrolling the area to make sure they were as safe as possible, he could spend all his time glutting himself on Sif's body. Not a bad way to while away the hours.

Even now, she sprawled across his chest while they lay on the couch, her hair tickling his skin.

As much as he loved the feel of being inside her, in a way the last three days had been excruciating. He'd been reminded too much of when their marriage had been good, before tragedy and betrayal had torn them asunder. The lines had been clearly drawn after that, and unless they were putting in a public appearance or fucking each other's brains out, they'd rarely spent any time together. He'd wanted it that way, but...the looming apocalypse had a way of blurring all those carefully constructed boundaries.

Shifting to the left, Sif settled her weight half against the back of the sofa, half on him. He stroked his fingers through her hair, contentment he didn't want to acknowledge winding through him.

Her question about why he'd never divorced her had been running through his mind on a loop. If he'd been completely honest, he would have admitted he'd never once considered dissolving their union. The possibility was there, of course, and he'd assumed that someday she would want to go through with the renouncement ceremony, but for himself? No. Not even at his most angry, his most agonized. Had that been a form of masochism, sadism, or both? Fuck, he didn't know anymore.

All he knew was that he'd been hanging on to this marriage for a long time, using it as an excuse to keep her tied to him, to fulfill his need to watch over her and keep her safe. He could have cut her loose, so why hadn't he? He wasn't sure he wanted to examine his motivations too closely. He had a feeling he wouldn't like what it said about him.

She stiffened beside him just as a familiar odor filled his nostrils. She whispered, "Someone's on my land."

In return, he hissed, "It's a giant."

Setting her aside, he jackknifed to his feet, adrenaline flooding his system. The bear in him bristled, and all his senses screamed a warning at the imminent threat.

"Shit, shit, shit." Sif scrambled up and dove for her clothes. "How did anyone find us? This place is shielded against detection."

"Possibly the same way I found out about it, back in the day. Sunstones—they're used for normal navigation, but they also refract off of magical shields." And, using that method, it had taken him several years of process of elimination to find this place. "What I want to know is how they got the manpower to find *your* shield in this short amount of time."

She paled. "It's Gymir. Outside. I can sense him now that I—"

Cutting herself off, she shuddered and looked a bit green.

"Now that you, what?" He shoved into his pants and boots, but didn't bother finding his shirt. It was somewhere in the kitchen, if he recalled.

"I bit one of his earlobes off." Her expression displayed her revulsion.

"Did you?" He chuckled softly and went to the bedroom. He tucked a dagger in his boot, grabbing his sword and war-hammer. "Good girl."

A thin smile appeared on her lips. "I have no regrets, but it wasn't pleasant. They might enjoy eating the occasional god, but the feeling isn't mutual."

"Ah…no." Even though some of the giants were quite bestial in shape, like the wolf Fenrir and the dragon Jörmungand, Thor had never had any desire to consume one of them. Sentient beings weren't on his menu.

"Be careful. I doubt I can use my little lava trick on an earth giant." She jolted at the crack of a tree limb, which sounded obscene in the quiet. Blanching, she held out a hand. "Come on. We can teleport out of here."

"Really?" He snorted. "You think I'd run from a fight?"

"He's not here for you." She jammed her fists down on her hips. "I get that you've taken on giants before, but it's better to face him when you have back up."

"He attacked you and he's here to finish the job. He won't stop unless someone makes him." Plus, Thor was spoiling for a fight. The bastard had dared to touch Sif—he had to pay. It was that simple. The bear within growled its support of that plan. But he didn't want her anywhere near here. She needed to leave now. He could sense the giant creeping closer. "*You* should—"

But whatever he was going to say was cut off by an inhuman roar. "Come out, Thor. It's time for a reckoning."

"Well, that clinches it." He gave her a broad smile. "He's not here for you, sweetheart."

"Nicely done." Despite her words, she didn't look impressed, just pissed. "He found you with me, and if you fight *or* kill him, then you're declaring you're the enemy of giants. Win or lose, he gets something he wants."

He countered, "And if I run away, I'm a coward, which makes me everyone's enemy."

"No one ever said giants were stupid, just evil. Damn it." She yanked her hair out of her face, plaiting it into a quick braid. "If you're not leaving, then neither am I. I'll stay out of the way, but I'll help where I can since he and I control the same element."

The front door exploded inward, a boulder ripping through her cabin. A shimmer of gold surrounded her, and he felt a crackle of her power. The boulder crumbled into harmless powder, and Thor used the dust cloud as cover to duck into the kitchen. He flattened himself against the wall, eased open the side door, and saw the giant approaching the front. Slipping out his dagger, he took aim and let it fly.

The blade hit its mark, embedding deep in Gymir's shoulder. The giant bellowed, his weapon dropping from suddenly slack fingers, and Thor grinned. That arm should be out of commission for a while. Excellent.

"Cheap shot, little god!" Gymir shouted, "A man of honor would face me."

"Repayment for the boulder," Thor said calmly, stepping outside. "And if you had any honor to speak of, you'd never have attacked an unarmed, untrained woman. Sif says hello, by the way."

"She dissolved my boulder," the giant grumbled. He bent down and picked up his spiked club with his good hand. The thing was massive, each spike six inches long.

This was going to be fun.

All the pent-up rage and frustration of the past days, weeks, months burst forth. No longer was he hiding behind subterfuge—this was as open a declaration as he could ever make and it felt fucking good. Wind whipped through the air, the clouds overhead turning dark and ominous. Sif might control earth, but thunder and lightning were his calling cards. The battle-fever flooding his body made his powers rage, and a storm brewed above them.

He held out Mjölnir and used it to beckon the giant forward. "Come, little boy, and take your punishment. No real man would behave as you have."

Gymir's face flushed red, from embarrassment or anger, Thor didn't know. Either would serve his purpose—to throw his opponent off-guard, to make him do something stupid. Thor focused on the giant's ear, and he laced his tone with mock-concern. "What happened to your earlobe? Looks like someone thought you'd make a nice snack."

That did it. The *jötunn* lifted his club and charged, a deafening battle cry ripping out of his throat. The bear within Thor roared in return, his fangs extending, the beast unleashing as he dove into the fight. Bringing Mjölnir up to block, sparks flew as the weapons met. The hit reverberated up Thor's arm, but one of the club's spikes broke off and flew into the bushes. Gymir retreated a few steps with a grunt, but rushed in again.

If it weren't for Thor's superhuman reflexes, he'd have been bowled over by this strike, which came straight for his head. For sheer strength, he was no match for a *jötunn*, but he was faster. He parried with his sword, dancing away quickly enough to save his skull. But the blade tangled in the spikes and a quick twist of Gymir's wrist sent the sword rattling across the ground until it slid up against the cabin's foundation.

Shit, piss, motherfucker.

Sweat slid down his face, stinging his eyes, but he didn't dare pause. The *jötunn* attacked again and Thor spun sideways. He extended his claws, slashing at the giant's throat. He sliced four neat lines along the other man's jaw, but missed the jugular. Gymir jabbed a meaty fist into Thor's ribs before he could leap out of reach.

It was the wounded arm, so the hit wasn't as forceful as it could have been, but Thor's breath still exploded out in a rush, and he stumbled back, pain shooting straight to his brain. The *jötunn* took advantage, smiling as he swung his club. The grin made his wounds gape, and Thor could see bloodied teeth through the shredded cheek. He blocked the club with his war-hammer, barely managing to miss the business end of the spikes.

The ground heaved under his feet, driving the giant back a few steps. He twisted at the waist and pointed his club at the cabin door, where Sif stood. "You're next, bitch."

"You'll have to catch me first." She blew him a kiss. "I'll be expecting you now, you filthy *jötunn*."

"I found you here." He smirked. "It's only a matter of time before I track you anywhere in any realm."

"Enough talk." Thor flicked his fingers, and lightning flashed down to strike the giant. Gymir screamed, but didn't drop. Smoke rose from his hair, his wounds blackened at the edges, and the stink of torched flesh flooded the air. But he was still on his feet. Damn, this bastard was fucking hard to kill.

They went after each other with renewed vengeance, their fight taking them from the edge of the yard back toward the cabin. Their weapons clashed again and again, sparks flying with every impact. They each got a few jabs in here and there, but neither opponent could claim a true advantage.

The ground quaked just a little, the consistency seeming to change ever-so-slightly. The *jötunn* began to sweat even more profusely, his jaw clenched. Thor realized Gymir was battling Sif to control the earth beneath them as much as he was battling Thor with brute strength. Good, if the man had his concentration split, he was easier pickings. Something that couldn't often be said about a giant. But it also meant Thor felt like he was fighting on shifting sand, and keeping his balance was an exhausting game.

He didn't know how long the fight lasted, but it felt like years. Time became elastic, stretching on forever. With the thunderclouds overhead, it was difficult to tell the time of day. He just wished the lightning had been a more effective tool. His muscles burned, his lungs were on fire, and he was soaked with sweat. He didn't know how much longer he could last, and only prayed his endurance would exceed Gymir's. They both seemed to be slowing, their breathing labored. They drew close to the cabin, and Thor saw the gleam of his sword in the dirt. He tried to push the fight in that direction, circling the *jötunn* to the left.

Gymir struck out with his club and Thor ducked just in time. The rush of air caused by its passing brushed against his face. The spikes slammed into the side of the house, embedding in the wood. Gymir lost his grip for just a moment, and it was all the opening Thor needed. He snapped up his sword, drove it into the giant's belly, and felt the tip rip through spinal cord. Gymir's knees buckled like a puppet with its strings cut. A shocked expression swept over his face, his eyes went wide, and then he toppled sideways.

Thor sagged, bracing his forearm against the cabin. "Shit."

Rocketing out of the house, Sif came skidding down the front steps. She didn't throw herself into his arms, which he was both glad and not glad about. "Thor! Are you badly injured?"

"No." He shook his head. "Bruised ribs, a few cuts and scrapes."

She sighed and pressed a hand to her chest. "Thank all the gods."

"Or just the ones who are on our side." He winked and she shook her head in return.

"That fight lasted the better part of four hours." Dark circles smudged under her eyes, and the skin around her mouth was tight.

Well, that took care of that question. Though he wasn't sure he'd truly wanted an answer. "It felt fucking long, but I wasn't counting the minutes."

"I was." She swallowed and nodded at the corpse sprawled near her porch. "What do we do with him?"

"Send him back where he came from." He rubbed at the ache in his ribs, the breeze cooling his sweat in truly uncomfortable ways. He needed a shower and a beer. Or mead. Or a shot of high-proof liquor. "I'm sure he has friends expecting him. We wouldn't want to disappoint them."

Her lips compressing, her brows winged up. "That would definitely send a message."

Calling down another bolt of lightning, he heated the head of Mjölnir and then struck a brand into the *jötunn's* chest. That should make it clear who'd sent Gymir to the underworld. Concentrating on the great palace of Jötunheim, Thor flicked his fingers and teleported the lifeless body to the king's dais. It would be difficult to miss that message.

Some of Sif's tension seemed to ease with Gymir gone. She eyed the hole his club had made in her wall. "I suppose we have to leave here."

"And never come back," he stated, tone implacable. "This place is no longer a safe haven for you. Get anything you want to take with you and let's be gone."

"My rune stones. I don't want anyone getting hold of them by accident. Everything else is replaceable." Regret made the corners of her mouth turn down, but she didn't protest. She was a practical woman by nature, and he'd always liked that about her. "I'll pack a few changes of clothes, too, just in case."

He watched her walk toward the door, saw how slow and tired her movements were. She may not have been involved in the physical fight, but she'd clearly thrown much of her energy behind keeping the earth giant from using his powers against Thor. "Thank you for your help."

Pausing, she glanced back. "I'm not much use in a battle, but I know my element. I'm glad that was enough. Some day, it might not be."

With that unsettling pronouncement, she disappeared into the house. He swiped a hand across his forehead, feeling shaky and clammy now that the adrenaline rush was crashing. There was no turning back now, not that he wanted to. Come what may, he—like Sif—had made the choice he could live with. But Gymir had come here for Thor, which meant the giants had decided he was a target too.

He didn't know how they'd found him so quickly or how many more might be coming to try their hand at assassination, but one thing was certain: the war had begun.

7

Gods, she was tired. It felt as if her bones had turned to lead, and every step was a marathon. She'd never tried pitting her powers against someone else's, and if she hadn't been so familiar with this particular patch of dirt, she might not have been able to counter some of Gymir's tricks, might not have sensed until too late the subtle shifts in earth he had tried that would have opened a sinkhole beneath Thor's feet.

The terror of those four hours was something she'd never forget for as long as she lived. One mistake and Thor would have died. Something inside her had shifted during that endurance test, maybe a realization of her own strength or just an end to her excuses. If she was going to die, or she had to watch Thor meet his end, she was going to be as brave as she'd claimed to be. She needed to tell him a few hard truths that she'd been holding back—about Loki and her, about how she'd done something horrible after Thura was murdered. Sif *might* even manage to muster the courage to tell Thor she still loved him, though she doubted once she'd imparted those hard truths that her love would mean much to him. She'd made mistakes she wasn't proud of, just not the ones he thought she'd made.

She needed to clear the air between them, once and for all.

Pulling out a leather satchel, she laid her box of runes at the bottom and tucked a small bag filled with various types of currency—including precious metals and gems—next to the box. That should get her anything she needed for a good long while. She stuffed some clothes and a few toiletries on top. Done.

It took an embarrassing amount of effort to slip the bag's strap over her shoulder, but she gritted her teeth and managed to heft it. She took a last, slow look around her tiny sanctuary. The place itself hadn't been as important as the peace she'd found here, but she'd loved it and would miss it. Thor was right, though—it was no longer safe now that the giants knew about it.

She stepped outside and found him sitting on her porch step, his weapons at his feet, his head bowed. "Are you sleeping?"

"No." He stirred and glanced back at her, the keen intelligence she was used to shining in his eyes. Rising, he slid his sword and war-hammer into their sheaths. "Are you ready?"

"Not really." She shrugged, wishing she could curl up and sleep, and when she awoke this nightmare would be over.

"Well, ready or not..." He stepped up and wrapped an arm around her waist. "It's time to go."

"Where—" The rest of her question was sucked away as he teleported them. She felt as if she were jerked forward into pure, utter darkness. In the space between heartbeats, they transitioned to another place.

Sunlight blinded her, and she held up a hand to shield her eyes. "Where are we?"

His voice rumbled in her ear, his breath ruffling the little hairs at her nape and making her shiver. "I thought you could always locate yourself on Earth."

"I could give you longitude and latitude, but that doesn't answer the question." Knowing she was somewhere in the Florida Keys was irrelevant—it was why he'd picked this place that was important.

"We all have our little getaways in the other realms. I have my hall in Asgard, a hunting cabin in Jötunheim, and a few spots on Earth. Before last year, this little gem is where I lived for the past decade." He smelled of heat and sweat and Thor, his warmth surrounding her. She wanted to sag against him, but knew he had to be as tired as she was, so she resisted. After a moment, he released her. "I don't have anywhere in Hel, but the underworld isn't a realm I have much interest in."

"You may not have a choice soon." It was important to keep remembering that, to know how precious time really was. That fact was far too easy for an immortal to forget.

"I'm not looking for real estate there any time soon, if I can help it." His shoulders straightened. "Despite what Nauma hinted at, the bottom line is, no one knows what's in the cards for any of us anymore. In some ways it's...a relief, really. I feel like I have some control over the future for the first time in ages. So I don't intend for either of us to die just yet. I hope you're okay with that."

"Totally okay. I'm in favor of not scorching and drowning my Earth, too." She let her gaze slide around the room, taking in her surroundings. It was a living room in shades of cream, white, and brown. White walls, cream furniture and tile floors, brown leather chairs. But the gorgeous woodwork was her favorite part. Pale honey wood lined each doorway and was inlaid into recessed panels in the ceiling. It was light and airy and nothing like the enormous fortress of Bilskirnir. He'd never invited her to one of his hideaways. Then again, until this week, he'd never been to one of hers either. Why would they take each other to their vacation homes? They spent as little time together as possible.

"Sugarloaf Key. About fifteen miles from Key West." He gestured to the wide expanses of windows. Like many homes in this area of Florida, the living spaces were on the second floor. So they had an elevated view of their surroundings—crystalline turquoise waves as far as the eye could see, and the muted roar of ocean penetrated the house.

The soothing sound did nothing to stave off her exhaustion, which hit her in a swift rush. She blinked, her eyes gritty, and her tongue felt thick in her mouth. "Pretty. The couch looks comfy. I need a nap."

"We can do better than that." Setting his hand on the small of her back, he guided her down a short hall to a room dominated by a massive bed. The frame looked as if it were constructed of recycled driftwood. "Here we are. Now, I'm going to spend some quality time with a bar of soap."

A tired laugh slipped from her as she dropped her bag. "Sounds kinky."

"Ah, well. I have to entertain myself somehow when you're sleeping."

"Resourceful man." She flopped forward onto the mattress, her legs not quite making it, but she didn't care. Sleep beckoned, and she couldn't resist its call.

She felt him tug off her shoes, lift her fully into bed, and tuck her in. That was nice. A little smile formed on her lips as she drifted in that place between asleep and awake.

At some point, she sensed the bed dip as he crawled in beside her. Peace wound through her, as if his being there was the last thing she needed to drop fully over the edge into oblivion.

8

Nightmares plagued Thor's dreams, as if the ghosts of his past had come back to haunt him. Every mistake he'd ever made paraded through his mind, and he relived the mortification of each one.

But then it got worse.

Suddenly he stood at a familiar set of doors, the entry to Valhalla. He could hear the sound of music and dancing inside. A feast hosted by his parents, and Sif was on his arm. Dread filled him, and he knew what was about to happen. He'd been to many such celebrations, but this one was different. This was the night when Loki had proclaimed—among other tawdry revelations about gods and goddesses—that he'd fucked Sif. The giant had come to make mischief in Asgard, and he'd succeeded.

Thor tried to stop his dream-self from entering the hall, from living through that moment again, but he couldn't save himself then or now. Instead, every moment passed in agonizing slow motion. He led his wife inside, Loki arrived shortly thereafter, and nothing had been right with the world ever since. Insults and barbs were thrown between Loki and the gods, the atmosphere growing thicker and thicker with animosity, though the *jötunn* seemed to enjoy himself to the bitter end.

Then it came, the moment he derided Sif's stainless reputation and said she'd strayed with "wily Loki."

Thor felt the twin blow to heart and gut now as he had then, crippling in its intensity. But for the first time, he pushed away his own anguish and focused on Sif's face. Her expression was full of impotent rage, grief, and shame. So much shame it made his soul ache. He'd always made assumptions about why those emotions would show on her face, but there was too much torment there and not enough guilt. Hers wasn't the manner of a woman who was humiliated about being called out publically for her misdeeds.

No, there was something dark and horrifying in her eyes. Something he'd never seen before or since. But she wasn't aiming that look at him. In fact, he remembered she hadn't met his gaze that entire night. He'd noticed her behavior was off, and had asked her about it, but she'd waved him away. Then Loki had showed up and the evening had spiraled out of control.

Thor's nightmare sharpened, and he grasped for the first time that his kind-hearted wife had leveled that venomous glare at Loki.

Not the look a woman gave a lover.

And something she'd said recently pinged in his mind—that she'd wanted nothing to do with giants after Thura had been murdered. So why would she choose to sleep with a giant less than a month after their daughter's death? He'd assumed it was revenge against him for not saving Thura, but Sif wasn't the type for self-destructive behavior.

So what had really happened?

He woke with a start, turning toward Sif in the dark. Moonlight played over her beautiful face, limning her in silver. She looked too peaceful to disturb, but he doubted he'd sleep another wink. Pushing himself out of bed, he found a pair of jeans in a drawer, yanked them on, and padded across the house to his office. He might as well get some work done if he wasn't going to rest. He rifled through his desk until he came up with an unused burner cell phone. Stripping it out of its packaging, he inserted the battery and turned it on. The screen lit and he made a call that would likely bounce around the globe a million times before it reached its untraceable destination. Just how he and his callee liked things.

The line clicked as someone picked up on the other end. "It's the middle of the fucking night. This better be life and death."

"Alfi," Thor said pleasantly, sitting back in his chair and smiling. "I'm so proud I raised you to be this polite when you have no idea who's on the other end."

Both Alfi and his sister Röskva had been his servants since they were children, and Thor had brought them up with all the love of a father, making them immortal. Röskva preferred Asgard, while Alfi roamed the Earth, gathering useful bits of information. The man grunted. "Who the fuck else would be calling me from an unlisted number at—*gods*—four in the morning?"

Well, he was in the same time zone as Thor, but that hardly narrowed down a location. "How am I supposed to know where you are?"

It sounded like sheets rustled and a mattress creaked. "Can't you track my rune stone? Or, rather, *your* rune stone?"

Thor propped his feet on his desk. "You mean the stone you destroyed last month and never got around to replacing?"

"Heh. Yeah. That one." A rough chuckle came through the phone. "The half-giantess who smashed it was...ah...well worth the effort it took to get her to talk."

"I don't need to hear about your seductive skills, Alfi." He smothered a snort. "What news do you have for me?"

"Hmm." Alfi scratched something loudly, and Thor didn't want to think too hard about which area of Alfi's anatomy was receiving attention. "Thor, my old man, you started a shit-storm with Gymir's death. Never did like that pompous asshole."

"He was a well-connected pompous asshole." It was the dead *jötunn's* friends Thor was concerned about now.

"I know." From the background, Thor could hear the blare of horns and a siren. Alfi was in a city—the sirens had a cadence of those in the U.S.—so Thor was guessing his servant was in New York. The man did enjoy the Big Apple. Alfi sighed, the exhalation sending static down the line. "Well, the asshole's pal Loki seems to be on the outs with his king, but no one's sure why. So, Mr. Trickster is hiding out with the fire giants. For now. I'm guessing the spat was over who's going to run the revolution because the king still sent a few giants to Earth afterwards. They have orders to assassinate you. You and Sif." A more cheerful lilt filled his tone. "So, how is my favorite goddess?"

"Exhausted." He briefly outlined her role in the fight. "She's sleeping now."

Thor could all but hear Alfi's admiring grin. "Ah, she's magnificent. They don't make women like her anymore. If they did, I'd be a married man."

"Sif's not available," Thor snapped, then felt a flush heat the back of his neck. Of course, that wasn't what Alfi meant, but Thor's knee-jerk jealousy told his servant far more than he cared for.

"So it's like that, is it? Good for you." Alfi's tone turned smug. "Röskva owes me money. She bet against you two ever reuniting."

"We haven't reunited," Thor answered stiffly.

"Your heart's more than halfway there, old man. I can hear it in your voice." Alfi sobered. "If you'll take another old man's advice…do yourself a favor. Swallow your pride and figure out how to get Mrs. Right back while you still have time. No one's future is certain now, and you haven't a moment to waste."

"Thank you for the reminder." Thor pinched the bridge of his nose.

But his servant was like a terrier after a bone. "Of all the women you've had in the eons I've known you, none has made you crazy the way she has. You love her. Always have, always will. Get her back, Papa Bear. And for more than just the occasional bang."

Ignoring the sting of truth that came with those words, Thor asked, "Do you have information that will actually keep us alive?"

"I have better than that." Typing on a keyboard rattled through the phone. "I'm going to send you a present."

"You don't know where I am."

"I can hear ocean waves. That narrows down your bolt-holes to…two. No, three." Alfi hummed to himself while he typed. "The weather in Florida's nice this time of year, don't you think?"

"Asshole."

He snorted. "Please, as if you haven't figured out where I am."

"That rat-infested eleventh-story walk-up you keep in Manhattan." Thor shook his head and wondered why he hadn't fired his insubordinate subordinate centuries ago. Mostly because the bear within considered Alfi a cub, and there was no changing that. Also, he loved the little pain in the backside.

"Yep. Expect a package sometime tomorrow. *Today*, actually, since it's bum-fuck early. In the meantime, go crawl back into bed with your gorgeous goddess of a wife." The line went dead.

"Helpful as always." He tossed the phone aside with a groan.

Booting up the computer he hadn't used in a year, he waited for about a billion updates to finish. Then he scoured news sites from around the world, looking for anything that might indicate what the giants were up to next. They were connected to elements, so he zeroed in on natural disasters. There had been nothing big recently, but he made a note of every minor earthquake and tsunami he found. He even checked the paparazzi rags that liked to report alien abductions—maybe someone had seen an oversized dino-man that only that type of news source would report on. Nope, bust. Just some blurry naked photos of actors cavorting in the Bahamas.

Boring shit, basically.

His eyes began to burn from lack of sleep and too many hours staring at a computer screen. He glanced up and saw dawn had come and gone. The sun blazed down merrily, the sky an eye-searing shade of cerulean blue. But he could see dark clouds gathering on the horizon, the kinds of tropical storms common to this part of the world.

Cocking his head, he listened for Sif. Mattress springs creaked as if she rolled over. Not awake yet, but stirring. He got up to make breakfast. He had a feeling they'd require some fortification for the conversation they needed to have about his memory-dream.

There wasn't much in the way of fresh food, and they might not be staying long enough to warrant resupplying. He had a box of just-add-water pancake mix and a bottle of unopened maple syrup. A can of peaches and two small bottles of apple juice completed his offering. Not fancy, but it'd do.

He made short work of preparing the food, loaded everything on a beat-up tray he had stashed in the back of his pantry, and went to the bedroom. The sight he beheld was almost a religious experience. Her body was bowed in a luxurious stretch that made his dick stiffen and his mouth go dry.

Her golden eyes opened and she smiled the kind of smile most men would die to have aimed in their direction. "Good morning. Or is it afternoon?"

He cleared his throat. "Not quite 10AM. You slept for almost fourteen hours."

Pursing her lips, she sat up. "I'm not sure whether to be impressed with myself or appalled."

"Impressed." He set the tray down and handed her a plate and fork. "I am."

"Food," she moaned, and the sound did nothing to ease his hard-on.

He picked up his own plate and stuffed down his pancakes while watching her eat, which was far more entertaining than the mediocre taste of boxed breakfast. She seemed to be enjoying herself, if the noises she was making were anything to go by. He'd heard her have quieter orgasms, and wasn't sure if he should be flattered or insulted.

"So," she said around a huge bite of food. "What's on the agenda today?"

"I called Alfi. He's sending us something he says will help us. After it gets here…we should stay no more than another day before we move on."

"So we're on the run for real." She nodded to her bag. "I have hard currency with me. Enough to hold us for a while before we need more."

"Unflappable as always." He saluted her with a forkful of peaches. "I have a cache here as well."

"Good. How's Alfi? Staying out of trouble?"

He grinned. "When it comes to him, *trouble* has such a varied meaning."

Shaking her head, she tsked. "And he was such a sweet child."

"Didn't he end up with us because he ate one of my goats without permission?"

She dimpled in a grin. "All right, so he's always had flexible morals. I adore him anyway. He's a loveable rogue."

Thor harrumphed. "He'd love to hear you say so."

"I'm going to tell myself you don't mean he looks at me in anything other than a maternal light." She licked the syrup off her fork.

"I had a nightmare last night." He either changed the subject or he was going to see what else that talented tongue of hers could do.

"I'm sorry." Sympathy shone on her features and she set aside her empty plate. "Was it some sort of prophetic dream? Are you developing new abilities?"

"No, I'm not a Seer. I wouldn't want to be. This dream was a memory. It was about the banquet. With Loki." *Come on, Thor. Use full sentences.* If he intended to talk about this he actually had to *talk* without choking on the words.

All the blood leeched out of her face, and she pulled her knees up to her chest, wrapping her arms around her legs. As close to fetal position as she could get while still upright. But her voice was calm and even when she spoke. "What about the banquet?"

"After the banquet, after he dropped his bombshell, I asked you if you'd been in his bed, and you said yes. At the time, that was all the information I thought I needed." He swallowed hard. "I've asked myself more than once over the years. Why him? How could you? I'm ashamed to admit it wasn't until recently I've begun to ask...*did* you sleep with him?"

9

Cold sweat made Sif's palms clammy, and she wiped them on her pants. Her stomach churned, and she was a lot less happy with her breakfast at this point. But she'd promised herself she'd be honest with him, and what had happened with Loki was on her list of things to talk about. She'd just thought she'd be the one to bring up the topic, thus giving her a chance to brace herself. No such luck.

"Did Loki fuck me? Yes, he did." She waited for Thor's explosion of rage.

But his eyes stayed steady on her face, not a single hint of judgment on his expression. "Were you willing?"

Oh, gods. There was the question he hadn't asked so long ago. Moisture stung the backs of her eyes. "Does it matter?"

"It does to me." He reached out and laid his hand on her foot, his touch hot against her icy skin.

"No. Sort of. I...don't know." A tear escaped to slide down her cheek and she swiped it away.

His fingers tightened around her foot. "That really says it all, doesn't it?"

"It was a couple of nights before the banquet. You were away from Bilskirnir, and Loki came to see you. I invited him to stay for dinner, playing my part as hostess in your absence." So many times, she'd wished she'd sent him away. She'd wanted to, loathing him because a giant just like him had murdered her daughter a handful of weeks before. But she'd known Thor would be upset if she was rude to someone who'd come seeking his counsel, and she hadn't wanted to deal with more strife in their relationship. Thura's death had already torn a rift between them. Too bad Sif hadn't realized the worst was yet to come.

"Go on," he urged.

"I think Loki put something in my mead that night, an aphrodisiac that made me...an animal. Violent and terrifying in my lust. So, did I go willingly to his bed? Yes. Was I in a state of mind to make a rational decision? No. The only choice I made that night was to have a drink with dinner. One drink, and my life was ruined. You know the worst part? I think he did it for *fun*, knowing I still struggled when dealing with giants. He thought it was a big joke." Her lips wobbled and it was all she could do not to crumble. Her nails dug into her legs as she tried to hang on to her composure. "But I wasn't entirely blameless."

"Yes, you were." Thor's gaze blazed so bright it seared into her, and for a moment, she'd swear there were tears in *his* eyes. "And if I hadn't intended to kill him already, I would now."

A laugh straggled out of her. "There's more, and this you might actually hate me for."

"I doubt it." His smile was self-deprecating. "Even when I thought you cheated, I didn't hate you. I thought I *should*, but I didn't have it in me."

That he was being so kind just made this confession all the worse. She'd once thought she'd rather die than tell him this, but it was a secret she'd held in for far too long. "I...hated you for not saving Thura."

"I know." His chin dipped in a nod. "I hated myself for a long time too. Aren't I supposed to be the champion? Yet what good was I then? I hunted down the bastard who took her, but she was already dead. I was too fucking late. Killing that giant was an empty victory when I knew I had to come home and tell you she was gone." His voice cracked, torment and self-loathing stamped on his features. "I will never forget the look on your face when you realized I'd failed."

Now it was her turn to reach out. She pulled his hand away from her foot and interlaced their fingers. "I expected you to be invincible, to conquer every problem with ease, and that was wrong. When you didn't live up to my expectations, and I lost my only daughter in the bargain, my mind spiraled down a dark hole that had no bottom. Of course you could have saved her, you just didn't want to. You didn't love her or me enough to do your best, to be the undefeated champion."

He made a choking noise, and she squeezed his fingers. "Let me finish. While I didn't willingly sleep with Loki, I also never tried to convince you I hadn't cheated on you. I found a way to get back at you for letting Thura be killed, even though it ate me up inside for you to think the worst of me." She shrugged, feeling helpless to explain her reasoning, knowing she'd been in such a bad mental space then that there really wasn't much logic. It was all lashing out combined with a sort of sick self-preservation. "At first, I didn't know how to tell you the truth about Loki because I wasn't entirely sure what had happened, why I behaved as if I were a willing bedmate when I knew deep down I wasn't. But he made some sly comment to me after his big banquet proclamation, and I...I was so disgusted and *ashamed* that I'd put myself in a position to be used by a giant. Then you demanded to know if I'd been in his bed, and the answer was yes. You didn't—wouldn't—listen to anything else I had to say after that. You left me and started sticking your dick in every interested giantess, and I was pretty sure your choice of lovers was a stab at me."

He winced. "It was, at first. I'm not proud of it, but you're not wrong."

"So my fury over Thura and then you having revenge sex with other women—well, I never bothered to tell you what really happened with Loki." She offered him a sad, anemic version of a smile. "By the time you'd calmed down enough to listen, I'd decided letting you think you'd been made a cuckold was your punishment. For failing, for leaving me, for not listening in the first place. I was just so angry at the whole fucking universe then."

He ran his thumb over the back of her hand. "I don't blame you."

"Thura's death wasn't your fault, for the record. There was nothing you could do. There was nothing any of us could have done." She leaned forward a little to emphasize her earnestness. "You'd trained her as a warrior and she was a grown woman, as capable of looking after herself as anyone. What were you supposed to do, chain her to your side? Keep her locked in a tower? No. What happened was terrible, but it wasn't your fault."

"Thank you. It took me a long time to figure that out myself, and I'll admit I still struggle with it. But hearing that you no longer blame me? It means a lot." His gaze never wavered from hers, his gratitude sincere for something so simple.

The gratitude shamed her even more. She could have told him this long ago, but she'd been too busy protecting herself, keeping those emotional barriers as high as possible. Of all the men in the world, he was the only one who could truly destroy her inside, and without the closeness they'd once shared, she'd been too afraid to admit anything. She didn't exactly look pristine when all the ugly facts were laid out, and he could have twisted the truth against her so easily.

If she hadn't already loved him, his next words would have done the trick. He brought her hand to his lips and kissed it as if it were precious, as if *she* were still precious to him. "What Loki did to you? It wasn't your fault either."

She closed her eyes, and more tears tracked down her cheeks. "Thank you. I...still occasionally have nightmares about it. Whatever he doped me with was like having some sort of out of body experience. I wasn't myself, I couldn't control what I was doing, but a part of me was aware the whole time, screaming in my head to make it stop. Just please, please make it stop."

That was the worst part, the helplessness, the violation of not only her body, but her will. The noxious feel of his breath on her face, his body pinning her down, his sex driving into hers. While her actions had been feral and wanton, her mind had recoiled from something she didn't want, would never want. When she'd woken the next morning alone, she'd retched, teleported to her healing spring, and scrubbed at the bruises he'd left as if she could wash them away. The spring had done its job, but the marks had gone far deeper than her skin and had taken far longer to heal.

"Sif." Thor hauled her into his arms, holding her so tight she could barely breathe, but it was exactly what she needed. He rumbled soothing noises in her ear as she sobbed harder than she ever had in her life. She cried for Thura, for Thor, and for herself. For all that might have been and never was. For all that was and shouldn't have been. She felt as if she was cracking open inside, as if the safe shell she'd built around herself was crumbling. It was exhilarating and terrifying.

She bunched her fingers in the front of his shirt. "It was almost a century before I let any man touch me again, and I picked a mortal because—"

"He wouldn't be able to overwhelm you or hurt you." His sigh ruffled over her hair. "That's why you've always chosen humans."

Nodding, she pressed closer, craving the warmth of his body. She'd needed to take control of her sexuality and sexual experiences after what Loki had done, and mortal lovers had seemed like the best way to ensure that. It might have taken her some time, but she'd refused to spend her life afraid of sex. Though only with Thor could she really let go and give up control. "The one immortal I've had in my bed since then was you. I just couldn't with anybody else. I couldn't."

He stroked her hair and rocked her. "Thank you for trusting me."

Tipping her head back, she met his gaze. "The trust wasn't voluntary—it was more subconscious than anything else—but I knew you'd never do anything I wasn't an eager participant in."

"Never," he agreed. He swiped the moisture away from her cheeks with the pads of his thumbs. "Sif, I—"

Whatever he was going to say was cut off by someone knocking on the front door. For a moment, she tensed, but Thor took a deep breath and didn't react. So he didn't sense a threat. Good. She let out a shaky breath. "That must be Alfi's present."

An odd expression crossed his face. "Yes."

She slipped out of bed and finger-combed her hair back into a ponytail, grabbing an elastic band from her bag. She was no doubt blotchy from crying, but the delivery driver was unlikely to care.

Thor moved toward the door. "Let me get it."

"Okay." That solved the strange-man-seeing-she'd-been-crying issue. "I'll splash some water on my face and then come see what Alfi thought could help us."

She took her time primping and dressing, figuring Thor would have to sign for the package and make polite small talk with the driver. When she headed down the hallway, she heard Thor having a quiet conversation with someone, but the voices were too low for her to pick out words. Wow, that was a chatty FedEx guy.

She entered the living room and froze. Three men stood in the middle of the room, two of them so tall their heads almost brushed the wooden inset in the ceiling. Thor was a huge man, and these men dwarfed him.

They'd been found again.

Icy dread ran through her veins. "*Giants.*"

10

"Half-giants," Thor corrected, coming to her side to take her arm, offering whatever support he could. "These are my sons. Alfi sent them to us."

"Why would Alfi do that?" Her normally rosy skin was paper-white, her eyes wide, and terror lurked within them. "You said you didn't know which side—"

"I didn't, but they went to Röskva, who went to Alfi." He kept his voice calm, knowing that having so recently dug up all the atrocities giants had committed against her and those she loved would make the wounds feel fresh. Having two giants, even half-giants, this close would be difficult. She'd seen their kind as absolute enemies for a long time, and had never seemed inclined to acknowledge the gray areas between their species. He understood why, but that didn't change the situation.

She crossed her arms, each palm grasping the opposite elbow, and gathered her composure. "I see. Röskva and Alfi believed your sons could help us?"

"Yes." He waved to the men dominating the room, and felt himself begin to babble to cover the weirdness. As if that were possible. "Modi is the darker one—he's half fire giant. Don't ask me why he thinks dreadlocks are a good look. Then Magni's got the pasty-pale blondness of his mother. They're about as opposite as they look too. It's only their blue eyes that tell you I contributed anything to their genetics."

His sons had spent half their childhood in Asgard and half in Jötunheim, and Sif had always been away when they were around because *Thor* was around. He didn't think she would have been unkind had she met his children, or taken out any anger over his infidelities on them, but he'd never had a chance to introduce them. While he wasn't ashamed of his sons, he wasn't proud of himself knowing that their conceptions had been part of his less-than-subtle revenge against his wife for a crime she hadn't committed.

"We've met," Modi said quietly, as if afraid to spook her. Of the two half-giants, he was the more introspective.

"I'm sure she remembers us." Magni's smile was cocksure. "We're hard to forget."

"Yes, you were at Valhalla once while I was visiting Freya." Her ponytail swished against her back as she looked between Thor's sons. "You were in a mock-battle against a group of berserkers."

"We won, too." Magni's smile grew. "Lucky they were immortal because we crushed them like—"

His breath whooshed out as his brother elbowed him in the gut. Modi hissed, "Shut up, idiot."

"Thank you for saving me the trouble, Modi." Thor rubbed his forehead, praying for patience. "Perhaps you should tell Sif what you told me."

"We talked about it." Modi gestured to his brother. "Which side we want to be on. We can see the signs the same as everyone else, and we've heard rumors of what's been going on with other giants. We want no part of it."

"Never did get a taste for human flesh," Magni chimed in.

"Or genocide," Modi added. "We like Earth just fine. No need to rule it or treat it as a feeding ground. Each race has its own realm, and it should stay that way."

"You've spent time on Earth?" Sif's question shot out like a bullet from a gun.

"Well...yeah." Magni looked at Thor as though he wasn't sure if he was putting his foot in his mouth. Again. "Father can morph into a bear, but we can morph too, in a way. We can downsize to human-form. Other giants and half-giants can do it too, but they don't advertise the ability. Makes it easier to walk around on Earth."

"Those of us that look humanoid anyway. A man-sized dragon is still a dragon, which would freak the fuck out of mortals." Modi shrugged. "They're a twitchy lot now that most of them don't believe species like us exist."

Sif's stiff posture had eased a bit since she'd arrived, though Thor could hardly call her relaxed. He was torn between wanting to protect her from what justifiably scared her, wanting to keep his sons from being caught in her prejudice, and knowing they needed as many allies as they could muster. The husband, the father, and the warrior were at odds. The bear was, for once, staying out of his inner turmoil.

"Frey's wife. She could downsize too, couldn't she?" Her eyes narrowed in consideration. "I always thought she was just petite for a giantess."

Modi nodded. "Yes, she could downsize too."

So could her father, Thor realized. That was who'd slammed into him while he was racing to save Sif at Valhalla. It was Gymir's blood he'd smelled.

Propping his fists on his hips, Modi continued, "Father said we should downsize before you came in so we didn't scare you by being all huge."

"But what would we wear?" Magni tugged at the bottom of his tunic. "The clothes don't magically shrink. Waving our junk at you would be just as freaky."

She snorted, but didn't crack a smile.

Modi slipped a bag off his shoulder and waved it in his brother's face. "I brought human clothes for us, dumbass. Did you think we were coming to Earth and staying this size?"

"No, I figured we'd teleport to our house in the Outer Banks after we checked in with Papa Bear. How does that make me a dumbass?"

"Children, please." Thor was getting a headache of gigantic proportions. He loved his boys, but they bickered like an old married couple. They took some getting used to. Not the first impression he'd have wanted them to make on Sif. Had he known they were coming, he would have threatened them with death and dismemberment to make sure they understood the need to be on their very best behavior. Instead, she was getting the unvarnished version of the halfling brothers. Outstanding.

"We don't have to stay long." Modi held up a placating hand. "We just came to say we're siding with you, with Asgard. We won't help our mothers make slaves of gods and men."

Magni's chin dipped in an emphatic nod. "We'll fight with you when the time comes."

Sif's gaze turned to Thor. "You trust them?"

Sliding his hands in his pockets, he considered how best to approach the question. Not so long ago, she hadn't been sure she could trust him. Did she really trust his judgment, especially when it came to his sons? He wouldn't, in her place. So he turned the question on her. "I think the most important question is: can *you* trust them? They're half-giants."

"Half-gods too." She uncrossed her arms, and he could see the crescent-shaped indentations where her nails had dug into her skin. Not a good sign.

"Siegfried and his cronies won't count them allies unless you do." He waited for that fact to sink in, for her to grasp just what kind of a linchpin she was in this operation. "We need all the help we can get, but you have to trust those on your team, or the battle is already lost."

He could see the conflict in her gaze, could see the internal war waging. All her old biases about giants cast against the two men standing before them, claiming not to support any *jötunn* apocalyptic schemes. Which would win—hope or hate? Compassion or bitterness?

She closed her eyes, swallowed, and then looked at his sons. "Thor trusts you and is ready to place his life in your hands, but parents can be blind to their children's flaws. I'll admit I have my own blind spots, though not those of a mother. So, if I'm going to put other people at risk by bringing you onto our team, then you need to convince me of why I should believe in you."

That seemed to stymie the men for a moment, and Thor waited to see what they would do. His sons were honest and honorable, and he knew they wouldn't have come to him until and unless they were certain about the choice they'd made. However, he wasn't going to try to force his conviction on his wife. She had to decide for herself. If she sent them away, they might have other uses during *Ragnarök*, but probably not in any direct combat. A shame and a waste of their skills, but such was life.

Modi moved forward, ducking his head as he stepped out from under the recessed ceiling. He approached Sif and dropped to one knee before her. When he held out his hands to her, she took them, though she appeared puzzled. His gaze was earnest and his voice firm. "I swear fealty to you, goddess Sif, and will do your bidding from here until the end days. I am yours to command."

Magic charged the air around them, the offer far more than a simple promise, but an unbreakable bond that would cause great pain to Modi if he violated it. Sif's eyes went round and her mouth fell open.

Shock rocked through Thor as well. He didn't know if what his son had just done was genius or the height of folly. Very few goddesses commanded warriors, unless those warriors were actually sworn to their husbands. What Modi had done was treat Sif as a ruler, a queen in her own right.

She stared at him for a long moment, assessing, but his gaze didn't waver. Finally, she nodded. "I accept your oath."

A glowing, bronze cord wrapped around both of their wrists, chaining him to her until the end of his service. Or his death. The cord sank into their skin and disappeared.

"My turn." Magni shouldered his brother aside and knelt in front of her.

She repeated the process with the other half-giant, and he arose with a wry smile. "I always assumed I'd be swearing fealty to Papa Bear someday. If he lives through this—and I'm going to make damn sure he does—but Odin either doesn't survive or never resurfaces, I figured Father would be the new ruler of the gods. My king." He rocked his hand back and forth through the air. "But you'd be his queen, so I'd have vowed my loyalty to you anyway. This is fitting, I think."

"Well said, brother mine." Modi clapped his hand on Magni's shoulder.

Thor blinked, glancing between his sons, and found them both nodding. He'd had no idea they assumed he'd ever ascend as ruler of Asgard. He'd been slated for death on the same day as his father, so it had never occurred to him what his life might be like after *Ragnarök*. There was no after. Until now. It was a heady thing to have a future to consider. He might still die, but *might* was a lot less rigid than *definitely*.

Before this moment, he'd assumed one of his surviving brothers, half-brothers, or nephews would have stepped up to take over. Likely, they'd thought so as well. Which meant they might have reason to conspire with the giants—to speed up and gain power for their own rule. And get rid of competition. Something to ponder later.

He gave Magni a hard look. "You can quit calling me Papa Bear, and try not to pick up any more of Alfi's annoying habits."

"Ha. Told you that would get you in trouble," Modi gloated. His brother punched his arm, but Modi shook it off and looked to Sif. "Shouldn't we join our friends in Virginia? We need a battle plan or Loki will pick us off one by one."

But she looked as overwhelmed as Thor felt. Her expression was composed, but he saw how she clasped and unclasped her hands, how she didn't meet anyone's gaze. She didn't know how to process this either.

He turned to his sons. "Give us a minute, guys. Why don't you go downsize and change into human clothes? Guest rooms are down the hall on the left."

"Sure thing." Magni linked his hands behind his back and stretched. "I wouldn't mind a dip in the ocean, either. Mom is a sea giantess, after all. There's saltwater in my blood."

"Fine." Thor waved them off. "Go."

Sif crossed the room and stepped out onto the balcony, propping her elbows on the rail. While the sky was still clear overhead, the storm clouds he'd seen earlier had unleashed themselves over the ocean in the distance. He'd normally kick back and enjoy the tempest, but he was far more interested in his wife than the weather. "Are you all right?"

"I have no idea." She dropped her face into her palms.

"I'm so proud of you, sweetheart." He laid his hand on her back. "I know how hard it was for you to put any kind of faith in a giant. Even a half-giant. It probably didn't make it easier that those particular half-giants are the result of your husband's infidelity. But you set aside your prejudice, even just this once, and that's huge."

"I could...*feel* their sincerity when they swore fealty. Almost like I could see straight to their souls." She shuddered. "That was a magic I've never encountered before. It wasn't comfortable."

"It might happen again, if things go the way I imagine they will." He rubbed slow circles up and down her spine. "You've made yourself into a lightning rod for this war. More might come to you because of what you did for Erik and Bryn."

"I helped a few berserkers teleport, that's all!" She dropped her hands and let her head fall back. "*You're* the lightning god. *You* should be the lightning rod here. There have been times when your popularity far outstripped your father's. Gods and giants should come flocking to you, not me."

Trying to keep his tone gentle, he replied, "You also lava-fried two *jötunn* assassins and helped me defeat Gymir. You were the first god or goddess to take a public stand. That's clearly not gone unnoticed. Also, your long-standing and well-known hate of giants means if you trust a *jötunn*, others will too."

"We'll see. Just because I accepted your sons' oaths doesn't mean I'd trust any other giants or half-giants. It would have to feel the same way." Her shoulders twitched. "Besides, I'm unconvinced events will play out the way you think anyway."

Fair enough. He was just guessing, but others could See far more than he. "You could ask Nauma if I'm right."

"Maybe I will." She pulled in a deep breath, straightened, and squared her shoulders before she faced him. "Something else that bothers me...your sons were right, you know. If you survive *Ragnarök*, you're the obvious choice to succeed Odin." Her throat worked. "In that case, it's probably best if we divorce."

"What?" There was a non sequitur he hadn't anticipated. He felt as if she'd opened up the ground beneath his feet, hurling him down a sinkhole. After all they'd been through, him becoming king was what would make her end their marriage? Despair tore through him, and he felt the bright future he'd just begun to imagine slipping through his fingers like loose sand.

Because the only future he could envision had Sif at his side. Despite everything they'd been through, there was no one who could ever come close to matching him the way she did. In bed and out of it. He braced a hand on the rail, trying to keep his knees from buckling. The bear within wanted to howl like a wounded animal. If he thought it would ease even an iota of his pain, he'd give in to the desire.

He wasn't interested in a divorce—he needed her back in his life. Not as an accomplice in a war that hadn't yet arrived, but as his wife, his partner in all ways. He loved her. He'd never *stopped* loving her, no matter what bullshit he'd told himself about duty and honor and her being under his protection.

"Divorce?" Words he couldn't stop ripped out of him, even if they weren't as diplomatic as they should have been. "No and no and *fuck* no."

11

Sif took a step back at the vehemence in his voice, jerking around and wishing she could flee. She headed for a set of stairs that took her down to the front yard. Her heart was so heavy it might have been a lead ball in her chest. Had he thought that offer had been easy for her? Gods, no. But the last thing a king needed was a queen he didn't really want. Better that he find a true helpmeet who didn't have all the baggage Sif did. Not just her personal baggage either, but the wreckage of their shared history.

She reached the yard, but didn't know where else to go. There was no escaping herself, so she stopped in the middle of the grass and stared out at the horizon. Thor came after her, a growl breaking from him. The breeze ruffled her ponytail and she dragged sea air into her lungs, trying to think about anything but the man vibrating with intensity beside her. She was so close to bursting into tears, and she'd cried far too much already.

"Did you hear me?" he demanded.

"I heard, but I still think I'm right." She didn't look at him, couldn't meet his eyes while she pushed for something she didn't want. That was the shitty part about being in love—wanting what was best for the other person over everything else. Even your own happiness. "A king doesn't need an estranged queen, Thor. You deserve better."

He went silent at that, so still he could have been a statue. She heard Magni and Modi clamor outside, but they didn't come toward Thor and her. There must be another staircase on the other side of the house. Thank gods. They might be bound to her now, but she didn't want to see them at the moment. The idea of any warrior being *bound to her* was so foreign, it was ludicrous, but it was a brave new world she was in. She doubted others would follow the half-giants the way Thor claimed, but who knew? If there were other giants—gods, it would be hard. Thor's sons she could handle *because* they were his sons. But…if others were as sincere and wanted to fight to keep Earth and Asgard safe, could she turn them away in good conscience?

No. They were in a war, and she refused to let her bias give Loki a single advantage. Sending away true allies just because of their race would be the kind of stupid mistake that could kill the gods' hopes of winning.

Lightning bolted across the sky in the distance, drawing Sif's gaze. "It's beautiful here."

Inane, but was there a non-awkward subject right now?

She felt his incisive gaze burn into her, but he responded anyway. "I knew you would like this place the moment I saw it."

The house sat on a part of the island that formed a small jut out into the ocean, surrounded by waves on three sides. To the left was the Atlantic Ocean, to the right was the Caribbean Sea, but those were human designations—it was all one massive body of water. The dramatic skyline was made only more so by the four distinct lightning storms that ringed the horizon. The low rumble of thunder in the distance was almost as constant as the beat of ocean waves.

Thunder and lightning, Thor's specialties.

Maybe his mood was increasing the storms, but he had to be in his element on days like this. Yet the lush grass felt right under her feet, the spongy texture of earth between her toes somehow soothed her soul. Flowers and palm trees lined the edges of his garden, verdant green spreading towards a small dock and the turquoise water beyond.

Somehow he'd found a place that suited them both perfectly. She tamped down on that disturbing thought. It didn't matter, since they were soon to leave, and likely wouldn't return.

He broke into her reverie. "I don't want a divorce. There's no one better for me than you. I love you."

If he'd punched her in the face, she couldn't have been more stunned. She looked up at him. "W-what?"

"You heard me." He arched an eyebrow. "I didn't stutter."

She hugged herself, hating that she had to ask the next question. "Is this sudden change of heart because you know now I didn't really cheat with Loki?"

Rubbing the back of his neck, he seemed to grope for what he wanted to say. "There's no way to answer that without sounding like a complete asshole. If I say yes, then it sounds like I'm happy you were drugged and raped. If I say no, then it sounds like the cheating didn't matter, and so why have we been separated all these years?" He let out a breath. "What Loki did to you...there are no words for how enraged I am at him or how sorry I am for what you went through. I'm even sorrier for the part I had in causing you pain. I wish I had asked more questions back then, and I also wish that we'd been in a place in our relationship where you felt safe enough to tell me the truth."

"Me, too. To all of that." She swallowed, her heart pounding against her ribs. "I'm sorry I blamed you for Thura's death for so long. You weren't the one who kidnapped and killed her, but since the giant who did was dead, and the loss still hurt so fucking much...I needed to direct that agony *somewhere*. So I held it against you, and that wasn't fair. You would have saved her if you could, and I know you loved her as much as I did. I'm sorry I ever thought otherwise." She shook her head. "Maybe I would have gotten past it sooner and our marriage could have recovered if Loki hadn't fucked me over, but that's something we'll never really know."

"I forgive you. For blaming me for Thura, for letting me think you slept with Loki." He stepped in front of her and cupped her face between his palms. "I shouldn't have walked away from our marriage, but I couldn't see past my own pain. Of all the things I regret in my life, that one stings the worst, because I could so easily have altered the outcome. There's a great deal I have no control over—no matter how much I might wish otherwise—but *that* decision wasn't one of them. I'll regret it forever."

"Don't. I don't want to be one of your regrets, Thor. I would never want that." Tears welled in her eyes, but she blinked them away. "I forgive you too. For everything. If we're killed in this war, I don't want either of us to enter the underworld filled with foolish wishes about all the things we should have done differently."

He rested his forehead against hers. "Whatever time we have left, I want you at my side."

So many terrible things had happened—a good number of which they'd done to each other—that she didn't even know how to hope he meant it. So she teased instead. "Even in battle?"

He swore, appearing tormented. "I—"

"Kidding. I'm kidding." She pressed a hand to his chest, enjoying the closeness while she could. "Physical combat isn't my area of expertise, and I won't pretend it is, but I can help our cause in other ways."

"Thank all the gods." A whoosh of air escaped him. "I don't think I could handle you being in the thick of battle, not unless you spend a few hundred years training with the valkyries."

She wrinkled her nose. "Not an interest of mine, and not something we have time for."

"No," he agreed. After a beat of silence, he jostled her. "You still haven't really given me an answer."

"Did you ask a question?"

His eyes narrowed, and he looked as if he wanted to shake her again. "Do you really want a divorce? I'm not talking about what you think is best for me, I'm asking what *you* want. Is there no chance you could ever love me again? We'll never have what we once did, but we're not those people anymore, so...we could have something just as good that fits who we are now. Does that sound crazy?"

It sounded too good, too right, too perfect. Too much like all her dreams had come true. She couldn't help but suspect it. "We've just been thrown together for an insane week. This is battle-fever talking. Or something. You *can't* still love me, Thor."

A muscle twitched in his jaw, and his eyes glittered like hard blue diamonds. "I can and I do. You can feel however you want, but I'll be damned if anyone tells *me* how to feel. I'm a grown ass man, and I've been around long enough to know my own mind. If I tell you I love you, I fucking mean it."

Okay, then. That was the fierce Thor she knew and loved. She almost smiled.

Almost. But too many centuries of telling herself her feelings were one-sided crushed any hope that wanted to sprout. "I'm scared."

"Of what? We can work through whatever it is."

"It's not that simple." She balled her hands into fists. "I'm scared that we're going to hurt each other again. More. I'm scared we're not good for each other."

"But you love me." His expression dared her to deny his words.

"Yes, but—"

"No buts!" Triumph shone in his gaze, and a brilliant smile lit his face.

She smacked a palm against the solid wall of his chest. "Despite what sappy human songs might tell you, love *isn't* all you need."

"Yes, it is." He snapped his arms around her waist and hauled her close. "Let me convince you."

His lips covered hers, smothering her feeble protests. She should try to push him away, but that wasn't what she wanted. Gods, she didn't even know what she wanted anymore. Could they really resurrect a marriage that had been more than half-dead for a millennium? Just like that? Kiss and make up? Or was it just about making the conscious choice to forgive each other for past wrongs and work through whatever problems came at them in the future?

That made sense, but her wits were spinning. His tongue teased hers, coaxing her to respond. Her breasts were crushed against his chest, and her nipples went tight. He eased the tie out of her ponytail, leaving her hair hanging heavy against her back. He kissed his way along her jaw, nipped at her earlobe, and slid his tongue down her throat in a hot, wet trail. Insidious heat slithered through her, stealing her will to resist. Her sex throbbed and she felt the lips of her pussy grow slick. Her thighs shook with the effort it took to remain upright, and when he bit her collarbone, her knees went weak.

She grabbed for his shoulders. "Your sons—"

"Are smart enough to know I'd kick their asses if they interrupted us now." His fangs pricked her flesh, which did nothing to ease her ardor.

"Well-trained," she quipped.

"Just how I like my warriors, but that's not what I want to talk about now." His hands snaked under her shirt, glided over her back, and then headed south to cup her ass through her pants.

Goose bumps erupted down her limbs, but she couldn't quite relax enough to let go. "We're in plain sight."

"I can fix that." He took her hand and drew her away from the house, not toward it. He wound through moss-draped trees and ferns until they were enclosed by balmy wilderness. His property went farther than she'd realized. When they reached a small open space, he dragged her down onto a soft bed of grass and moss. "Here. Our reunion should involve naked writhing against the Earth with thunderstorms in the sky, don't you think?"

"I haven't agreed to a reunion." Though her heart fluttered at the sweet possibilities he was offering her. The chance to change their fates, to try again as older and wiser people. It sounded amazing. And frightening.

He just chuckled, his tone taking on the deep, wicked note he used in bed. "I do love a challenge."

Kneeling over her, he shucked his clothes and then went to work on hers. He plucked open the buttons on her shirt, spreading it wide. He made an appreciative noise when he saw she wore no bra. Bending down, he suckled her nipples one at a time. She shoved her hands into his hair and tried to hold him close. He batted each tight crest with his tongue, swirling around the tip, then shoving her sensitized flesh against the roof of his mouth. She choked on a breath, her fingers turning to fists.

He let her nipple slide free and blew a cool stream of air over her damp flesh. She gasped and shuddered, her torso bowing in reaction. "Thor!"

"Yes. Scream my name. That's so fucking good." He wrestled open her zipper, hooked his fingers into the waist of her jeans and panties, dragging both garments down her legs and leaving her as bare as him. The humid air curled over her skin, making her painfully aware that they were outside where anyone could stumble across them. Somehow that only increased her desire.

He slipped his hands up her thighs, pressing his thumbs into the thatch of hair that shielded her sex. He stroked her clit, and fire licked over her skin. Shivers of climax built in her belly, the feeling so exquisite her knees drew up, clamping them around his arm. Her hands scrabbled for something to anchor her as the storm began to foment inside her. Her fingers gripped the grass beneath her and her hips rose and fell to the rhythm his hands set for her.

"Open for me, sweetheart."

She parted her thighs, giving him all the access he could want. He took advantage, moving between her legs and easing his weight onto her. The head of his cock slipped along her slit before he pierced her in one swift thrust. Orgasm exploded through her, shocking in its intensity, dragging her under in a tumbling riptide of ecstasy. Her mouth opened in a silent scream, her sex milking the length of his dick.

She hadn't even floated down to reality when he rolled them onto their sides facing each other. He pulled her leg over his hip, holding her wide for a deeper penetration. He sank himself to the hilt, the rough hair at his groin stimulating her clit. She grabbed his shoulder, her nails digging into his skin. "Gods, *Thor*."

"Convinced yet?" His tone had gone silky smooth, pure temptation.

"Sex has never been a problem for us." She moaned when he thrust at just the right angle to hit her G-spot. When the man set his mind to convincing a girl of something, he didn't take half measures.

"Neither has love, but they're both a good place to start." He grinned, powering into her slowly, but with enough force to make his breathing hitch as he spoke. "It was trust that killed us, but I promise not to fuck that up again. I promise to ask questions if there's ever a reason to doubt you again. I promise to believe you over anyone else."

"Even if I told you the sky has pink and gold polka dots?" She was ridiculously proud of herself for coming up with a coherent reply.

"Mmm. Gold, like my beloved Sif." He reached between them to rub her clit. "Pink, like some of her most interesting parts."

"Thor!" she gasped, and he chuckled wickedly.

He leaned in to brush a kiss over her mouth, their lips clinging. "I love you, my goddess."

Emotion swamped her, and it was all she could do not to sob. "Don't."

"Too bad. I do anyway." His hips drove forward, his body as relentless as his words, demanding everything she had to give and more. "And you know what, Sif? You love me too. You hate the idea of us being apart any longer just as much as I do. You'd have tried to get rid of me days ago if you didn't want me around."

"You wouldn't have gone, anyway." She tightened her leg around him, moving with him as he plunged into her pussy. The scent of crushed grass and her own wetness reached her nose, sensation piling on top of sensation.

"No, I wouldn't. Because I love you, and the idea of anyone hurting you is more than I can bear." His gaze locked with hers, and she couldn't look away. His expression was mesmerizing. All the armor that used to hide his feelings from her had fallen away, and she could see everything. His passion, his determination, his uncertainty, and something far sweeter, something she hadn't seen on his face in more years than she could count.

Love.

Her heart tripped, her nails scoring into his shoulder. It was one thing for him to say he loved her, it was another thing for him to offer any sort of vulnerability, opening himself to the kind of hurt and pain they'd caused each other before. He'd put his life on the line a million times, but he'd only ever put his heart on the line with her. To do it again, after all they'd put each other through…he was nothing if not brave. Was it any wonder she adored him?

His movements grew rougher, faster and she could see his restraint slipping. She clenched her pussy around him and a groan exploded from him. "Sif!"

"Yes," she purred. "Say my name. That's so fucking good."

"You little witch." He laughed and shuddered against her. "Tell me you're close."

"I'm close." She dug her heel into his flexing butt and her fingertips into his arm. "Just keep doing exactly what you're doing, only a little harder and deeper."

"Deeper?" He grabbed her ass, pulled her tight to the base of his cock, and ground his pelvis into her clit. She broke, screaming and shaking, climax crashing in one massive wave that swallowed her whole. Pinpricks of light burst behind her lids and tingles swept down her skin. Her pussy contracted around his dick again and again and again, and he kept fucking her, dragging out her orgasm to the point where she wasn't sure if she should beg him to stop or never to stop.

His big body locked in a tight line, and his hot come flooded her sex. His hand tightened painfully on her flesh, and she was pretty sure he'd left bruises. Totally worth it. He gave a choked cry and a final shudder, jutting into her one last time. Chest heaving, his grip on her backside eased, and he relaxed into the bed of moss. His cock softened inside her, but they were pressed so close together he stayed nestled within her. That was just fine with her. She stroked his arm, his back, everywhere that she could reach. Somewhere in the middle of their wild coupling, hope had managed to take root in her soul, and she'd begun to believe he might be right about them. The world might get a second chance, why shouldn't they?

His eyes opened. "I love you, Sif."

"I love you, too." She cupped his jaw, unable to stop the moisture that gathered on her lashes.

"Do you actually want a divorce?" His palm swept up and down her back. "Please say no."

"No," she whispered. "I never did."

"I know I have no right to ask, because I left you the first time around, but...stay with me. I need you." He squeezed her nape.

She laughed, the sound waterlogged. "If there's one thing a goddess who's all but faded from human memory learns, it's that no one really needs you. Everyone can muddle along just fine without you."

"*I* need you," he insisted. "Losing you now would rip my heart out."

The same words he'd used so long ago, in a far worse context. The same words she'd so recently used to justify her choices. She closed her eyes, tears leaking down her cheeks. "Thor."

He continued to press his point home. "You saved Bryn to give Erik something to fight for. So give *me* something to fight for, too. I'll make it worth your while."

"You have your sons." She sniffled, the sound loud and inelegant.

"No, *you* have my sons. They're yours to command." He laced his fingers with hers and brought them to his mouth for a kiss. "Our lives are in your hands."

"Ha." She shook her head. "You wouldn't let me boss you around."

A single brow lifted. "Is that what you want? A husband you can control?"

"No." What would she do with that kind of man? Die of boredom, probably. If she wanted an easy ride, she'd hop on a merry-go-round. Earth goddess or not, she was a Viking. Weak men would never be attractive to her.

"Then what do you want?"

"You." She offered him a crooked grin, feeling as if she were standing on a steep cliff and one false move would send her plunging into the abyss. But no risk meant no gain, and she'd wished for something like this for so long, she'd forgotten what it was like not to be haunted by helpless longing. "And I want to save the world, and have Odin and Freya come back, and live in this house with you for a few hundred years, when we don't have a death sentence hanging over our heads."

A beatific smile flashed across his face. "That sounds pretty damn good to me too. With two additions."

"Oh?"

"First, this is an exclusive reunion. No other lovers for either of us."

Easy enough. If she had him full-time, why would she want anyone else? She was glad he seemed to feel the same way though. Starting off on even footing would help them move forward. "I can do that."

"Next...a little girl, with your eyes and your smile."

Those damn tears came rushing back to her eyes. "*Oh*."

His fingers stroked through her hair. "Too soon?"

She shook her head, swiping at her cheeks. "I'd like more children. No child would ever replace Thura, and I'll probably be insanely overprotective, but I realized quite some time ago I don't want to give up on motherhood. I just...it never felt right to have any other man but you father my children. And things were way too complicated between us for me to ask you to be my baby-daddy."

"True, but things have changed." His cock swelled inside her, making them both moan as he thrust deeper, reseating himself in her pussy. "You have no idea how much it turns me on to think of you all ripe and round with my child. Let's get started."

Clinging to sanity, she swallowed. "But...Modi and Magni are going to wonder what became of us. Aren't we supposed to be teleporting to Bryn's farm soon?"

"The apocalypse can wait a little longer."

She chuckled. "But you can't?"

"No." And he rolled her underneath him and proved it.

THE END

About Crystal Jordan

Crystal Jordan is originally from the San Francisco Bay Area but has lived and worked all over the United States as an academic librarian. After many years of wandering, she returned to her home state and now resides in southern California with her husband. An award-winning author, Crystal has published paranormal and futuristic romance independently and with publishers such as Harlequin, Kensington Books, and Entangled Publishing.

On the Prowl series
Claim Me
Take Me
Need Me
The Between series
Between Lovers
Taken Between
Twilight of the Gods series
Reclaimed by the Immortal Viking Wolf
Reclaimed by the Immortal Viking Bear
In the Heat of the Night series
Total Eclipse of the Heart
Big Girls Don't Die
It's Raining Men
Crazy Little Thing Called Love
Wereplanets series
In Ice
In Heat
In Smoke
In Mist
Wereplanets anthology

Please enjoy this excerpt from Claim Me

Antonio watched the men circle his mate from atop a building far above the alley they'd cornered her in. A few nimble leaps brought him to the end of the shadowed corridor. He jerked his clothes off and dropped them as he ran, shifted into his Panther form to let his black fur blend into the night, and stalked the men as they had stalked her.

The predators became the prey.

He ran his tongue down a long fang, anticipation and rage boiling hot in his veins. They would pay for scaring her. God and all the saints couldn't save them if they harmed her.

It had taken two days to track her scent after he'd sensed her in the city. And now he'd found her. Nothing compared to the ice that froze the blood in his veins when he heard her first scream, the terror of seeing men hunt her. Yes, these men would beg for his mercy before the night was through. A growl rumbled from his chest as he moved down the alley, his claws clicking on the pavement.

When one of the men grabbed for her, a roar ripped from his throat. Everyone froze, turning in slow motion to stare at the newcomer. A Panther. He bared his teeth and watched the man closest to him turn ghostly pale. He could smell their fear, taste the tang of it on his tongue, and he took a small amount of satisfaction in that.

This close, even his rage couldn't cloud the fact that the men weren't human. They were Panthers, like him. Worse, they were from his Pride. The Ruiz brothers—Javier, Felipe, and Roberto. His own people, under his rule. Why would they hunt a Panther female? If she belonged to another Pride and was visiting his territory, then her Pride leader would hold him responsible for any harm his people caused her. Not to mention she was his mate and he would shred them alive for hunting her in the first place.

She screamed, and the frozen tableau broke into chaos. Antonio lunged forward, slicing his claws into Roberto's calf. He went down with a spray of blood and saliva, squealing and clutching his leg.

Antonio leaped over the fallen man to sprint forward, intent on reaching his mate. Felipe shifted to Panther form, hissing a warning, but it meant nothing to Antonio. They were past the point of warnings. A single leap forward and the two of them clashed midair, claws and fangs tearing into each other. Antonio slashed across the young Panther's face and he rolled away with a whimper, his black fur matted with dark crimson blood.

Antonio's tail whipped around as he sprang for Javier. The man—barely more than a teen—tried to climb the wall, but he had no more chance of escape than Antonio's mate had. Antonio dragged him down to the ground, his fangs digging into the man's jeans. Both front paws planted on the younger man's chest, making him wheeze, and Antonio shoved his face into Javier's. A growl vibrated his vocal cords, and what little blood was left in the man's face fled. His bloodshot eyes went wide with horror.

His mate's soft cry reached Antonio's ears, jerking him back from the edge of feral. He shuddered, fighting the instincts of his Panther nature. He turned toward her, wanting to comfort her and soothe her fear.

But she wasn't looking at him—she snarled at Felipe, bracing her back against the wall as she hissed deep in her throat. A purr rumbled his chest at her courage.

Javier took the opportunity to speak. "Please, sir. Listen to me. She doesn't deserve protection. She's a—"

A roar ripped free from Antonio's throat as he transformed into his human form. He hoisted the shorter man up by his T-shirt until they were nose to nose. "*Silence!* The three of you will be in my study when I return to the mansion. Is that clear?"

"But how long until—"

"Obey me. You won't enjoy the consequences if you don't. But I will." He dropped Javier to his feet. The younger man scrambled away and ran. His brothers had already disappeared.

He turned back to his mate. "Are you all right?"

"Yes. You?" She shoved her dark hair out of her face, her fingers sifting through the streaks of blond that shot through the long strands. He soaked in the details of her, taking in every curve of her face and body. Her chocolate-brown eyes searched him and they went wide when she saw the straining erection jutting between his thighs. Shifting back had left him naked. A wry smile pulled at his lips. He was going to have to figure out where he'd dropped his clothes and hope some vagrant didn't steal them before he got there. For the moment, he focused on his mate.

She sucked in a quick breath when he took a step toward her. Swaying on her feet, she stared at him for long moments. The silence stretched to a fine breaking point. She shook her head, pressing the heel of her hand to her forehead. "It can't be."

She'd finally sensed it—that they were mates.

"Oh, but it can be. It is." Stalking forward, he backed her up against the brick wall. His nostrils flared to catch her sweet scent, the one he would become addicted to. He had no doubt she had the same adrenaline humming through her as he did, and it morphed into something hotter, more carnal. Anger and fear still pumped through his system. His shaking fingers fisted at his sides. His eyes narrowed at her and a dart of excitement flashed through her gaze. The delicate smell of her wetness filled his nostrils. It was heady. She swallowed, her lids dropping to half-mast.

She released a breathy laugh, and naked want shone in her gaze. "I don't believe it. We can't be mates."

"Let me prove it to you," he growled. His hands wrapped around her waist, lifting her against the rough brick. Her legs curved around his flanks, she arched against him, and made him snarl with his need. She drove him wild. Jerking her dress up, he found her naked underneath. Perfect. He pushed forward, his hips fitting into the cradle of hers. The blunt tip of his cock rubbed over her slick folds. Her gaze flashed with the same desire that burned in his veins. "Your name. Tell me your name."

Her little pink tongue darted out to slide along her lips. "Solana."

She whimpered, tightening her legs about him. He groaned, but held back from plunging his dick into the snug fit of her damp pussy. Barely. "Yes or no, Solana?"

Her hands reached for him, fingers burying into his hair. Choking on a breath, she arched her hips toward the press of his cock. "Yes."

He thrust hard and deep. She screamed, the slick muscles of her pussy clenching around his dick. He groaned, hammering his hips forward. Her back arched, and she shuddered around him. He held on to his control by the tips of his fingers as her orgasm fisted her sex around his cock again and again. She was so responsive, so amazing. He kept pushing into her until her moans caressed his ears and she moved with him toward another orgasm. A tear leaked down her cheek and she hissed softly. Her head rolled against the brick wall, and her eyes slid closed. He wanted her gaze on him, wanted to see her come apart in his arms. "Look at me, Solana."

She moaned, but didn't obey him, so he seated himself as deep as he possibly could and stopped moving. Her brown eyes flared open. "Don't stop."

"I won't." He withdrew halfway and plunged back in, starting a slow, hard rhythm. She whimpered, clamping her knees on his hips, but she kept her gaze locked with his. Passion flushed her face, made her dark chocolate eyes shine. She was so beautiful—the most beautiful woman he'd ever seen. His mate. A grin curved his lips. "Tell me you want me."

A deep blush raced up her cheeks, her fingers tightening in his hair. She glanced away. "I'm doing it with you in an alley. Do you really have any doubts?"

He smiled at her. "Ah, but I want to hear you say it."

Clamping her pussy around his cock, she pulled a groan from him. A hot, purely female grin flashed across her face as she locked her gaze with his. "I want you. I want you to fuck me hard and fast."

He choked on a breath and gave her what she asked for. The scent of her, the damp feel of her around his thrusting cock drove him right to the edge of his control. His fangs extended and he knew his eyes had turned the deep gold of a Panther's as he held himself back from shifting. The sound of her demanding he fuck her harder made his head feel as though it were going to explode. And if he was lucky, he might get fifty more years of this with her. A purr tangled with a groan in his throat. "You make me crazy."

"*I* make *you* crazy? Do I need to mention we're in an *alley* again?" She laughed, and it made the soft skin of her belly quiver against his. His breath hissed out.

He rotated his hips against her, and she shivered. The urge to finish the mating swamped him. To bite her. To make her his forever. Mate.

"No mating. No biting." She pressed her lips to his before he could take what he wanted. Her tongue twined with his, and their kiss was as harsh and demanding as their coupling had been.

He drove into her soft, willing body until she strained against him, until all he could think about was the orgasm just beyond his grasp. Fire crawled over his skin, settling deep inside him. The muscles in his belly tightened as the need to come overtook him. When she pulled her mouth free, her cries of passion rang in his ears, spurring him on. She twisted in his arms, sobbing as her pussy milked the length of his cock. A harsh groan burst from his throat as he froze, every muscle in his body locking as he jetted deep inside her.

They clung to each other in the aftermath of orgasm, their breathing nothing more than rasps of air. The instinct to finish the mating still clawed at him, but he forced himself to ignore it, to savor the feel of her in his arms. His mate. Unclaimed, but his.

She stirred against him, pushing at his shoulders. They both groaned when he pulled out of her. Her muscles clenched around his dick in one last spasm, and he fought the urge to shove back into her, to thrust his cock deep and sink his fangs in her flesh until she knew she could never be parted from him.

Dropping her feet to the ground, she slid out of his embrace and stepped away from him. She smoothed her dress down around her thighs, not looking at him. "I don't even know your name."

"Antonio." He stepped in front of her, silently demanding she acknowledge him, what they had experienced together this wild night. "I am Antonio Cruz."

"Cruz?" The color leeched from her lovely face. "Esteban Cruz's heir?"

Arching a brow at her reaction to his name, he shook his head. "Not heir. My father died four months ago."

"Ah." Her shoulders drew into a tense line. Obviously, his father had made no friend with this woman. "I'm afraid I don't keep up with Pride politics."

"You weren't at the loyalty ceremony. I would have remembered you." He might not have been able to resist taking her then and there. His cock swelled again.

Her arms folded protectively around her waist. "I'm not a member of your

Pride."

"Which one, then?" Once they were mated, she would have to leave her current Pride to join his. Unless she was a Pride leader herself. Then, well, things would get complicated. But the only Pride in the world with a female leader right now was in Australia...and she was well into her fifties. Definitely not his mate.

"None of them." She lifted one shoulder and let it drop.

"No Panther is without a Pride." It just wasn't done. They found strength in numbers. Without the Prides, they had to hide who they were from everyone, and in cat form were the prey to any human with a gun.

"This one is." She turned away, ghosting down the alley.

"Wait." He took a step after her, confusion flooding him at this new turn of events. "Why?"

She didn't turn around, just paused for the briefest of moments. "Why no Pride? I was part of your father's Pride, but I left when I came of age." Bitterness edged her soft voice. "Or I was invited to leave."

He had no doubts about his father's ruthlessness and need to control everything and everyone around him—including his heir—but the more members a Pride had, the more prestige for the Pride. Bigger was better. "My father wouldn't do that."

"Even to a non-shifter?"

His mouth opened and then snapped closed as shock rocked through him. He watched her slip away, disappearing into the cool mist of the San Francisco night.

Dios mio. Nausea fisted his gut. A non-shifter. A Panther shifter unable to change forms. They were second-class citizens in the Prides, treated as nothing. Less that nothing, depending on the Pride leader's attitude toward them. So much of what made a Panther a Panther remained a mystery, including what made a non-shifter unable to change forms. Some of the older, more superstitious Panthers thought non-shifters were a curse upon a Pride.

Scientists believed that panthers were any large cat that was black, usually a genetic mutation of a leopard or jaguar. The average human thought panthers were a separate species all to themselves. The average human was much closer to the truth than they knew. While leopards and jaguars *could* be all black, a true Panther was a shapeshifter able to transform between animal and human forms.

Some thought it was a demonic curse, others thought it was a blessing from a benevolent god. The truth of their magic had been lost long ago. Now it didn't matter why—they just needed to survive.

Contrary to popular legend, a wereanimal's bite wouldn't turn someone in to a shapeshifter. If only it were so simple to keep the population alive. Panthers had to breed in their animal form, and humans couldn't be turned into Panthers. Survival was a constant struggle. It might be easier if they could breed without being mated, but they couldn't. Panther children were rare and highly prized. That the Cruz family had *four* children was almost unheard-of among the Prides. If anything, one or two was much more normal.

The Ruiz family was another with exceptionally high breeding rates—and the Ruiz brothers' actions toward his mate made sudden, sickening sense. She must have come and gone in his Pride while he'd been fostering in South America. With his very conservative father as a Pride leader, he didn't even want to imagine what she must have been through. And what more would she have to go through now that he had discovered what she was to him?

He swallowed. His mate couldn't shift, couldn't have children. And he was the Pride leader. God help him.

What the hell was he going to do?

www.ingramcontent.com/pod-product-compliance
Ingram Content Group UK Ltd.
Pitfield, Milton Keynes, MK11 3LW, UK
UKHW040904280225
455691UK00005B/352